THE GHOST OF GLENGULLION CASTLE

A MURDER MYSTERY SET IN SCOTLAND

ADRIANA LICIO

The Home Travellers
Press

THE GHOST OF GLENGULLION CASTLE
A Murder Mystery Set in Scotland

Book 6 in the *The Homeswappers Mysteries* series
By Adriana Licio

Edition I
Copyright 2023 © Adriana Licio

Cover by Wicked Smart Design
Editing by Alison Jack

CONTENTS

THURSDAY
NIGHT

"So, are we all agreed?" I asked them once more.

I was feeling a little tired by then. Improvising quite a few extra preparations, on top of the daily running of the place, had taken its toll. Not to mention getting ready for the fair. Now, if you consider we may be young at heart, but somewhat older physically, you will surely understand that 10 hours of solid work followed by this meeting had made me feel a little exhausted long before I could call it a day.

Then I gazed at them. As one, my friends and faithful members of the Pensioners' Posse – we call ourselves the PP as it trips off the tongue so much more easily – shouted "YES", their faces bright and filled with determination. And he was looking approvingly at me. I know he doesn't agree with me a lot of the time, however much he tries to hide it, but I like to work with him by my side. Ours is what you might call a dialectic relationship. It's just a friendship, mind you, but a good strong one, giving me both new ideas and energy at all times. And quite a few laughs besides. Even tonight, despite the situation being rather serious, what he presented to us had been ingenious and hilarious at the same time. When he'd shown us what he could do, he'd had us giggling like naughty schoolchildren, which is something most of us haven't been for five, six or even seven decades. Time is definitely a traitor, but don't let me get started on this topic.

"Then that's all, folks," I said, smiling a little wickedly, I must confess. "Let's give them a welcome… Tobermory style."

And with that, the meeting was finally over, and so was my long day.

FRIDAY

1

WELCOME TO TOBERMORY

Concetta Natale Passolina, simply known as Etta to her friends, felt immensely grateful. She appreciated the solid asphalt where her feet stood, felt happy to be in a car park. Her stomach might still be rotating like a washing machine, but at least the spin cycle had ended. The turns were less violent, the knots were loosening. The air was finally reaching her lungs and properly oxygenating her blood after the sense of constriction that had prevented her from breathing freely and deeply. Even the nausea was leaving her in peace, though at 10am, she found it impossible to appreciate the smell of fish and chips coming from the kiosk ahead of them.

"How can Scottish people eat fried food at this time of day? Dora? Leon? I'm talking to you," she addressed her two companions. But neither answered.

Leon the Basset Hound had long lamented the fact that humans are far too lazy to pronounce names of more than two syllables, even one as noble as Napoleon. Resigning himself to the indignity of never being properly addressed, he was turning his head this way and that, his nostrils quivering, busy taking in all the new smells. The pungent scent of diesel from the nearby quay; the delicious aroma coming from the fishing nets. The overall local odour was so different from what he had experienced on Skye, where a mixture of sea breeze and mainland held many delights for a dog's keen olfactory senses. Here in Tobermory, on the island of Mull, it seemed the sea note was dominant.

And talking of dominance, Leon had work to do. Taking in the smells of all the dogs who had dared to visit the car park in the last 48 hours, he was anxious to mark his new territory, and to do it categorically. But first, his smart brain needed to classify the scents of he-dogs, his future subjects, and the lovely she-dogs whose hearts this valiant Basset was ready to conquer.

The third member of the company, a pleasantly rotund woman with a salt-and-pepper fringe, was the only one acting out of character, Etta thought. Dorotea Rosa Pepe, simply known as Dora, had not once clasped her hands at the marvel of it all. Not on the ferry from Oban when they had passed Duart Castle on the way to Craignure, nor during the 40-minute drive from the harbour at Craignure to Tobermory, nor now, when they had finally reached their destination, the breathtakingly pretty seaside town of Tobermory, for their latest home swap. Of course, a car park, with its odours of fish and diesel, might not be the best of places to indulge in fanciful dreams, even for her most romantic friend. Still, it was rather unusual.

"Shall we go?" the woman asked Etta, clearly feeling her intense gaze.

"Of course, I can't wait to steady my legs on this beautifully firm asphalt and concrete. This fresh air is making me feel alive again."

"Oh, come on, Etta, we left the boat almost an hour ago. And anyway, it wasn't such a bad crossing…"

"No, if you like feeling as if the world is coming to an end," said Etta, who felt seasick even when getting into a bathtub. At least that got a laugh from Dora.

They moved on, leaving the car park to walk along the

succession of brightly coloured buildings facing the sea that had made Tobermory so famous.

"How lovely," said Dora. "I think it will be nice to live here for the next few weeks."

"I wonder what the country house we're staying in will be like." Etta never bothered to look at the details of their forthcoming home exchanges, leaving it to Dora to do all the planning, make or answer invitations, close agreements, decide the itineraries. Those things would make Etta anxious – too many decisions to take, too many guidebooks to read. Life was already complicated, so why create more trouble for herself when Dora seemed to enjoy the organising as much as the trip itself?

"It *seems* a very fine place," Dora answered, a bit too vaguely for Etta's tastes.

"So, where are we heading now?" Etta asked.

"To the Tobermory Fish Company. I've ordered one of their seafood platters for our dinner." Moving forward, Dora led her companions into a neat shop that looked almost like a boutique. A family business since 1971, the sign proudly stated. The ambience was friendly, the staff chatty and welcoming, inviting the newcomers to try a couple of oysters. Etta declined with horror.

"Not at this time of day!" she exclaimed. "Not after having ridden the wildest waves in a nutshell."

"What nutshell? It's a proper ferry." A man in a wheelchair, who had entered the fish shop behind them, laughed at Etta's protestations.

"Try explaining that to my stomach!" Etta retorted.

"Is that an Italian accent?" The man's strong arms skilfully moved the chair closer to Etta. He had an unlined face and a pleasant voice that exuded a deep sense of calm.

"It is, but that's not my fault. It's my father's or my mother's, whoever decided I should be born there a few decades ago."

"Are you tourists spending a few days on the island?"

"We're not really tourists," Dora said, always proud to explain their way of travelling whenever she had occasion to do so. "We're swapping our home in the south of Italy with a woman from Tobermory, so we'll be staying at her house for a few weeks starting today."

"That's a superb way of travelling," acknowledged the man. "I guess it means you get a taste of living like a local?"

"That is exactly why we love it so much. Are you from Tobermory yourself?"

"I wish! No, I'm simply on an extended holiday with my wife," and he pointed to a tall woman busy checking the plethora of fish on display at the counter through round glasses with thick black frames. "We're from Manchester, but we fell in love with the island of Mull years ago and hop on a ferry any time we have an opportunity." He moved his chair towards the window and indicated a tongue of land overlooking the sea. "There, before the hill starts, among that group of houses. We've rented a flat there. It has a lovely view and it's easy for me and my wife to get to the pier and Main Street. We enjoy exploring the area and I value my independence, too. Where are you staying, if I may ask?"

Etta hesitated. She didn't have a clue. "Somewhere close to Tobermory. I guess in the countryside."

"Yes," confirmed Dora. "We're at Glengullion House."

"Glengullion House?"

"That must be the castle," said the wife, joining her husband. She was someone you could not help looking at. Tall and slim, she had wavy hair that was more salt than pepper and cut in a layered bob barely covering her ears. The combination of her starkly framed round glasses and lips coated in bright pink lipstick suggested a sophisticated yet outgoing personality.

"Castle?" asked Etta.

"It's a large house," explained Dora.

"You mean Eilidh McGullion's place, don't you?"

"Indeed," Dora confirmed.

Husband and wife exchanged a puzzled look.

"Well," said the woman after what felt like an awkward pause, "what can we say? Welcome to Tobermory and have a nice stay. I'm Sandra, by the way, and my husband is Grayson."

"Thanks," said Dora, shaking hands and introducing herself, Etta and Napoleon, the Basset relieved to be credited with his full name for once. "I hope we will see more of you during our stay."

"I'm sure you will," said Grayson, but his demeanour seemed to have changed. He glanced again at his wife, but she simply shrugged as if to acknowledge her reluctance to say or do more.

The woman who'd served them checked in with Dora to make sure she had everything she had ordered.

"If you don't mind," said Dora who, at times like these, when faced with her daily tasks, could be more practical than dreamy, "we will pay for our stuff now, but fetch it on our way back. We're walking Main Street and have some more shopping to do."

Seafood platter paid for and stored safely in the fishery, they continued their walk, slowly as Monsieur Leon had to sniff each lamppost, tree trunk, blade of grass, or anything else that emerged vertically from the ground, and mark it with his own scent. What a demanding job this was. It involved a meticulous chromatography process that would have graced the most advanced test labs, followed by a very precise aim at a particular spot, usually at a ridiculously vertiginous height for a Bassett. This in turn required the acrobatic prowess of a gymnast, all for one long spritz of pee. Only then would he move on with the satisfaction of a craftsperson assessing the successful completion of one of their creations.

For the humans, there was a wealth of independent shops; a public house; a couple of fine churches, one of which had been converted into a gallery. But Dora resisted them all, until she came to a stop in front of one named "Tobermory Chocolate Shop."

A chatty lady welcomed them in and was more than happy to explain how she and her 'better half' had created the factory back in 1991. It had been hard going at first, as new beginnings are always meant to be hard for some reason.

"Maybe it's just to test us to see how determined we are to pursue our dreams," she mused.

"How do you make your chocolate?" Dora asked, her keen love for the dark stuff written in her glowing face.

"We select the best natural ingredients from suppliers who care about their products, and all the chocolate is tempered and hand dipped in our lab. We started with just the dark variety, but have grown our selection to include white and milk, fondant, fudge, fruit and nut centres, bars, and truffles, of course."

"It's all very well now, in the height of the tourist season," said Etta, looking at the number of patrons checking the shelves and asking questions of the other staff, "but winters must be a sorry time, stuck in such an isolated place." In her mind's eye, she visualised wild storms ravaging the town and leaving the island isolated for months.

"Not really," said the woman with the smug grin of someone who knows better than the naive person in front of her. "We're grateful for the tourists who visit for the major part of the year, but winters… winters are for us. It's the islanders' time."

"What do you do in winter?" Etta asked in disbelief. "Don't you get cut off from ci… the mainland?" She realised in the nick of time that suggesting Tobermory parted touch with civilisation might be a bit too rude, even for the outspoken Etta.

"Not at all, it's really not as bad as you may imagine. And even if we did get cut off, it's the time of year we dedicate to our own community. After a busy tourist season, we're free to organise things for ourselves, get together. We have a theatre company and an incredible number of associations. Whether you're keen on wildlife or acting, knitting or photography, you can be sure we have a group for that."

"And it's also the time for organising celebrations, entertainment and charity events," said the man beside her, breaking off from serving a couple of customers to join in the conversation.

Etta was deeply struck by the enthusiasm in their voices. "Do you mean you're happy to live here?"

"Let us say…"

"…we wouldn't change Mull for anywhere else in the world," the man finished the woman's sentence while filling a bag with chocolate seahorses, shrimps and cute little mice. The two looked at each other with a harmony and complicity that suggested he was the better half the woman had mentioned earlier.

Scottish people are so proud of their country and lifestyle, thought Etta. And as much as she tried to keep her thoughts in check, *he* made his way through the thick spider's web of neurons. Inside Etta's brain, electricity ran through the firing synapses and buzzing chaos that sounded like 1,000 crickets, and *his* image popped into her mind. His loud velvety laugh; his eyes scanning that Scottish landscape he was so fond of.

Rufus McCall was just a source of trouble for Concetta Natale Passolina – the sort of trouble she had managed to keep at bay for most of her life. Until very recently. When Fate had decided she should meet this proud Highlander during a cèilidh in Luss on the banks of Loch Lomond, while she and Dora were hiking the West Highland Way.

Through the chirping crickets inside her head, Etta became aware that the chocolatier was speaking to her.

"So, where are you staying?" she asked Etta, maybe for the third time. As Etta gasped for words, embroiled as she was in her silly thoughts, Dora came to the rescue.

"At Glengullion House. Just outside Tobermory, as I understand."

"You mean the B&B above town?"

"No, the actual house."

"The castle?"

Dora hesitated. "That's the one, I think," she replied eventually.

"Are you sure it's open for visitors?"

"We got in touch with Eilidh McGullion. She's a member of the Homeswapping International Circle, as are we…"

"Homeswapping?" asked the male chocolatier, looking puzzled.

"You know. We stay in someone else's home and they stay in ours."

"I thought Eilidh was in London with her daughter, Elizabeth," said the wife.

"That's correct, we're doing a non-simultaneous swap as she wants to take a holiday later on in the year. I believe right now, she's helping her daughter find somewhere to live in London. It will be a friend of hers called Edwina who will show us around later on today."

"But are you staying at the castle? As in… sleeping there?" the woman asked, a strange worried expression spreading across her face.

"That's correct," Dora answered.

Etta harrumphed. "What's wrong with that?" she demanded, pulled back to the present by evidence of doubt triggered by the mention of their accommodation for the second time since they had arrived.

"Nothing wrong. Really. It's a lovely historical property," but why did the man's facial expression say otherwise?

"There will be a farmers' fair on the grounds tomorrow," added the wife.

"Yes, Eilidh mentioned that in her emails." Dora nodded. "We're very happy this is taking place while we're here."

The conversation went on a little longer, but as it had done with the couple in the fishery, it felt stilted now, husband and wife seeming to send private messages between each other. Finally, Etta and Dora paid for their chocolates and moved on.

"What weird people," commented Etta once they were outside.

"No, they're so sweet with their love for the island. Not to mention their skill with chocolate," said Dora. Then she stopped in front of one of the few white buildings in among the multicoloured row. "This is the Co-op. Shall we have a cup of coffee before doing our grocery shopping?"

"Indeed," said Etta, her eyes piercing Dora. She felt there was something fishy her friend was hiding from her – fishier even than the harbour they had just passed.

2

THE SPIRIT OF THE PLACE

Despite her misgivings, it seemed that luck was a little bit on Etta's side that day – and Leon's. On the way to the café, Dora stopped in front of a building, the ground floor painted red in contrast to the grey of the first floor and surrounding the dormer windows of the attic. White stonework framed the windows with irregularly sized rectangles, making them look uncannily like huge Lego bricks.

It was a bookshop, with tantalising displays along its frontage. But before Dora could either lose herself in hand-clasping rapture or disappear into the shop for a long – a very long – browse, she was stopped in her tracks by a sign. And Etta silently blessed that sign, because it read 'Closed. Back soon'.

"Such a pity," cried Etta, sounding as false as a gold tooth. Hands unclasped and books unbrowsed, Dora followed her two companions to a small café along the harbour. Leon, as ever, was served first with a bowl of water, and then the teenage waitress asked if she could bring him a little toast to eat.

"Only if you're going to bring us something, too," snapped Etta, "like two cappuccinos and a couple of those doughnuts…"

The girl promised she would take care of them, but still, the toast arrived before the doughnuts did. Etta sighed. If you travel with a dog, you have to get used to the idea that you will always come second, no matter what.

Once their order arrived, Etta decided the time had come to quiz Dora about their accommodation.

"Are we really going to live in a castle for a month?"

"Well, it's not really a castle. It's more like a sort of large house…"

"Thank goodness!" said Etta gratefully. "All the Scottish castles we've visited so far have been so cold and draughty, I'm sure they wouldn't make decent accommodation. For ghosts maybe, but not for living human beings."

"The Scottish castles we've visited so far have mainly been museums or ruins of some sort. They must be very different if people still live inside them, I'm sure they have all sorts of comforts…"

"I'm not so sure. Remember how Scottish people have a worrying tendency to sleep with their windows open, even in the middle of winter? I doubt they would realise there was a draught, used as they are to sleeping in the worst of weather."

"But we're here in the middle of summer."

"A Scottish summer is nothing like a normal summer anywhere else. It takes a rare combination of stars to align for the sun to shine for more than a few hours without a deluge of rain. But as we're staying not in a castle, but in a real house, there's no need to worry, I guess."

Instead of replying, Dora bent down under the table to make sure Leon was satisfied with his food. Which, of course, he was, but didn't he deserve a doughnut too?

"That'd be no good for you," Dora explained patiently. Leon, once again betrayed by a canine's supposed 'best friend', turned his back to her and curled up for a nap. When the pain of life gets too much to bear, dogs sleep to forget.

They returned to the Co-op supermarket in Main Street of Tobermory. Dora, the organiser, had planned to stock up on groceries there so they'd be set for a few days in their new home. Leaving Leon tied up by his leash outside, they worked through the long list of things Dora insisted they needed. By the time they finally emerged from the shop, they found a man and a woman surrounding the hound, the woman bending down to caress and console him.

"He was worried you had abandoned him," she explained. Appearing to be slightly older than Etta, the woman had a sweet round face which clearly expressed all the emotions going on inside her.

"It'd more likely be the other way round," Etta answered. "We fear the dog may leave us for whoever offers him the juiciest steak."

"But he looked so sad." Despite being in at least her seventh decade of life, the woman looked almost childish as her eyebrows frowned and her lips twitched.

"Bassets are born actors," said the man beside her. His face reminded Etta of a balloon, wide at the top part and narrowing almost to a point at chin level. His short hair was very white, contrasting with his tanned skin, and looked suspiciously like a wig.

"Oh no," protested Dora. "He's just a sensitive soul."

"That's absolutely true," Etta spoke at the same time as Dora. "He's such a talented actor, he would do anything to grab people's attention."

The man smiled at them.

"You have plenty of shopping there. Are you moving to Mull to live?"

While Dora explained the home swapping thing for the umpteenth time, Etta casually wondered if they should print the info and simply hand out leaflets whenever they were asked about it. They'd save a lot in time and energy. Not that Dora ever seemed to tire of spelling out the wonders of the scheme, every time wording it in a slightly different way.

"And who are you swapping with?" the man asked.

"Eilidh McGullion, do you know her?"

"Of course, we all know each other in Tobermory, and most of the island too. But you don't mean you're staying at the castle, do you?"

"Well, sort of…"

"Goodness!" replied the man. His small mouth gaped open, showing teeth that seemed too large to fit inside. The woman with him seemed oblivious to the conversation and continued to pet Leon.

"What's wrong with Eilidh McGullion's place?" Etta snapped, unable to let this latest expression of disbelief pass unchallenged.

"Well, there's nothing wrong with the place, except… are you going to sleep there as well? I mean, as in spending the night?"

"No, we're only sleeping during the day. In the evenings, like any self-respecting vampire, we'll go human hunting, returning at dawn with all sorts of morons in our large jute bag."

The man laughed at that. *On the whole,* Etta thought approvingly, despite her increasing misgivings concerning their accommodation, *the Scottish people might get touchy when you mention certain things about their history, but overall they have a good sense of humour.*

"Okey-dokey, I guess I deserved that," the man said. Then he stretched out his hand. "By the way, I'm Tom, born on the island about twenty, maybe thirty years ago. And this is Letitia, also from Mull, and just as young as I am."

The two women shook hands with them, laughing and declaring they were a similar amount of decades young.

"But why do people here in Tobermory seem to be shocked when we mention we're staying at Glengullion?" Etta asked bluntly.

"I don't want to worry you," Tom explained. "It's just that

the old building might not be in such good shape, never mind everything else."

'Not in such good shape' was too much for Etta, to the point she didn't even question what Tom meant by 'everything else'.

"You mean the building is cold and draughty?"

"Well, I'm an old man. I don't want to alarm you... two young women like you, you might be fine there. I just find it weird that Eilidh would use that place to welcome friends, that's all."

Etta treated Dora to the dirtiest, scariest look she had given her in the past year, since their home-swapping adventure started.

"From the pictures we saw, it looked a nice welcoming place," the rose-tinted spectacles woman stuttered.

"Aye," said the man, "it might look nice... to passers-by."

Dora sighed. Etta banged her forehead with her hand. One month. They would be stuck in the coldest castle in Scotland for a whole month!

"Did Eilidh mention anything else?" asked the man.

"Well, all the walks," said Dora. "The large park surrounding the house, with deer visiting at the end of the day..."

"No, I meant... did she mention *him*?"

"Him? Who's him?"

"The... how can I say this? The night guest."

The two women looked at each other, neither understanding what the man was on about.

"Well, you know what Scottish castles are like. They never come... empty."

"You don't mean a ghost?" asked Etta incredulously.

"Hmm, I'm not sure you can call him that exactly. But I guess to that extent..."

"Oh, the ghost. He's scary, isn't he?" Letitia was now all ears, giggling as she spoke. Etta laughed too, although far more cynically.

"That's just superstition, pure and simple, born from

centuries of living far away from land," and she threw her arms in the air, as if Mull was as isolated in the middle of the Atlantic as Easter Island in the Pacific. "I can see the need for all kinds of beliefs, and you Scots do have a tendency to be rather imaginative. But it doesn't matter, because I don't mind ghosts. What I'm worried about is catching my death of cold in a huge draughty place." And her eyes bulged at poor Dora like two boulders jutting out from a mountain.

As if sensing the tension growing between the two women, Tom took his leave, hastily explaining to Letitia that Leon had to go with his owners. The woman looked almost heartbroken to leave him. As for Etta, had she not been so mad, she would have realised how mortified her friend was. But Etta was Etta, and the only thing she could think about was how to face a month living in a refrigerator. It made no difference to her if it was dressed up as a cottage, a manor house or a castle. Not even collecting the platter from the fishery, containing all sorts of delicacies from the sea, sweetened her up. As they walked back to the car park, Dora listed them all: oysters, langoustines, fish pate, mussels, smoked salmon and trout, along with oatcakes, bread and dips. But it was useless.

Etta was simply too furious for words.

3

IT NEVER RAINS, BUT IT POURS

The route to Glengullion, Dora was soon to realise, was one of those windy, steep one-lane-only country roads that Etta had learned to fear. And it showed as she drove more tensely than usual, her hands clinging to the wheel for dear life, the car juddering and jolting as she changed gears.

"At least you can't forget whether you're driving on the right or the left," Dora would usually joke, but this time she remained silent under the weight of her own guilt. The now gloomy sky was a perfect companion to her sinking mood.

How could it possibly be so bad? the poor woman wondered. She had studied the photos, the descriptions, and it had seemed such a fine place. A wonderful surprise, she had thought. She wouldn't tell Etta that Glengullion was a real castle; she'd simply call it a house, and then enjoy her friend's delighted astonishment when they got there and Etta discovered what a stunning place was to be their residence for the month.

To tell the *whole* truth, Eilidh had mentioned the place was not in a perfect state of repair and that some of the rooms were closed as it was too difficult to maintain such a large property. But the pictures she had shown Dora were of a nice apartment within the castle that had a cheerful living room, comfy bedrooms and a quaint, if small kitchen. Of course, Dora had mostly been attracted by the parkland, the garden, the views onto the sea from the cliffs, but she was sure the interior hadn't looked as bad as the locals were suggesting. Or, as sometimes happened, had her imagination taken over and she'd seen only what she wanted to see?

After looking forward to it for so long, she was now dreading the moment of their arrival. Recently, she'd had reason to fear that their travels could soon come to an end, but this! Now, this could settle things for good. How could she have been so careless with a swap that would last not a weekend or even a week, but a whole month?

So concerned was Dora, she forgot to look at the satnav on her mobile. She had set it to mute because Etta found the 'stupid AI voice', as she called it, confusing; it made her anxious with its "In two miles, turn left, but for now, keep on the right bearing slightly left" announcements. Their usual method of navigation required a silent phone, with Dora attentively watching the map on the screen so she could translate the complicated instructions into simpler ones such as "Turn left here" or "Keep going straight ahead". But on narrow country lanes, things were a bit more complicated. The satnav couldn't discern properly between real roads and dirt tracks totally impracticable for their old Fiat 500. The straightest road to the castle, as far as the satnav was concerned, passed through fields of grazing sheep, which wasn't a viable option.

By this time, Etta was so nervous, she was pushing hard on the brakes, stalling the engine, and changing gear while the car was revving madly. Dora and Leon's bodies were thrown forwards and backwards so many times, it felt like they were riding in a bumper car. And now…

"Maybe we'd better do a U-turn," Dora said hesitantly. "I'm afraid I think I might have missed the turning earlier on…"

"U-turn, my tooth! Can't you see how narrow this track is?

How ever am I going to turn the car around? Let's keep going, this blooming road must lead somewhere!"

'Somewhere' is a relative concept anywhere, but much more so in the islands of Scotland. The one-lane road went on forever. Well, almost forever, which might have been preferable as after one more bend and one more hill, it came to a dead end, their way blocked by a low stone wall as grey as the clouds suspended over their heads. Apart from two women and one dog, the only other living beings were cows to the left and right, along with more cows to the right and left.

Etta breathed deeply, as she always did when she was trying to keep herself from exploding. That was a worrying sign, indeed.

"Dorotea Rosa Pepe, I don't want to be nasty, but you will have to understand we're no longer two adventurous youngsters. We made it, I don't really know how, all the way to Scotland – to the Highlands of Scotland, then on to a totally isolated pea of an island. Now, having successfully done all that, was it necessary to end up in a forgotten-far-from-anywhere-and-anyone place in the depths of the countryside? Couldn't we just have stayed in Tobermory? Wasn't that enough? I'm sure no one else from Castelmezzano has ever attempted anything like this."

The problem with Etta was that her rants tended to gather momentum. Dora had exited the car to help her manoeuvre it out of the cul-de-sac it had arrived in, and while she gave precise instructions as if Etta were driving a bulky campervan rather than a small Fiat, she could hear Etta's comments coming out through the open window. And they were harsh, even for the perennially hot-tempered woman. But you know what? When you're in trouble, that's when life hits you even harder. It's nothing personal. Just Murphy's law.

When Etta had somehow managed to turn the car, Dora jumped back on board, feeling her eyes getting watery, but determined to fight hard to keep any tears back. She turned her head. At least Leon was looking peaceful, but maybe he sensed there was something wrong with his gentler biped as he sat and leaned his head over the hammock covering the back seats to get closer to Dora's face. In a rare show of generosity, he gave it a long, rough lick; he would tolerate kisses and hugs from bipeds, but would never usually return such mawkishness. Proud dog that he was, it simply wouldn't do.

Dora looked gratefully at him, feeling she could put up with Etta's tantrum a little longer, but then BANG! The explosion not only happened, but it was much more violent – and physical – than she had foreseen. It was followed by a huge bump as the car jolted forward, then screeched awfully as Etta pushed hard on the brakes. Leon would have landed in the anterior part of the car, were it not for the hammock preventing him doing so. As for the two ladies, their bodies were thrown forward to be halted abruptly by the seatbelts. It was only because the car was proceeding at a very low speed that they were at least spared the airbags.

"Wha... what now?" cried Etta as she recovered from the shock.

"What was that bang?" For the first time, Dora wondered if the explosion of sound might not have been created by Etta's rage after all.

"Is the dog OK?" Etta asked, unable to turn round, stuck as she was between the tightened seatbelt and the steering wheel.

Dora managed to look to the rear seat and sighed in relief.

"Yes, he's fine. He looks as shocked as we are, but he's fine."

Acting on a silent mutual accord, they slowly, slowly got out of the car.

"It's raining," said Dora.

"Just drizzle," said Etta. Studying her side of the car, she added, "Everything seems to be fine."

But the car leaning over on the passenger side spoke volumes.

"The tyre..." said Dora.

Etta came round to her side. "I can't believe it!" This time, it really was Etta exploding. Kicking the tyre, stomping her feet, she shook her fist at the threatening sky. "The wretched tyre has burst and we're out in the middle of nowhere!" All around them, the indifferent cows kept grazing, beyond the animals a few trees. Otherwise, they were surrounded by rocky fields and bogs. The countryside was too desolate and far from civilisation to offer any comfort.

Turning back to the car, they located the spare wheel in the boot, which in their ancient Fiat was actually located under the bonnet. Etta even managed to find a long heavy tool, and they looked at the mysterious object as if it were an alien weapon with unknown powers.

"I guess we're supposed to lift the car with this."

"That's the jack, then, and we use the contents of that bag to remove the flat tyre," said Dora, pointing to a black faux-leather bag next to the spare tyre. Etta bravely opened the bag and extracted more obscure tools one by one. She handled each as if weighing up the value of rare findings on an archaeological dig.

Dora leaned back inside the car and came out with the instruction manual. She read how to change a tyre silently, but then got confused and decided to read it all aloud, with the result that Etta got just as confused. They bent their heads over the manual together and desperately tried to match each strange word to the array of weapons and the flat tyre.

"I can't see the wheel bolts," Dora said finally after much hard thinking and looking at the flat tyre. "How can we possibly do this without them?"

And they both got down on their knees, looking for an explanation that didn't come.

"My goodness," Etta cried after a few pointless minutes had passed. "We really *are* all alone in the middle of nowhere!"

All of a sudden, the old expression 'it never rains, but it pours' decided to take itself literally, and the drizzle turned into a deluge. Not the gentle rain you hardly notice, but a real downpour with thunder and lightning.

"Oh, Etta, I'd say this is not our lucky day," said Dora as they quickly clambered back into the car. In reply, Etta said something that cannot be repeated, the gist of it being it was their *unluckiest* day.

The car was unusually dark, as if they had entered a cave.

"Gosh!" cried Etta. "What now?"

"We've left the boot open. I'll go," and out into the storm Dora went, heroically managing to close the thing. Maybe later, she would have to check she had closed it properly, as the wind was rather powerful.

"We'll have to wait for the blasted rain to stop," Etta said once her friend was safely back in the car. "I doubt we will ever be able to use that jick… jack… whatever you called it to unscrew the mysterious nuts we can't find. But in the end, even if we manage to get our spare tyre in place, I don't think we should attempt to drive the blooming car. What if the wheel decides to go on a ride on its own and leave the car and the three of us for good?"

"I think we'd better call Eilidh's friend, Edwina, and see if she can send someone to the rescue. She will be worried that we're not there yet."

"How will you explain where we are?" said Etta. "There's not a single signpost worthy of the name."

"With the help of the satnav, I could send her our position…"

"Bless you," said Etta. As she had always refused to even look at the satnav, she was far from knowledgeable about what it could do. But when Dora tried to make the call, there was no signal. And to add insult to injury, a roaring clap of thunder made the car windows rattle as if they would blow out at any moment. In fact, the whole car shook, and the brave Bassett forgot all about his pride and, with an unexpected agility, jumped over the hammock to land on Dora's lap, trembling with fear. He must have done something truly awful if the sky's owner was so very mad at him. But what?

"Switch off that wretched thing in case it attracts the lightning to strike us dead."

Dora switched off the phone, gently pushing the trembling Leon to the floor. His 30kg weight was not a joke, especially when they were stuck in a small and ancient car. She petted him and whispered reassuring words, only to be the one to jump from her seat whenever the lightning split the sky in front of them with its sinister forks and the thunder detonated explosions as if it was madder even than Etta.

"This must be the end," Dora heard her red-haired friend whisper. Etta's face was so concerned, her brows so furrowed, her huge red-framed glasses so low on her nose, it looked like she too might jump on Dora's lap sometime soon.

They closed their eyes and took each other's hands, clasping them over Leon's head *Thelma and Louise* style as they waited for their final moment to come. Such was the intensity of the terror that had seized the trio, such was their despair, that their three brains decided, as one collective intelligence, that the best way to deal with the catastrophe at hand was to shut down. Soon a deep, thick sleep overtook them.

4
_____

KNOCKING ON HEAVEN'S DOOR

"KNOCK, KNOCK, KNOCK!"

"Come in," cried Etta, startled into wakefulness but keeping her eyes closed, determined not to see if their situation was still as bleak as it had been. *Shouldn't we be the ones knocking on Heaven's door?* she wondered.

"KNOCK, KNOCK, KNOCK!"

Irritated by the persistence, she found the courage to open one eye, and was surprised to find out it took a car to reach Heaven as they were clearly still in their Fiat. She opened both eyes. Outside the car was a strange grizzled and bearded angel, wearing a green windproof jacket. He made a rolling motion with his right hand, which Etta took to mean she should lower her window. Manually, of course, as it was an old car.

"Hello," she said unusually shyly, not sure how she should address the heavenly creature.

"Hiya, it looks like you've got a flat tyre," fittingly, the angel had a Scottish accent.

"I know," replied Etta. Just her luck: even her admission into Heaven was flawed.

"If you want, I can help you change it."

"Well, that'd be great, though I never thought we'd need a

car here." She got out and looked around at the brilliant expanse of bright green grass. The sun was shining and the hills rolled down to the bluest sea she'd ever seen, a smattering of islands dotted in the distance.

"On the contrary, you desperately need a car in this part of the world. There's *some* public transport, but it's limited and depends on where you're heading."

The fresh air defogging her thoughts, it finally dawned on Etta that the angel might be as much flesh and blood as she was, and the green Heaven around her might have previously been hidden under the gloomy grey rain clouds.

Dora emerged from the car, a smile printed on lips that articulated an enthusiastic "Hello!" as a border collie materialised from the fields behind the man and ran to greet the two women.

"WORF!" protested the proud Basset in the car. Was someone stealing the limelight from the one and only brave hero of Mull? The border collie put her legs up on the passenger window and the two dogs smelled each other. Leon decided to growl a little, just to establish the hierarchy. The border collie barked happily in protest; clearly, she was not taking him too seriously.

One moment…

She…?

This was a *she*-border-collie. Leon immediately changed his entire demeanour. As Dora let him out of the car, more sniffs were followed by invitations to play and run around. Not an easy task for a short-legged Basset to keep up with such a lively and fast she-doggie, but Leon did his very best, only drawing the line at running as far as she did.

"So, where are you heading?" asked the angel… I beg your pardon, the Scottish man. He had secured the car in place by pulling the handbrake higher and jamming stones behind the wheels, and now he was placing the jack and removing the hubcap, finally revealing the elusive nuts and bolts to Dora and Etta.

"Glengullion Castle," said Dora instinctively. Etta glared at her. So the fibber had known all along the place was nothing but a cold, draughty castle! "I believe that's what you locals call it," added Dora hurriedly, but she was too late to sound convincing.

"Glengullion? Then I should have left you where you were!" For a moment, the angel turned into an angry devil. His smile disappeared, leaving a stern grimace.

"What's the matter?" asked Etta, more hurt than annoyed this time.

The man shook his head. "Ignore me, I'm being stupid. You're probably nothing to do with the silly woman."

"Eilidh McGullion, you mean?"

"Aye, her."

"Has she done something bad to you, if I may ask?"

"Only ruined my life. But here you go," he said, lowering the car to its natural position, removing the jack and placing what was left of the flat tyre back in the car. "You'd better get it repaired properly as soon as you can. Here in the countryside, you never know when you might need a spare tyre again."

"Wait," Etta called to the man, who was already walking away towards the endless fields of cows. "How do we get to the castle?"

"Go all the way down this hill. Shortly after the small bridge, turn right. There's a sign, but you may have missed it in all the bad weather. The road isn't paved, but it's driveable and it will take you all the way to the wretched place."

"Do we owe you anything? Is there something we can do to repay your kindness?"

"Aye, give that woman a brain transplant."

"Leon, come over," Etta called authoritatively to conceal her surprise at such a blunt answer. As someone who didn't ever mince her own words, she wasn't aware how shocking her plain speaking could sometimes be, except when other people did exactly the same back to her.

As for Leon, he merely troubled himself to raise his eyes to

ADRIANA LICIO

the tougher biped of his, but that was all. He had no intention
whatsoever of leaving the cutest lassie-dog the Scottish islands
had to offer, energetic as she was. Turning his back on Etta, he
trotted behind the border collie, his ears flapping up and down
merrily.

"Dora! That dog of yours is pretending he can't hear me."
Leon instantly became Dora's whenever he disobeyed Etta,
which was quite often.

"I see trouble ahead," said Dora. "Maybe we should let him
run around for a while, as he won't come to us right now."

So, there they stood in the middle of nowhere, leaning
against the wet car, their eyes following the hound who seemed
to have forgotten he was a hound and was trotting and running
around behind his agile new friend.

"There won't be enough food to satisfy him tonight if he
keeps this up," said Etta.

As for the man, he went about his business, completely
ignoring both women and dogs. He slowly approached each of
the cows, passing his hands over their coats, whispering a few
words that the animals seemed to enjoy. He checked their heads,
around their ears, their eyes, legs and udders. When he was
satisfied, he moved to the next one and started the process all
over again.

The border collie seemed to be sprinting and galloping in all
directions, but now that the man was further away from them,
the two women could see that the dog was actually running in
large circles around the former angel, every now and then
wagging her way over to him to get her share of caresses. At
times, she pretended to charge the two women, only to wag her
tail when she got close to them. And all the while, a short-legged
Basset was doing his utmost to copy her.

"Gotcha!" said Etta, catching Leon by the collar as he
followed his companion. Leon pretended to be offended by the
brutal seizing and resisted Etta's efforts to return him to the back
seat of the car – never an easy operation when the Basset

30

wouldn't cooperate, but Etta managed somehow. He would never admit to the truth, but Leon was exhausted and was actually grateful to Etta for rescuing him. Still, that collie was a charming she-dog. His eyes didn't leave her sleek form until the car rounded a bend and she was no longer in sight. He'd find her again, he promised himself as he cuddled up for a good, restorative nap. Of course he'd find her! Didn't he have the very bestest nose on the Scottish island?

5

GLENGULLION CASTLE

More little roads, more drystone walls, more rocks later, the Fiat 500 passed one more line of trees, rounded a final bend and the view suddenly opened up on to grassy plains, the sky and ocean a backdrop to the most romantic honey-coloured stone building with grey slate roofs.

There could be no doubt it was a Scottish castle, consisting of a rectangular keep surrounded by a multitude of turrets with conical roofs and crow-stepped gables, adorned with tall, narrow windows, quoins and corbels. The sight was so breathtaking, it instantly reminded Dora of Sleeping Beauty's castle in illustrated books for children.

"But that's a real castle," cried Etta, in such a state of wonder that her foot pushed against the brake, causing her two passengers to be jolted forward and abruptly returned to their seats. Dora beamed, finally satisfied with her decision, her hands clasped, her eyes full of delight.

"You knew all along, didn't you?" asked Etta.

"Well… it was meant to be a surprise. I was sad it had been spoiled by people's reactions in Tobermory."

"That didn't spoil anything, actually. I never thought it would be this lovely, I imagined some austere pile of stones…"

"Scottish people can be very romantic, you know. They call this the Scots Baronial style, and it's similar to the Royal Family's Balmoral Castle. Just a wee bit smaller."

"And much less grand, but infinitely cosier, I'd say."

"The best wine comes from the smaller barrels." Dora quoted an old Italian saying, never more proud than when she managed to please her friend.

"Will we be staying here? For real?" Dora nodded gleefully. "Let's go, then," and such was Etta's enthusiasm that she stalled the engine once more.

As Etta parked in front of the central tower, a tall, slim woman with a poker face and piercing grey eyes, dressed in a severe wool tweed softened only by a silver Gaelic brooch, was waiting for them. She must have spotted the car as it emerged from the woodland.

"Hello," said Dora in a friendly tone, getting out of the car. "You must be Edwina."

"I am," said Edwina, scrutinising the two women with her icy stare. She had to be older than Etta and Dora, but she stood straight and stiff. Her high forehead below a back-combed grey bob, her facial muscles, the line of her lips and her long eyebrows seemed to be motionless. "I take it you're the guests from Italy."

"Exactly. I'm Dora, this is Etta, and the gentleman getting out of the car is Leon."

"I see. You know, then, that Eilidh is away for the next week at least, so she asked me to show you to your rooms."

"Do you do the housekeeping for her?"

"No." The woman, if you could read her at all, seemed to be offended by the question. "But the castle is old and rambling, so she wanted someone to show you around."

"If it is too much trouble, we'll show ourselves around," said Etta, clearly already fed up with the woman's stuck-up ways.

"Trust me, it'd be better if you come with me." The woman turned her back on the main tower and led them to one of the smaller turrets on the left. They entered an austere stone passage that led to a dark, narrow spiral staircase.

"Three storeys up, no lift," Edwina announced. "Old buildings can be rather tiresome."

Even the romantic Dora gasped. It was not only due to the prospect of the narrow stairs, but coming from the sunny outdoors, she felt chilled inside as if they had moved underground.

"Wait," Etta suggested. "We'd better bring a few bags from the car, save ourselves having to make too many ascents." So back out into the welcome sunshine they went, fetching as much as they could manage to carry from the car. Edwina didn't offer to help with the carrying, and Dora noticed the scowl her friend sent the stiff woman's way.

It was a hard job to manoeuvre the luggage up along the narrow stairs, to the point that even Edwina offered to take the smallest, lightest bag. The only one who really enjoyed the climb was Leon. He loved musty odours of any sort, and besides, he didn't have to carry any luggage.

When they reached the second floor, Edwina announced, "Let's stop here before moving upstairs so I can show you the kitchen that you can use to prepare your meals."

They entered a large dark room that made Dora and Etta's hearts sink. There was a severe stone fireplace so tall that the two women could have stood inside it, leaving room enough for a couple more people. A dirty old kitchen stove may have been white in the past, but was now an unpleasant shade of yellowy brown. A tall and narrow window was covered by an awful mustard-coloured curtain, making sure no sunlight whatsoever disturbed the gloomy interior. The huge dark pine cupboard looked as if it would open to reveal a dead body rather than cooking utensils, while a low stone sink and a few rundown chairs around a heavy square table completed the cheerless picture.

"The fridge," and Edwina pointed to a small appliance that,

like the cooker, might once have been white. It at least had the advantage of being so noisy, it drowned out any inadvertent exclamations of shock that might have escaped from Dora and Etta's lips. "Make sure you keep all your food either in there or in the cupboard, so it's safe from mice."

"You mean there are mice scurrying around?" Dora asked, horrified.

"They tend to abound in old places," was the cool reply.

"Do you ever light the fire?" asked Etta, rubbing her hands up and down her arms as if to ward off the cold dampness from settling into her bones.

"Not in the kitchen. You'd need to burn an entire tree each day just to get a modicum of warmth. Let's go upstairs to your rooms," and turning on her heel, Edwina stalked out of the kitchen, leaving the small bag she had been carrying to add to Etta and Dora's burden. Dora wanted to turn tail and run. Her shoulders sagged under the weight of her mortification and guilt, all her daydreams and happiness having left her. Etta stared at her, but for once bit her lip as if to remind herself to be patient with this hopeless friend of hers.

Up they went in total silence. In the third-floor corridor, they passed a decrepit grandfather clock that looked as ancient as the castle itself. Etta wasn't pleased.

"I hope it won't chime every hour throughout the night. I hate that!"

"It's not worked for decades," Edwina replied sharply, looking Etta up and down. Then she opened the oak door in front of her and showed the trio from Italy into a large room. A mahogany four-poster bed was dressed in heavy tartan fabric. In the corner was a fireplace of a more normal size than that in the kitchen, but no fire was laid. At least, Dora noticed, there were a few logs in an iron basket next to it. A bureau stood to the side of a window covered by a curtain in the same dull blue and green tartan as that on the bed, and a bulky chest of drawers and a cumbersome wardrobe that could pack in even more bodies than the kitchen cupboard completed the dubious delights on offer.

"I thought you might want to share this bedroom, keep each other company," intoned Edwina. "But one of you could use the smaller bedroom on the other side of the hallway if you prefer."

"Oh no, we will stick together," Dora replied hastily, not daring to think of spending the night by herself in such a grim place, especially when she looked up at the large portrait between the fireplace and the window and met the mean eyes of a severe looking man wearing a green and blue kilt. Behind him, people dressed in tatters on whose faces she could read despair stood beside the smoking remains of their houses. But what impressed itself upon her the most was the cruel smile stretching between the long sideburns, the icy glare in the man's grey eyes and the smugness on his face.

"Who is he?" gasped Etta, following her friend's gaze.

"That's Lord McGullion, the man who built the castle."

"He's got a rather cold expression. And who are those poor people behind him?" asked Dora.

"Their houses were burned down the day the man decided he wanted to build his castle. The elderly, children, pregnant women – all were left without a roof over their heads in a single day."

"How could he enjoy living in the castle after causing such pain?"

"He had very little time to enjoy the castle. An old woman from the village cursed him, told him he would never live in the castle, but would be condemned to walk the place forevermore after his death."

"What?" asked Dora, not too sure she'd understood – or even wanted to understand – the second part of the curse.

"I don't know what it means," said Edwina with the smug grin and complacent nod of the head of someone who's heard the very question she'd been waiting for. "All I can tell you is that Lord McGullion died in strange circumstances just a few months after he and his family moved here. An old suit of armour in the Weapons Hall fell, the mace hitting the man's head. It is also said that his spirit never left the castle, as many people – those brave enough to spend the night at Glengullion," the smug grin widened, "swear they've seen him time and time again."

Dora wowed. Usually, she would love a good ghost story, were it not for the fact that the place was far too spooky. And worse, she was going to spend a whole month of nights right here. The painting unnerved her. There was something weird about it, as if the man's cold eyes were alive and looking straight at her.

As for Etta, Dora noticed her eyes had left the painting and were taking in Edwina. There was something triumphantly disdainful behind the woman's grey eyes, as icy as Lord McGullion's, that was too challenging even for Etta to gain any satisfaction from dismissing her story as rubbish. Instead, Etta turned her attention back to the accommodation.

"Will we have to go outside to use the toilet or is there a chamber pot under the bed?"

Edwina pretended to be horrified. "Of course, there is an en suite," and she showed them to the facilities adjacent to the bedroom: a brown bathroom suite that looked like it hadn't been modernised since the 1970s. "During your stay, you can also use the reading room on the ground floor. I left some logs next to the fireplace, and you can get more from beside the stables in front of the castle. I will show you the reading room if you so wish."

"Please," said Etta.

Down the spiral staircase they went, returning to the small hall on the ground floor and continuing into an equally narrow corridor. On either side of the corridor, niches contained different marble busts, their cold faces lit sinisterly from below.

"These are all the descendants of the McGullion clan."

In the upper middle niche, Dora started as she recognised the laird whose portrait she had encountered upstairs. Again, although the face was rendered in marble, she had the same feeling of the eyes not only staring her up and down, but also following her. Even when she reached the end of the corridor and glanced back, she saw the cold marble face still glaring at her. She hurried into the room that Edwina, Etta and Leon had just entered, anxious to catch up with the others.

The reading room was the nicest they had seen so far. Panelled oak walls housed shelves and cabinets filled with books, while the room itself offered a tartan sofa, an old piano, a small card table and, most gratifyingly, a fireplace of a normal size. It was by no means a cheerful place, but it was definitely less disquieting than the upstairs rooms.

"Is this all we're allowed?" Etta asked. "A whole castle, and we only get three rooms?"

"The other parts of the castle are being restored," said Edwina. "It's rather a large place to manage for a family that's no longer rich."

"The thing is," Dora finally found her voice, "the pictures Eilidh showed me were quite different…"

"What pictures?" Edwina asked suspiciously.

"The ones on the Homeswapping International Circle website."

"I don't know what to say. Does the castle look different?"

"No, the outside of the castle looks exactly the same. It's just in the pictures, the rooms seemed more…" Dora had to make a great effort to find the appropriate words, but then even she gave up any attempt at tact and diplomacy as disappointment ebbed from her guts. "Just lighter, cosier, more cheerful, I guess."

"Well, I don't know what kind of pictures Eilidh sent out. All I know is she's very good with her camera, and with those little tricks she calls post-production work…"

"Post-production my tooth!" Etta – just as Dora had feared – exploded. "If she's shown photoshopped pictures that are not faithful to the real state of the building, we will bring the issue to the attention of the circle… ouch!" The last cry was due to a powerful kick in the shin by Dora, who thought Etta had gone too far.

"You're free to do all that," said Edwina indifferently. "Anyway, Eilidh will be back in a week's time. Should you decide to stay, you'll be free to discuss any issue you have directly with her. I hope you will enjoy Mull in the meantime."

She reached the door, then turned back to add a parting shot.

"There are candles in the card table's drawer. You'll want to take a few upstairs with you in case of a power cut."

"Do they happen frequently?"

"Not frequently, but they happen." Then, as if she was suddenly worried or repenting of being so cold, or both, she hastily added, "And try to avoid the smaller bedroom."

"Is there a ghost?" Etta asked cheekily.

"It seems Lord McGullion used the room as his personal study."

Before leaving, Edwina asked if they had her phone number, just in case, and Dora replied that Eilidh had supplied it. It seemed now that her time in the castle was coming to an end, Edwina felt more communicative, as she also announced that the next day, the farmers' fair would be held on the castle grounds, so they were not to worry if they saw goings on and a continuous stream of people in the main gardens. Their part of the garden, Edwina explained, along with the castle's inner gardens would be undisturbed if they preferred to stay away from the locals.

"Oh no," Dora said, "it'll be fun to meet people and get to know them, and we can buy some fresh produce."

The light-hearted answer was maybe not to Madam's tastes, as the door was shut behind her with a powerful slam!

6

AN EERIE NIGHT

The good thing about Scotland at this time of year, Etta thought, was that even at nine o'clock in the evening, there was still plenty of daylight left. The two women, after much scrubbing and cleaning followed by many trips to take their shopping to the kitchen, the rest of their luggage up the spiral staircase to the third floor, decided to have their dinner in the reading room.

Etta had initially rumbled, "By the time we carry it down there from the kitchen, the food will be cold." But she was wrong, it was still warm and the fire was crackling pleasantly because even in July, an old castle in Scotland can be cold. The seafood platter starter had proven to be divinely good, and Dora had made an exquisite fish soup that warmed their souls even before it warmed their stomachs. Leon had loved his share immensely and confirmed that a little slice of smoked salmon on toast was an enticing appetiser before a meal of fish. He then found the stone tiles next to the fire gorgeously warm as he snuggled down for a nap – Bassets instinctively know how fundamentally important a good sleep is for tough adventurers. From the library shelves, Dora had chosen one of the 44 *Scotland Street* volumes by

Alexander McCall and was reading aloud for the enjoyment of Etta.

It was into this comfortable scene of relaxation that Leon suddenly raised his head and launched a deep growl towards the window.

"What were you dreaming?" Etta asked him, smiling. "Of chasing some fierce enemies and rescuing the most charming she-Basset?"

It happened at times that Leon would dream too intensely, waking up enacting a ferocious fight only to find out all was peaceful and safe around him. In those instances, as the women gently teased him, he'd wag his tail, feel just a little silly and let them have a good laugh safe in the reassuring knowledge they had a valiant warrior watching over them.

This time, though, Leon continued to growl.

"Come on, Leon, stop pretending. We're just reading a story about a silly dog being lost and found, but we're not laughing at you. We know full well the dog catchers would never dare take you..."

"Shhh!" Dora silenced her friend. "What was that?"

"I didn't hear anyth..." but then, Etta did. Very slowly, very softly, "Too, too, tooo" followed by a deep and booming "TOO, TOO, TOO, TOOO".

Then silence.

"The piano?" Etta asked, looking at the instrument on the other side of the room.

"But its lid is closed."

Again, the tune played, slowly, then just a touch louder. "Too, too, tooo." Pause. "TOO, TOO, TOO, TOOO".

There was no doubt now: it was coming from the piano.

"I know that tune," whispered Etta as more notes came out, following each other as if elfin hands were tickling the ivories.

"Bach's Toccata in D minor," said Dora.

"But still, the piano lid is closed," the two murmured in unison, and then they got up in perfect synchronisation. Leon, still growling, joined them, staying well behind their legs. Courage should never be confused with recklessness.

They moved a few steps towards the piano, which was apparently at rest – apart from the running melody.

"*Shall we open it?*" Dora's eyes telegraphed to Etta without her pronouncing a single word.

"*NOOO!*" Etta's wide bulging eyes telegraphed back. She turned around and went over to the card table, next to which she'd seen a long pole of the type used to open and close curtains hung too high for hands to reach. Returning to her starting position, she manoeuvred the stick under the piano lid and, after a few failed attempts and in perfect time with the deep final note of the melody, slammed it open.

After a silent pause, the music began again with a blast of lighter notes. To their horror, the two women could see the piano keys moving up and down as if invisible hands were playing.

After the *toccata* comes the *fugue* – *fuga* in their native Italian – which means flee, and that's exactly what they did. They rushed into the corridor, Dora feeling the cold observation of McGullion's marble bust, and up the stairs, not stopping until they reached not just their bedroom, but their bed, diving beneath the blankets as if only there could they feel in any way safe. Leon, who had turned into the Carl Lewis of Bassets, jumped right under the covers with them.

Only when their hearts had stopped galloping in their chests like a herd of wild beasts during the migration in the Kenyan Masai Mara could their lips finally utter a few words.

"Under the blankets, we can't see him," said Dora.

"But HE can locate us," Etta continued her friend's train of thought.

"Shall we have a little peep around just in case?"

"OK, but let's do it together," and slowly, slowly, slowly, two heads came out from under the blankets. The room, as ugly as it was, didn't look any worse than it had earlier in the day. The fire was lit, the wardrobe closed. On the desk were some familiar photos and postcards Dora had placed to make the room feel more homely.

Maybe *whatever-it-was* had decided not to follow them upstairs.

But when Dora looked at the painting, she gave a gasp.

The cruel man had winked at her!

She cried out and called for Etta's attention, but her friend was not to be fooled this time.

"It's ugly, but it's definitely just a painting. I can't see anything wrong with his eyes. It must have been your imagination."

"No, it wasn't. And I'll tell you more, it's not the first time he's been staring at us. This afternoon, his eyes followed me when Edwina showed us around the room."

"I'm looking at him now and can't see anything wrong with it… I mean, him," Etta corrected herself just in case the ghostly aristocrat was touchy.

"I know, it's fine now, but two minutes ago, he winked at me. I'm telling you!"

"OK, we will check the room. In fact, that would be a good idea before we lock the door for the night."

"Should we spend the night in the castle at all?"

Etta looked at the fire, at the blankets, as if weighing up her options.

"It's better than sleeping in the car or getting lost on the way back to Tobermory."

Dora nodded hesitantly, but couldn't help asking her next question.

"Locking the door… will it stop him?"

"Not sure. I'm no expert, but it will certainly make me feel a little better."

They climbed out of bed.

"woooRFFF!"

The two women were startled, their hearts skipping quite a few beats, as Leon protested the fact they were both abandoning him, leaving the safety of the bed for the uncertainty of the room beyond. The women stared at him, hissing at him to be quiet.

"Or you will be left on guard outside the door, all alone," Etta added cruelly. But that long, loud bark, rising in volume, had really scared her. What if the ghost had been reminded there were living people under his roof?

They listened tensely for a few moments, but nothing happened. They checked that the wardrobe was empty, that no one – human or inhuman – was hiding under their bed, then moved on to the bulky chest of drawers and decided to push it in front of the locked door as an extra level of security, even if they might break their backs under the strain.

"If *he* manages to move the chest, at least it will make some noise," Etta said, the underlying text "That is, if he doesn't walk through solid objects" remaining unspoken. But in the face of extreme horrors, one has to put up some defences, so Etta was determined to delude herself that a locked and blocked door would keep them very safe indeed.

It was then that they heard it.

DONG! DONG! DONG...

The pendulum clock in the hallway was chiming. Dora counted the strokes.

"It's midnight!"

"At least the sun will rise early."

"The shorter the night, the better. But didn't Edwina say the clock was broken?"

"Never mind what she says."

Dora ventured over to the window. Looking out, she saw a ghostly face peering back at her from a window in the round tower opposite.

"Look, Etta, it's dreadful!" she cried.

Etta was just in time to see the floating face before it disappeared into the darkness.

"Whatever that was, we'd better get back into the bed," she said. "We just need to do one more thing first," and with a pole similar to the one she had used for opening the piano downstairs, she now hooked the lower corner of the tartan curtain and lifted it over the painting. With some effort, she managed to drape the curtain over the frame until the whole face and part of the body of Lord McGullion was covered.

"I feel better now," said Etta, satisfied. Doing practical things helped her drive fear away. All the same, once the three were back in bed, she repeated a reassuring mantra.

"This will pass. Everything, good or bad, comes to an end, and this will too."

SATURDAY

SATURDAY
MORNING

I disliked that woman from the first moment I set eyes on her. So opinionated. If I had any doubts about what we planned to do, they fell away when I spoke to her. I mistrust those green feline eyes. They seem to notice every detail. Yes, she surely is a real nosy parker. The other woman seems like a puppet in her hands. OK, she might not be inherently bad herself, but how does the old saying go? Birds of a feather flock together. No matter who we are, we're all responsible for the choices we make when we select our friends.

As for Mr T, he did an excellent job last night. I can't wait to speak to Mrs Opinionated now. But I mustn't be so impatient, and besides, all my energy today will be devoted to the fair. We need to speak to as many people as we can. Not only locals, but tourists. They should know what is about to happen. We can't lose it all, not now we're finally poised to reap the fruits of our years of labour.

And Katherine? My dearest Katherine... I owe it to her. I'm so sorry Eilidh is giving it all up, but young people today are so stupidly selfish. That Jeremy is no help, just a spineless idiot, but at least he's not an obstacle either. With time, I'm sure I will be able to convince Eilidh, but right now we're in the middle of an emergency.

Extreme situations require extreme remedies. I confess I can't wait *for tonight. They will see what they are up against and this time, they will be leaving the island for good, along with their stupid plans.*

Goodness! It's time to go.

7

THE GLENGULLION FARMERS' FAIR

They fell asleep only once the dawn broke, and when they woke up much later, it was almost nine o'clock. Now, with the sun filtering through the window, even their room seemed serene and normal. Definitely still cold and draughty, but there was little to remind them of the horrors of the night.

The two women looked at each other, both wondering if they had fallen prey to some form of hysteria. A ghost? In the 21st century? It made no sense.

In the spirit of their newfound courage, Dora removed the curtain from the painting, looking immediately as if she regretted doing so. Lord McGullion really did have a scary face, his eyes and countenance were so cruel, but in the end, even the imaginative woman had to accept that he was no more than an image on a painting. His grim stare was as immobile and frozen as that of any other portrait in any art gallery the world over.

As for Leon, after indulging in a good lie-in nestled in the bedlinen, he decided he deserved, in this order, a short morning walk, a breakfast worthy of the name, and then a longer walk to explore his new realm. To make his feelings clear and ensure his requirements weren't – heaven forbid – overlooked, he launched into his customary trio of barks.

ADRIANA LICIO

"Worf, worf, woRRRRf!"

"I'm about to prepare the breakfast," Dora reassured him.

"And I'll take the dog out to do his business," offered Etta. "But first, we will accompany you to the kitchen." She nearly added, "To make sure everything is OK in there, and in the castle as a whole," but she didn't want to discuss the night's happenings before she had drunk a good cup of coffee.

They moved the chest of drawers back to its usual position and were slowly opening the door when all of a sudden, a powerful "WORF!" filled the room behind them. The two women slammed the door shut in panic.

"What was that for?" stammered Etta.

Dora burst out laughing. "Just Leon expressing his impatience at how slow we are this morning!"

"That dog will be the end of us," snapped Etta, wrenching the door open and glaring at the quadruped.

Leon who, when the women had been startled, had scampered to the far end of the room, fearing something terrifying had happened, now marched ahead of them and left the room, his head and tail up. Blue blood ran in his veins, and it showed. Or at least, that's what the hound thought without any pretence at false modesty.

Everything was fine in the kitchen and Dora felt happy to be left there all alone. In any case, Leon's appetite was such the two were back by the time the brown bread from Tobermory's bakery was toasted and the coffees were ready. Placing everything on a tray, Dora had carried it all downstairs to the reading room, not particularly enjoying traipsing up and down the narrow spiral staircase, but conceding that it was better than eating in the dark kitchen. At least the piano was silent and still, remaining as inanimate as the portrait in the bedroom.

"Perhaps we should bring the toaster, the kettle and all the cups and spoons down here, so whenever we want a hot drink, we don't have to climb all the way upstairs," she suggested.

Etta was relieved, not so much at the practicality of the idea itself, but more because of the cosy familiarity of the suggestion. She'd always admired Dora's organisational skills. In any house, she'd improve the way things were done, devising a continuous but never bothersome process. If the universe tended to entropy, Dora was insurance that things would be sparkling clean and well organised, no matter what. Where Etta had bouts of energy, when she'd clean and sweep and do her best in a once-in-a-while heroic but exhausting effort, Dora would create systems that almost seemed to take care of themselves. Where Etta would cease and desist when faced with ineluctable disorder, Dora found it a challenge to discover new ways to do things more efficiently.

"How profound I am this morning," muttered Etta to herself.

"What?"

"Nothing, I just love this biscuit. What is it, by the way?"

"It's from the local bakery," said Dora, the words not sounding as enthusiastic as Etta would have expected from her friend. "It's an apple crumble biscuit with oats and cinnamon. Delicious, isn't it?"

"I forgot to mention, when I was out with Leon, we found a few signs for walks where the forest starts. One shorter track goes to the stone circle, the other mentions a lighthouse... that's a good thirty-minute walk, but we should go there some time."

"Of course, dear," was the distracted answer.

Etta looked at her friend and finally had an epiphany. Possibly her mind had become more acute than usual because of the adrenaline that must be running through her body. Dora's eyes, above that shy smile, were not sparkling. She had not reacted to discovering they were close to a lighthouse, any more than she had reacted during the journey to the island at the prospect of visiting Iona or going on a whale-watching tour. She had not clasped her hands in one of her long enraptured trances, even when faced with the garden's grass shining under the sun, the honey-coloured walls of Glengullion Castle with its turrets and gables, the ocean at its back. She had reacted to all of that, certainly, just less keenly than usual. It was as if everything in Etta's friend had been dialled down.

Yes, there had definitely been something weird about Dora recently, but even Etta could not put her finger on what it was. Maybe the sensitive woman had had a premonition about their stay at the castle and the night ghost? Dora was the kind of creature who could sense things long before Etta's rational mind could grab, analyse and explain them.

But what exactly was the premonition about? Was something evil threatening them?

∽

AFTER A QUICK BREAKFAST, THE TWO WOMEN WENT OUT TO EXPLORE the fair. During her short walk with Leon, Etta had noticed the stalls had already been set up, the farmers were putting the finishing touches to their displays and the crowds were flocking in.

They had just entered the area of the garden earmarked for the fair when they came face to face with Edwina in her tweed. On the lapel of the jacket, she had pinned her silver Gaelic brooch with its beautiful flowing lines. This was the only concession to frills and frivolities in her clothing, but no such concession found a place in her words.

"Good morning," she said, scrutinising the three of them as if she were a CT scan machine.

"Good morning," said Dora with a light smile.

"Good morning," said Etta, her tone defiant.

"Did you sleep well?"

"Very much so, thank you," Etta answered almost before the question was out. The woman looked a little startled. Maybe Etta's reply had been too emphatic. Or was the woman expecting an altogether different answer?

"Do you have any plans for today?" Edwina asked.

"We want to explore the fair, then later, we will have a little walk through the woodland," said Dora. "Etta informs me there's a path leading to a lighthouse…"

"Be careful, that path is a little unstable. Make sure you don't fall into the sea," and with that, Edwina disappeared in the direction of some stalls in the distance.

"I can't stand that woman!" Etta cried.

"I know, she's quite abrupt. Is this why you didn't tell her what happened last night?"

"I'm sure she would have laughed at us," Etta admitted. "And I couldn't give her that satisfaction."

"You're right, she would have asked us what we expected from an old Scottish castle. Still," said Dora, looking at the idyllic building at their back, "what do you think about last night?"

"Same as you," said Etta, following not only Dora's gaze, but also her train of thought. "Now that the sun is shining and people's chatter is filling our ears, it seems incredible."

"Did we imagine it all?"

"We were tired, it had been a long day – the driving, the sea crossing, the road, the stupid tyre…"

"The shock of finding the accommodation was so very different from what we were expecting…"

"What *you* were expecting. I thought we would be staying in a normal house."

"Still, I thought it'd be a… *normal* castle."

"Edwina's cold welcome…"

"The cold in general. Just a hallucination of some sort, then?"

"Maybe, but let's see what happens tonight before jumping to conclusions."

"I wish Eilidh had been here to welcome us. She sent me such a nice message this morning and confirmed she will be back next Friday. I didn't dare mention our misgivings about the place on WhatsApp…"

"Well, you could mention that a proper heating system would have been very much appreciated."

"You're right, but I still find it so hard to tell people what I should tell them."

"That's why we love you, you're such a gentle soul," said Etta, hugging her friend.

"Oh, Etta," said Dora, moved.

"Worfff!" Leon approved.

"But now let's see what this fair is all about. I need to walk a little in the sunshine as my legs have gone stiff with cold," added Etta hastily. She could never be sentimental for too long without starting to feel awkward.

They had not walked far before they recognised the man who had come to their rescue the previous day, along with – to Leon's delight – his lively border collie. His stall was rather small compared with the others, but a colourful rubber cow on the side caught the eye, as did the tall brown truckles of cheese behind him. On the counter in front of him, one cheese had been cut open to reveal a light creamy colour inside, and a wooden chopping board was filled with bite-size morsels to try.

He greeted the two women with a friendlier manner than when he had left them the day before, introduced himself as Josh McIntosh and his dog as Bree and, as the collie joyfully teased Leon, invited the two women to try his cheese. After introducing herself and Etta, and gesturing at the Basset bounding after the new love of his life, letting Josh know the dog's name, Dora did as invited.

"This is so very good," she said, her eyes half-closed as if to enhance the experience. "So nutty and aromatic…"

"That's because our cows are free to graze for a good part of the year. You'll get a slightly different flavour depending on the season the cheese was made."

"It really reminds me of my grandfather's cheese," said Dora. "The milk went almost straight from his cows to the vat."

"That's very much the same for us, we don't pasteurise our milk for cheese making. I don't want an industrial product but an artisanal one, with more flavours and more variations, and much healthier as its micronutrients haven't been killed by some industrial savagery..." The man stopped his speech abruptly, as if aware he had revealed his views more than he ever intended to.

Dora smiled at him. "You're absolutely right, and I'm sure people with a vision like yours can do so much for the island in general. We don't need just one more anonymous cheese on a supermarket shelf..."

"We weren't expecting to see you on the castle grounds," Etta interrupted. "Not after what you said about Eilidh."

The man showed them the label on the cheese form. It had the castle logo on it and indicated its contents was Glengullion Cheese.

"You work for Eilidh?" Etta cried in surprise.

"I joined her aunt, Katherine McGullion, a couple of years ago, and got hooked on the job. I really wasn't a nice person then..." he grinned guiltily. "Not that I believe I'm a wonderful person now, but I'm much better than I was. But that's another story. Katherine hired me for a cheese-making project, we researched cow breeds that could live on the island where pastures are not as abundant or as lush as on the mainland. We tried, we failed, we learned a lot, we failed again, then we discovered some Swedish cow breeds were adapting quite well to our soil. We found the right type of hay for their winter forage and realised that our cheese was no longer too hard and dry. It had no cracks, and tasted neither too sharp nor too bland. In fact, it was... it was... well..."

"Tasty and magnificent!" said Dora.

"Yes, exactly. That is... I hope so," the man flushed and stammered as if a big tough bull had turned suddenly into a shy calf.

"Is Eilidh's aunt on these grounds today?"

"Katherine passed away a year ago and that stupid woman took over."

"Well, you can still continue your project with her, I guess..."

"No, you're very wrong," the bull instantly returned with all its vigour, kicking a milk bucket against the rubber cow. Luckily, it was empty. "You see, the first thing she decided to do..."

"Josh! JOSH!" Edwina was calling for him from another stall a few metres away.

"Let me see what she wants. Sorry if I... scared you. It was nothing against you." Before rushing over to Edwina, he put the bucket back in place and pressed a packet of cheese into Dora's hands. Then he ran, Bree bounding joyously after him.

The friends had no time to comment on the man's weird behaviour before a woman came over to them and got down on her knees, fussing Leon as he wagged his tail in welcome.

"Hello, cutie, do you recognise me? Such a good boy, you are." As she turned towards them, Dora and Etta recognised the sweet round face of Letitia, the woman they had met with Tom outside the Co-op in Tobermory. Once she had paid proper homage to Leon, the woman got up, staring at the two women blankly.

"Hello," Dora said, warmly as ever. "How are you?"

"I'm... I'm fine, I guess."

Etta felt sure that although the woman had recognised Leon, she hadn't a clue who his two bipeds were. It was happening again – people only had eyes for the dog.

"Are you here by yourself?" Dora asked.

"No, I'm with Edwina and all," and she indicated towards one of the stalls, but they couldn't really see it through the crowds. "You can come over if you wish."

"We'll certainly do that at some point," said Etta.

"I'll get back to them, see if they need me," said Letitia, turning away. "Be sure to bring the dog with you."

"More likely it will be the dog bringing us with him," Etta answered, and finally the woman relaxed enough to laugh.

8

NOT IN MY BACK YARD!

A s they walked around, the next stall they came to was run by Sandra, the woman they had met in the fishery the previous day. She was selling beautiful framed landscape photographs. Possibly of Mull, they were rich with atmosphere and colour. In a corner of the stall was a small selection showing weddings on the island, and another included portraits of the young and the elderly that seemed to Dora to look into her heart.

"Those are beautiful!" she exclaimed.

"Indeed," even Etta had to acknowledge that.

"Thank you," said Sandra, a large smile on her bright pink-painted lips. "I'm glad you like them."

"But I thought you said you were just tourists on the island. How come you have a stall of your own at the fair?" Etta couldn't help asking.

"That's true, we are visitors, but as my husband Grayson mentioned, we tend to spend a lot of time on Mull, and we want to be a part of the community as much as possible, participating in local events."

"Are you a professional photographer?"

"I wish!" the woman replied with intensity. Wearing a flat Trinity wax cap and enshrouded in a brown leather raincoat, she was definitely conforming to the country stereotype. "I'm a photographer in my spare time, but I'd love to turn it into a profession. It would give me more time to spend with my husband and organise things, not to mention that I simply love to go picture hunting!"

"But?" asked Etta, too used to hearing the flip side of the coin from people to wait for Sandra to get to the point.

"But, as with most things we love, it's hard to make them pay the bills. So I work as an assistant for a large company, but as a part-timer, I tend to get more holidays, which I mostly spend on Mull. It's such a wonderful place, we'd do anything to keep it unspoiled." She spoke the last bit passionately, as if Etta and Dora were threatening to do just what she feared. Behind her round black glasses, an unblinking stare seemed to challenge them. Then her eyes flitted to another stall in the middle of the crowd. And Etta spotted a wheelchair. Grayson was evidently over there.

"Has your husband got a stall of his own?"

"No, he's running that one with other people. Other volunteers who are determined to defend the island no matter what."

"Sandra," a voice called from behind Etta and Dora, "I was just looking for you. I've brought my daughter to see your wonderful photos, as she's getting married in the autumn... I hope I'm not intruding?"

"Not at all," Etta said. "We were just leaving."

"See you later," Dora added.

Sandra said bye to them, then greeted the two newcomers.

"We won't be short of people to talk to in this place," said Etta.

"It really is a happy community of welcoming folk," agreed Dora.

"I'm not actually too sure about the 'welcoming' part. They're very chatty, but it's like they resent us for being foreigners."

"Do you think so?" Dora was getting used to falling from the clouds whenever Etta tried to remove the rose-tinted glasses through which she viewed the world.

As they moved on, a young lad who was distributing leaflets didn't hesitate to place one in each of their hands.

"Discover the new face of Mull," read Dora. "The new jobs and opportunities the new development will create for all the islanders. Join our presentation at noon in the castle grounds. Gary Mason."

"The 'new' word is rather overused," Etta commented dryly, turning the leaflet to see a computer-generated image of Glengullion Castle towering above a large swimming pool and golf course. Various smiling people milled around, dressed in fanciful summer hats and posh sundresses as if they were on the French Riviera.

"Oh!" Dora gasped, not sure she liked what she was seeing.

"Gosh!" cried Etta enthusiastically. "Why didn't Eilidh mention we should have waited a couple of years or so before visiting? It seems they intend to turn this place into something good."

Dora looked at the picture, then at the castle as it was, and shook her head, not convinced.

A woman with curly reddish-brown hair that was turning silver approached them. Thick-lensed glasses didn't prevent her grey eyes from shining and twinkling as she, without preamble, tore the invitation from Dora's hands and replaced it with a new leaflet. With the energy, and speed, of a rabbit in a field of carrots, she turned to Etta, who only just managed to save her own copy from the brutal attack.

"Don't bother with that rubbish, come to this instead," the woman said, holding up her leaflet and tapping a few lines of text on it. This was not a beautifully designed invitation with a nice photograph on the back, but a simple A5 sheet printed in black and white on a basic photocopier. Even someone as accommodating as Dora would have resented the brusque intrusion, had it not been for the fact that the woman had two captivating dimples which, along with her curly hair and rosy-apple cheeks, made her look like a grown-up version of a cherub. She stood in front of them and explained her point of view in such a broad Scottish accent that the two women weren't able to decipher much. All they really understood was that her manner might be overbearing, but her intentions were good.

After an uninterrupted two-minute flow of words, the woman stopped to draw in a breath. It was at this point that doubt finally struck her.

"You are nae Scottish, are ye?"

"No, we are…"

"Foreigners!" The woman went on, evidently making an effort to speak something that resembled English a little more. "You didnae… didn't understand much, did ye?"

"I'm afraid we're still completely in the dark," replied Dora, laughing.

"Oh my, my husband David always tells me I should calm down. But there's so much to achieve, how can I be calm? Look, there are some very nasty people over here who want to brainwash the locals into believing that it'd be *wonderful* to create a luxury hotel and spa, or whatever they call those stupid fashionable places where you enter exhausted and leave fit and well, but with your bank account much thinner, right here in the castle."

"That's the way of the world nowadays," said Etta pragmatically.

"Maybe, but not on our island, not in our castle!" Another torrent of not-so-connected words flooded the two friends. "I'm not too good at explaining it, but such a project would in the long run sweep away our small indie shops and replace them with designer clothing stores for the rich and upmarket restaurants that serve you the smallest bite of food in a huge dish and charge you 50 quid to leave you starving. Not to mention they would take the castle away from us."

"Doesn't the castle belong to Eilidh McGullion?" When the woman paused to breathe and get some oxygen into her lungs, giving Etta just enough time to pose her question, she jumped in.

"The silly child! She should know better. Money isn't everything in life. Not to mention poor Josh... and us. What about us?"

Now the two women were staring at her as if she were a lunatic, not wanting to provoke or encourage her. At least the woman still had enough of a hold on reality to read her audience's faces.

"Och, I have nae made myself clear, have I?" She shook her head and, before anyone had time to answer, she found the solution. "Come along. Tam... I mean Tom will explain it all. Come along!"

She gestured towards the stall where Grayson's wheelchair was surrounded by a group of people. The two women glanced at each other and decided by tacit agreement not to contradict the woman. At least she was taking them towards the crowds rather than to an isolated spot. If she turned on them, the other people would surely help them to deal with her.

As they walked the 10 metres to the stall, the woman made sure to squeeze as many words in as she could.

"I'm Debbie, by the way. I attend to the elderly in Tobermory and just beyond, though David says we're getting old ourselves and will soon need someone to take care of us. But I'm not afraid of getting old, I've lived my days to the full. I've lived on a magnificent island in a stone cottage. And I've helped so many people's parents, I've no doubt they will help me when the time comes."

Those words, maybe the most understandable the woman had spoken so far, sent shivers down Etta's spine. She dreaded the very thought of getting old, not to mention the fact she had hardly done anything to help anyone, so was sure no one would give her a cent in her dotage.

Do something about that now! she told herself. Maybe she still had time to become as nice and helpful as Dora was, at least in their own village. She felt many people there had a reason or two to give her a wide berth, and that included her former students, who numbered more than a few. So her allies among the younger generations would be hard to find.

When they reached the stall, Debbie touched one man on the shoulder.

"Tom, I think you need to speak to these two tourists."

Turning at Debbie's words was the very same balloon-faced man Etta and Dora had met outside the Co-op on Tobermory harbour. He looked startled as he recognised them.

"Och, Debbie, they're the Italians I was telling you about," the man had clearly wanted to whisper, but caught up in the surprise of the moment, he spoke louder than he had intended.

"Are you sure? They seem such nice people." As she said this, Debbie turned her lively blue-grey eyes on Etta and Dora as if to spot any dark secrets they were hiding. As used as she was to being on the other side of such an encounter, Etta felt like the guilty pupil who'd played a nasty trick and was trying to appear innocent in front of her strictest teacher.

Tom shook his head, and then muttered something between an embarrassed hello and a valiant attempt to camouflage his gaffe.

"So, how was your night at the castle?" he asked.

"It was freezing, exactly as I had feared a Scottish castle would be."

The two Scots exchanged glances, seeming rather disappointed with the answer. It was unlikely they were merely fearing the guests might have caught a bad cold.

"I hope you found the castle to be fine in all other respects," said Tom.

"Fine is possibly stretching it too far…"

The two Scots beamed.

"…My friend and I thought we'd have a larger and more luxurious flat."

The beam vanished instantly, leaving Etta wondering if she had imagined it.

"But how about you?" she asked, trying to peer beyond the two people in front of her to where others were queuing to sign a piece of paper on the stall. "What are you doing?"

"We're gaining signatures from both locals and visitors to Mull so we can petition the authorities to stop this folly."

"What folly?" asked Dora.

"The spa, the golf course, the castle sale..."

And then, Dora and Etta recognised the woman in front of the folks lining up to sign. Edwina was coordinating the petition with her usual determination, but without the stiffness and air of superiority she'd used with them.

9

THE STONE CIRCLE

E tta and Dora looked at Edwina, and how transformed she was. True, her lips were still pressed tightly together when she wasn't speaking, but she explained the petition and handled questions with a patience she hadn't shown before, nodding and even smiling every now and then, while inviting more people to join the queue to sign. Letitia was helping by distributing leaflets. She sent her ethereal smile in Etta and Dora's direction, but didn't acknowledge them, possibly because Leon, lost in a forest of human legs, was not in her line of sight.

Not far from Letitia was Grayson in his wheelchair, doing pretty much the same as Edwina: encouraging people to sign the petition, explaining the hows and the whys. He recognised the two women and moved towards them, asking the folks he was talking to, to excuse him for a moment.

"Hello, ladies," he said with a grin. "Such a fine day, isn't it?"

"Fine indeed," the two women replied, unable to make sense of the feeling of challenge they received from everyone they spoke to.

"See how many are queuing to sign our petition," he said while Tom looked on in obvious approval. "People don't like the proposal. At all."

"Well," said Etta in her best Miss Contrary tone, which came so naturally to her, showing both Grayson and Tom the spa leaflet that Debbie hadn't managed to tear from her hands, "let's see what people who attend *this* think. Maybe they prefer the comforts of a well-maintained property to one that's obviously falling into disrepair." And with that, she turned her back on the two men, secure in the knowledge that Edwina had been close enough to hear too.

"Etta, was that really necessary?" asked Dora, scuttling after her with Leon.

"What?"

"Provoking them like that."

"They have to learn to accept that life is not all dreams and flowers. But mostly, they have to learn to treat foreign guests with respect." Then, thinking of Tom's curious words, she added, "Whether they're Italians or not."

"I can't understand what they've got against us, just because we happen to be Eilidh's guests."

"That's our biggest transgression, in their eyes at least." Etta felt anger brewing from the inside.

"Do you think last night's… events might have been caused by a real ghost?" Dora asked, despite the fact the two friends had agreed earlier that the night's frights had all been a hallucination.

"I don't believe in ghosts," Etta's answer was as firm and solid as Josh's cheese.

"But what should we do now?"

"There's nothing like the light of knowledge and information to defeat ignorance and superstition."

"You mean you want to go to the midday presentation?"

"Of course," replied Etta wryly.

"It's not yet eleven, what should we do till then?"

"Let's join the crowds, visit the stands and keep our ears open. This place is full of malevolence, but of a very human kind. Nothing to do with the other world."

And so they did. Although their ears didn't catch anything suspicious, their eyes loved the homemade garden decorations, the knitted goods, the wealth of produce made by local hands using ingredients from the island.

"They certainly don't lack creativity and imagination," said Dora, sounding impressed. "Don't you think that biscuit jar with the island otters on it would be just perfect for our kitchen in Castelmezzano?"

Etta looked at the jar critically. She had the hard job of acting as a filter when Dora was on the hunt for souvenirs, otherwise there wouldn't be enough room in their small Fiat for any passengers, human or furry. But in the end, even Etta had to concede it was a beautiful object, which had the merits of being both attractive and useful.

Unexpectedly, though, Dora waved her hand dismissively, turned her back on the biscuit jar, and moved on to the next stand, a strangely sad expression on her face. The woman was definitely behaving weirdly – was she dreading the moment when they would have to return home? But that would be so very unlike Dora, the woman who had an enviable ability to enjoy almost anything in life. And that included departures and arrivals, and all that happened in between. What was going on?

Dora didn't give her friend the opportunity to ask. Possibly aware she was under scrutiny, she changed their plans.

"On second thoughts," she said, "let's not bother with these stalls. There's still an hour before the presentation, so shall we take a short walk and make this dog happy?"

Etta was surprised, but nodded in agreement. "I'm afraid the lighthouse might be too far for us to walk there and back in an hour, so shall we visit the stone circle? The sign said it was just a 15-minute walk, so we'll have plenty of time to get back for the presentation."

"Great!" said Dora.

They left the chatter of the fair behind and took the path through the woodland. Dora hurried along the path, following the signposts. Etta followed on, bursting to ask what was wrong with her friend, but a rare dose of empathy hit her.

Be patient, old hag, she reminded herself as they walked towards the cliffs. *Give the woman time to speak out, as I'm sure she will when she feels ready. I just need to let her know that I'm here whenever she needs me.*

DESPITE LEON'S LONG PAUSES FOR SNIFFING AND PEEING, THE PATH soon led them to a clearing where the trees thinned out, making room for 15 standing stones dominating the Gullion Peninsula. From there, they could see it all: the castle behind them, the sea ahead, the nearby cliffs. And then Dora gave a small cry of delight.

"The lighthouse!" She pointed at a white building in the distance, below the succession of cliffs where tongues of land jutted out above the water. "Glengullion is such an incredible place, it really has it all: a castle, a lighthouse, standing stones…" As she spoke, they moved towards the circle. "Don't you get a weird feeling from them?" Dora asked her friend.

"Like what?"

"It's as if the stones are emanating a sort of power."

"Miss Pepe, please! Don't let your imagination run wild, it's just not on. Stones are stones. They might be an important testament to the past, but that's that. Actually, if you compare them to Greek temples or Middle Eastern architectural gems or Roman cities, they're pretty daft."

"I wish a certain Mr McCall could hear you right now!"

"Never!" Etta quickly pulled back. "He's so proud – and touchy – about Scottish history, but still. It doesn't take much skill to plant a stone in the ground, does it? It's not as if they built the Giza pyramids."

"When is he coming to visit Mull?"

"He suggested the week after next. He's babysitting his

grand-daughter next weekend, but he should be free from a week Monday. We'll have to find him a good B&B, I daren't have him stay at the castle."

"But we have a spare bedroom…"

"I told him we have always stayed in very nice homes through home swapping, and he seemed so sceptical. If he should come to the worst place we've ever ended up…"

"You know, today I feel much more kindly disposed towards the place. Maybe it was just tiredness yesterday. Maybe it's not as bad as it seemed."

"Humans have an innate tendency to adapt to the most adverse situations," said Etta preachily, pushing her large red-framed glasses up her nose in her best schoolmarm pose. "It's very useful for survival purposes, but we shouldn't forget what we were expecting, the unwelcoming accommodation or the frights we had last night, whether real or imagined. No, I don't think he'd like it here at all, even though he is used to cold draughts."

They had been circuiting the stones while talking. Dora couldn't resist touching some of them, possibly thrilled to think that other hands had done the same for millennia. Then, having completed the short circuit, the two women were attracted towards the centre of the circle.

Etta looked uneasily at her friend, sure she was feeling some kind of weird magnetism, but after rebuking Dora for her flights of fancy, Etta decided to keep those feelings to herself. But a mysterious force was definitely drawing her to look down at her feet. There, in the very centre of the stones, something had been written in gravel. And it had nothing to do with Celtic symbols or runes.

"*Stay away from evil.*"

The two women started.

"Was it there when we arrived?" asked Etta.

"I'm not sure," Dora replied. "For the most part, I've been

looking at the stones and the views. But all along, I've had – and I still have – the uncomfortable feeling of being watched."

"Leon doesn't seem to mind," Etta said. The dog was peering out at them, each time from behind a different stone.

"Maybe he can't smell the supernatural," suggested Dora.

"Whatever the case," said Etta, looking back at the path they'd come along, "it's time to go. We don't want to miss the noon presentation. I have to say, I never thought an island counting barely 3,000 souls would have so many events going on."

"Neither did I, but I agree. Let's go."

10

ISLAND OF MULL FOR THE FUTURE

E tta, Dora and Leon walked back to the castle, where signs led them to the "Island of Mull for the Future" presentation. This was to be held in the back gardens, on the far side of the building to the main entrance and the door to Etta and Dora's accommodation, but closer to the castle than the area occupied by the fair in the wider park.

Almost all the rows of chairs were occupied. In fact, more seating was being brought in as if the organisers hadn't expected so many people to show up. At the same time, technicians were rushing round in a frenzy, busy checking that microphones and video projectors were working properly.

A short, sturdy man, dressed in a light-blue suit and white shirt, was going up and down, giving directions to all personnel. Then he turned to face the audience and gave them a large smile and a nod. He had silver hair with a tuft going from one side of his head to the other, which looked suspiciously like a toupee. It was so stiff and dense, it was very unlikely to be real. A goatee beard failed to hide two long dimples on either side of his face, but they made the man look more sly than friendly.

"Ladies and Gentlemen, good afternoon. I'm very pleased to see how many of you are curious about our project and have decided to join us for this event. Let me explain how it came about."

He paused and looked around. It was evident he loved to be on stage, to perform and play to an audience.

"Presently, Eilidh McGullion, the legitimate owner of the castle, is away in London, setting the foundations for her new life. After her return, we will give a talk together in Tobermory Hall in a couple of weeks' time. But yesterday, I learned that a few elderly people were getting worried and anxious about our proposal, and I knew I had to do something to put their minds at rest. You see, I'm a man of action, and this is what has brought me here. But I won't bore you with how a boy from the poor streets of Glasgow came to enjoy a successful life. Let me just leave you with one clue: it's to do with my proactive attitude to life. 'Improve whatever can be improved all around you' has been my motto since forever.

"About a year back, one of my many good friends was passing through Mull, and he sent me a snapshot of a beautiful castle and gardens on this amazing Scottish island. His wise words were, 'This place will end up in ruins soon, Gary, unless you intervene.'

"No more than two weeks later, I was here. I met a clever young lady who had just inherited the place. We spoke, I gave her my best advice... Mind you, she's a capable – a *very* capable – young woman, but the task of maintaining the castle was just too complicated, the obstacles too innumerable.

"So yes, I gave her my best advice, but around nine months later, she called me again and she said, 'Look, Gary, I'm very grateful for what you've done for me, but I have a young daughter to think of. I lost my husband, so I want to support and be close to my daughter. The task here at Glengullion is overwhelming and it seems to me I've made no progress at all. At the same time, I don't want to sell off the family inheritance. I'd love to leave it in good hands, more capable than mine, that will revive both the property and the grounds.'

"Truth is that my wife and I had just decided it was time for me to cut down on my working hours, so I could be free to spend more time with her and our children. But I simply couldn't resist Eilidh's plea. And my wife, who's ever supportive, told me… what did you tell me, honey?"

A tall, slender woman, a good thirty years younger than Gary, got up from the front row, moving like a supermodel. She wore a skin-tight purple dress and frighteningly high heels, strings of pearls of various lengths cascading on to and around her generous bosom. She pushed back her long, wavy hair with a sophisticated sweep of her left hand. When she spoke, her voice was deep, languid and breathy.

"I said that I knew you would have no peace, nor would you give me or the children any peace, until you had this sorted. We know you, Gary. We've come to accept that you've got to keep going. If we kept you for ourselves, it would be so very selfish of us. You're so needed by so many…"

He grinned. "Marrying and having a family with Gary Mason is not a task for the faint hearted. I love you, honey, for your generous nature, but let's not bother these people with our family issues."

"Most of the menfolk," Etta whispered into Dora's ears, "don't seem that bothered by having to listen to – and look at – Mrs Mason." As if to prove her point, she gestured towards Leon, who was gazing at the woman with an expression of adoration, as if hanging on her every word.

"It took me three months and the right business partner, but in the end, we had our plan on the table. Ms McGullion couldn't believe her eyes at the beauty of it all. But she was even more excited at the opportunity it represents not only for the town of Tobermory, but for the whole island of Mull.

"Now, I don't have the final renderings and models that we plan to show at the official presentation, but since last night, my staff have worked hard to put together a few things to show you. They've worked all night, had the printing facility open early this morning to create the posters and the leaflets you hold in your hand. No, it's not easy to work for me, but they have fun, they tell me, and the satisfaction of seeing dreams coming true, the impossible coming to life."

He turned towards a projector screen that had been erected for the occasion in the shadow of the castle. He pressed a button on his remote, the screen went pitch black, but music surrounded the audience from four, maybe even six different speakers. It was jangly celebratory music, as if everyone's favourite sports team had just won an important match. Then words appeared on the screen:

"Mull, the most beautiful island of Scotland."

Images taken from a drone showed the island emerging from the morning mist, and then the footage ran along its breathtaking coastline, cutting to the wildlife, the island of Iona, Tobermory harbour, the crumbling Aros Castle, then focusing in on Glengullion Castle. The man called Gary stopped the video at this point.

"Should we leave Glengullion to the mercy of the elements, like Aros?"

Many in the audience cried, "Nooo!"

"You are right, my friends, we can do much better. But I have one question for you. Are you ready to share your treasures with the rest of the world, or do you want to keep the island all to yourself?"

"Share, share."

"We need visitors."

"We love respectful tourists."

The cunning man held up his hand to silence the audience, focusing on the last speaker.

"What did you say, sir?"

The young man, looking confused and a little intimidated by Gary's steady gaze, muttered, "We love tourists…"

"No, young man, you used another word."

The man stuttered, "We love respectful tourists…"

"You're very astute, thank you. Here is a man," Gary turned his attention back to the entire audience, "who has the power to create visions. We don't want any old tourists arriving on these shores, the ones who consume vast quantities of fish and chips and cheap beer, throw their litter on the ground and leave with nothing more than a few selfies. My friends, you're paying taxes to clean up after these eejits, for public transport to ferry them around the island, and what do you get in return? Nothing.

"What you need are *respectful* tourists who enrich the island by investing their money in a holiday to remember right here on Mull. Because, believe it or not, money is important. It's essential if we want services, well-kept roads, schools and nursing homes, efficient public transport, hospitals. And to earn money, we have to attract investment, invite well-known companies to come and open businesses here.

"Now, a warning!" Gary boomed. "If you're weak of heart, if you're afraid to dream, you'd better leave, now. Because, my friends, I'm going to show you what's gonna change over the next couple of years, and trust me, it's revolutionary." He paused and looked around. "Is no one leaving? Are we all Bravehearts? Let's go, then."

And with that, he pressed the play button on his remote. The screen went black again, the celebratory tune played, then words burst out on to the screen, each statement fading to make way for the next.

"Welcome to Your Island Retreat!"

"Regenerate Your Spirit!"

"Relax Your Mind!"

"RESET!" This last word appeared in giant characters occupying the whole screen, lingering for a few seconds before the screen went dark again. Glengullion Castle appeared, looking magnificent in its sun-kissed grounds, but with a few buildings superimposed along the sides, a swimming pool on the front lawn, a golf course stretching away to the cliffs, tennis courts just waiting for new balls, please. It was an excellent computer graphic, simulating what could be. And then the view changed, as if the camera of the present day was moving into the interior of the future to show the completely renovated inside: a luxurious restaurant, spa treatment rooms, a mahogany staircase and a breathtaking sparkling reception hall. Bedrooms so fanciful one could almost imagine one were in Dubai.

The public gasped, some in pleasure, some in horror. Others just gasped in surprise, unsure how they felt about the proposal.

"Now, my friends, I'm by no means an expert when it comes to hospitality, and the wisest thing you can do when you're facing a new challenge is to find a partner with the expertise you lack. The good news is that I've found the best hospitality group operating in the international markets. I can't name them yet, but yes, they're a celebrated Italian group, and these are the kind of things they do."

The next video came with a cheesy feel-good soundtrack. There were interviews with customers enjoying breaks in properties run by the mysterious partner investor, being massaged, lying in hay or covered with chocolate. A woman getting out of a hot jacuzzi declared how her stay had allowed her to overcome the stress of being a successful actress in Hollywood. A man in his forties with the physique of a Greek god said how he was ready to return to his chief executive position and achieve the best results of his career. A woman in her fifties with unnaturally plump lips and sculptured cheekbones was interviewed while eating three small colourful morsels from a plate that could easily have contained 30 times that amount of food, saying how her intestinal biome had benefited from her special diet and she felt as if she was 20 again.

"Lock up your boyfriends, you youngsters, I'm back," she trilled, grinning in a way that Etta found rather disgusting.

"Wish I'd known in my younger years that a healthy intestine… I beg your pardon, a healthy intestinal *biome* was all I needed to conquer a man," she muttered in Dora's ear.

"The positive thing is that you know now," replied Dora with a grin.

More wonderful locations, more VIP interviewees, more jewels and dresses and sports and beauty treatments later, the video finally ended, the cheesy tune fading out. There was a smattering of applause from some people, which was possibly not as enthusiastic as Gary had expected.

"I know what you're thinking," he said. "That's all too good to be true, but mark my words, this is *exactly* what is going to happen right here, not in a decade, but within the next two years, starting from when we get our permits granted. Are there any questions?"

A few people asked for more details about the project, how many customers the castle could welcome in a year, if Gary planned it to be open in the offseason. For each question, Gary had a reassuring answer. The proposal partners would increase the location capacity to welcome more people in the high season, but the castle would be open 365 days a year so the island would not be abandoned during the dark winter days. Christmas would become an integral part of the area's marketing season.

A hand had been up the whole time Gary had been answering questions, but its owner had remained ignored. That was until the young assistant scanning the audience and holding a microphone out so individuals could ask a question pretended not to see the waving arm once too often. As he walked past, Edwina stretched out her leg, the young man stumbled and, with a fluid manoeuvre, the feisty woman grabbed the mic.

"Hello, Gary," she said, her amplified voice ringing out across the gardens. "First of all, thank you very much for showing us exactly what we do *not* want this island to become. Lock your VIPs and big companies up tight, keep them all to yourself, keep them wherever you want, but do NOT bring them here. We have nothing to share with them."

"You can't speak for the whole island," sneered Gary. "How

can you refuse such an opportunity on behalf of everyone on Mull?"

"What opportunity, Gary? We know what the folks who come to these spas are like. They join an exclusive club and they will stay in that club. They will spend all of their money in your hotel, never buying chocolates at the Tobermory Chocolate Shop, nor ordering a seafood platter at the pier, nor indulging in coffee and cake in town. They won't take one of our whale-watching cruises, as I've no doubt your company will provide them with a luxurious yacht and all kinds of amenities, all at an overinflated price. They will come and they will go without contributing anything to the island. And for this, we have to give away Glengullion Castle which is such an important part of the heritage of Tobermory and Mull."

On hearing applause that was rather more enthusiastic than his presentation had received, Gary bowed his head at the audience. As confident as a tomcat about to pounce on his prey, he got ready to make his summing-up speech in front of his very own judge and jury.

"I have three main objections from the thousands that pop into my mind. Firstly, did you say heritage? This castle is falling into disrepair, in case you haven't noticed. Two, the castle, I'm sorry to have to inform you, is the private property of Ms McGullion, who's free to dispose of it any way she wants, whether you like it or not. Three, I'm talking jobs! Year-round jobs that will ensure people will not leave the island, but will actually stay and prosper."

"Jobs?" Edwina's high-pitched cackle was worthy of a West End portrayal of the three witches in *Macbeth*. If they had ever laughed, that is. "You mean as cleaners, bartenders and waiters? I'm sure the higher-paid positions will be filled with people that you will recruit from your inner circle."

"I didn't know you were an industry expert. But please, could you explain to me what *you*'d do with this place? What kind of jobs would *you* create? How would *you* stop depopulation?"

"Depopulation?" Tom sprang to his feet and turned to the audience, taking the mic from Edwina. "That's the problem when you have a one-size-fits-all approach. Let me inform you, Gary, that the population of the island has been *increasing* in the past decades. That *local* businesses have done so much for the island that it is doing well and thriving. That it is now exporting quality products well beyond the UK. We have plenty of excellence of our own. We're not talking on a generic multinational scale, we're talking about great handmade products, and the satisfaction and joy of working in a small, friendly environment!"

"I'm still waiting to hear what your plans are for the castle."

"A number of us want Glengullion Castle to become a retirement home," Edwina took the mic back. "And we will have part of the castle restored for visitors, so as to pay for the property's maintenance. We already have the nicest café imaginable on these grounds, and Josh McIntosh is striving hard to produce the best local cheese ever. We plan to add more projects into our portfolio, like a rose garden nursery and forest development. All these small projects will create jobs for the locals in an integrated and sustainable way, and the castle will still be a place of enjoyment for the whole community."

"Josh McIntosh, I see." A sly smile dawned above Gary's goatee. "Would you remind me how many cows he has? Five? Ten? I can see how that's going to have a real impact. But, correct me if I'm wrong. This retirement home – you mean for yourselves. You've earmarked the best flats in the castle. You don't want VIPs coming to stay because… you plan to keep the castle for yourselves!"

"Not only for ourselves, but for a number of the local elderly. And we will be paying a regular rent, part of which will go to cover the expenses of upkeep, and part to pay the rent for the elderly people who can't afford it."

"You selfish woman! You want to deny a bright future for the island to satisfy your personal gain. That's disgusting! I can't find a more appropriate word."

"You know perfectly well that's not the case, so don't try to turn the tables in your favour..."

"The last word is Eilidh's. All you have to do is make her a more generous offer than mine." The man laughed. "You'll have to sell a little more cheese."

"You talk about disgusting – you're the most disgusting person I've ever met. Watch your back, Gary. Be careful, because you're being far too provocative for my liking."

"Is that a veiled threat?"

"Nope, it is an openly declared threat. The sooner you leave the island, the better it will be for us *and* for you." With that, Edwina got up and left, her cheeks red with fury. Etta, looking on with a newfound respect for the woman, could almost hear her teeth grinding. Tom accompanied her, but when he reached the last row of seats, he turned to announce an alternative presentation at 3pm.

"Please, come along and see that we don't need this folly. This spa, golf course, fine dining madness could be created anywhere on the planet, it has no roots whatsoever in the local history or island culture. We, on the other hand, want to do things with and for our people."

"I'll be there. How could I miss the fun?" said Gary with a grin, but it was easy to see he was just as furious as Edwina. He was merely pretending to be cool. Certainly, his wife wasn't about to console him. She was far too busy enjoying a drink with a smartly dressed young man who seemed to have all her attention.

11

MULL FOREST CAFÉ

When Etta and Dora left the presentation to return to the fair, all around them, they overheard a variety of comments. Some people were backing Edwina and Tom, but the majority seemed to be arguing that it'd be a pity to miss out on such a wonderful opportunity.

"What opportunity?" the first group would demand. "Edwina's right. All this land would be inaccessible to us, and the trickle down of wealth to the locals would be no more than crumbs."

"I'd rather have retired people living here and be able to show the castle to my children's children than suffer those RESET goons hogging these beautiful grounds for themselves."

"You're right in theory, but look at the practicalities. Eilidh planned to do so much to renovate the castle, but after just one year, she's had to give up. It's too tough to keep a property of this size well-maintained *and* make it pay for itself."

"The castle needs a big investment. At least Gary's proposal means the place would be saved from falling into ruins."

The discussions were becoming rather animated, Etta noticed, but at least these people were talking about something that really mattered to them, evaluating the pros and cons of each solution. Indifferent, they were not. And that in itself was a positive thing indeed.

However, one of the unfortunate facts in life is that not all positive things lead to positive outcomes. And as Etta was soon to find out, it appeared there could be such a thing as caring too much.

But for now, she was blissfully unaware. And she was hungry.

"It's time for a little lunch, surely?" she suggested.

"I know the perfect place," answered Miss GoogleMapsIncorporated, leading her friend through the beautiful park, then turning a corner to reveal what had been hidden behind a small hill and a copse of oak trees.

No, Etta hadn't expected that. Not only a few paces from Glengullion Castle.

ON THE TOP OF A HILL OVERLOOKING THE SEA AND THE CASTLE, Dora recognised the white frame of a building in the shape of a traditional barn. She had seen pictures of it many times while planning their stay in Mull. In the long winter months, she had dreamed of this moment, when she'd walk in for the first time. Yes, she already knew that the walls were all made from glass panels, but now she could spot the greenery and vegetation growing inside. Seeing the café for real totally blew her away.

"A greenhouse!" cried Etta.

"A café inside a greenhouse, it's sooo lovely!" cried Dora. Even she had not imagined the café would look *this* nice.

They wandered around the area for a while, walking all the way up to the cliffs to take in the view, to breathe in the scent of the ocean as if they could never get enough of the breezy air, especially on such a lovely sunny day. But it was that very fine air that made their stomachs grumble. The two exchanged meaningful looks and headed for the café.

The greenhouse contained wooden tables, some large and some small, with wicker lamps suspended above that looked like birds' nests. Potted plants nestled in every nook and cranny. Most of the vegetation was vines with brilliant large leaves, climbing up the four corners of the building to form a large canopy covering the entire ceiling, shading the interior from too much heat during the sunny days of summer. Overall, the impression was of entering a tropical jungle embraced by lianas; only the unexpected fragrance of baked goods reminded them that even if this were the Garden of Eden, people still loved their food.

They sat at one of the small tables with a view over the green fields and the sea in the distance. A marmalade jar had been filled with the prettiest arrangement of fresh flowers, which Dora noticed to be different on each table. Sweet peas in shades of white and light blue, purple giant allium, gaudy zinnias, and some small, shy white flowers to accompany the bold cornflowers.

After much browsing through the menu, Dora chose a crispy filo parcel stuffed with roast squash, kale and Hebridean blue cheese, served with a fennel and red onion slaw and home-grown salad. Etta seemed unusually undecided, but in the end went for homemade Yorkshire pudding, mackerel pate, celeriac and horseradish remoulade with watercress salad.

It must have been just before two when Dora recognised Gary Mason and his wife, getting up from one of the tables and leaving the café. She pointed them out to Etta, who simply nodded, too busy welcoming the waitress arriving with their lunch dishes. Each was a real feast for the eyes as well as the taste buds. Leon got salmon and mackerel toast, which he had conceded was quite a nice treat while he was waiting to be served a full meal back at the castle. And as for dessert, the choice of cakes and pastries was overwhelming to say the least.

"We're lucky living so close by, we have the chance to try

them all. Let's make sure to come here every other day," Dora said, biting into her apple and caramel tarte Tatin.

"So true," answered Etta, taking a mouthful of her lemon-flavoured baked New York cheesecake, made with both blueberry jam and fresh blueberries. However, both were still wondering what the carrot cake would have tasted like. Even as they ate, their eyes wandered over the selection of homemade apricot and pumpkin-seed flap jack, chocolate brioche, cheese scones, brownies and lemon drizzles…

The same waitress who had taken their orders explained that the place was run by four women. When Etta and Dora looked towards the open kitchen ahead of them, they spotted four no-longer-very-young ladies chopping and cooking and garnishing between a laugh and a spot of banter. The two friends finished with a cappuccino and Dora handed Leon a piece of cheese she had saved, knowing the dog's habit of looking at her, even after the most filling meal, with imploring eyes.

"Is that it?" his gaze would beg.

"Nope," she'd answer. "There's one more morsel, dear, but this is the very last."

They lingered over their cappuccinos, chatting over inconsequential things and occasionally dozing off for a few minutes. Finally, Etta looked at her watch and gave a little scream of alarm.

"It's almost three," she cried. "We need to move, fast!"

"Why?" Dora answered languidly, perfectly happy to stay put and enjoy the café's atmosphere.

"Have you forgotten? Edwina and her friends are having their presentation at three."

"Do you really want to go? It will be pretty boring."

"Boring? You don't want another dreadful night at the castle, do you?"

"Of course not, but what's that got to do with attending the presentation?" Even as she was asking, Dora was getting up ready to go with her friend.

"I told you, knowledge is power."

With a supreme effort, Dora followed Etta out of the café, throwing a last glance at the barn as they walked away, then locking eyes with Leon, who agreed with her. He could hardly imagine a better place for an after-meal nap.

They had just reached the gardens at the back of the castle, which were closer to the café than those at the front, when from an open window, a woman's scream rose above any other noise. It chilled Dora to the bone, as if all the horrors of the previous night had returned.

12

AN UNFAIR TIME FOR DEATH

"What's going on?" cried Dora.

"WoooRRRRRf!" barked Leon. Before either of the two women could even think of keeping hold of him, the dog was already heading round the side of the castle towards the main door.

Dora looked at Etta. Etta looked back at her.

"We have no choice," said Etta. "Let's follow him!"

"After all," muttered Dora, trying to reassure herself while keeping pace with her friend, "what self-respecting ghost could possibly be on the prowl while the sun is still shining?"

The main door had been left ajar, but coming out of the bright summer sunlight, the two women felt like they had been plunged into gloom. It was only as their eyes grew accustomed to the dimness that they could appreciate the majestic hall, its chequered floor and walls panelled with dark oak displaying a variety of swords and other medieval weapons. Where the wooden panels ended, the wall continued, painted a deep red, and here were more weapons, hunting trophies and a number of paintings of hunt scenes. In the depths of the shadows on the right-hand side was a large mantelpiece with a portrait above it.

To either side was a suit of armour, and in front of it were two figures on the floor.

Etta and Dora froze to the spot, despite the fact the hound was already next to the fireplace and repeatedly glancing at his two humans, wondering why they were wasting time lingering. The friends swallowed a few times before moving forward, each hoping to take strength from the other.

"WOF!" the dog barked as a warning that his patience was running out. Upon hearing the bark, one of the figures on the floor turned and cried out again.

"HEEELLLLP!"

Now, the two women ran, fast. It seemed at least one of the figures was human after all. More precisely, it was Sandra, bent over an immobile shape wearing a light-blue suit. Around this figure's head, blood had spread out into a dark pool.

"I think he's dead," said Sandra.

Dora dropped to her knees to feel the man's pulse. "I'm afraid he is." She gently turned his face towards her, only to cry, "Goodness!"

"Gary Mason!" Etta cried just as loudly.

"He must have fallen and hit his head against the hearth," Sandra said.

Etta shook her head. "You need to view him from here," and with her chin, she pointed just beyond the body. There, a mace was lying on the floor. The suit of armour on the other side of the fireplace was holding a similar mace at head height, as if ready to strike out at any enemy foolish enough to come near. But the suit on the near side had an empty arm raised in the air.

"It fell on his head," Sandra suggested as her hand moved towards the weapon.

"That's for the police to say," said Etta gravely. "No, don't touch it. I actually hope we've not already contaminated the evidence. Dora, accompany Sandra outside. I will call for the police and make sure no one comes this way."

~

THE POLICE AND THE PARAMEDICS ARRIVED ALMOST IMMEDIATELY. After all, they didn't have far to come as both had been present at the fair. The local constable who arrived first asked to speak to Etta and Dora, giving Sandra a little time to recover from her shock. She calmed down only when her husband joined her.

While the interrogations continued after the constable had spoken to the three women who'd found him, involving other people who'd interacted with Gary, the crime scene was cordoned off. A pathologist arrived and Etta tried to find out the estimated time of death, but the police officer ushered her away, telling her that kind of information would not be made public yet.

As they wandered around, Etta and Dora overheard a few comments from people who had been near the castle when Sandra had found the body. But they didn't amount to much. Some reported seeing Mason's staff leaving the premises at about 1.30 to have lunch in Tobermory and two separate people had witnessed Gary accompanying his wife to the car park at 2pm. Shortly afterwards, they saw him heading towards the castle, alone. Not much to go on, for the keen amateur sleuths.

Things became even more frustrating later on in the day when the CID arrived from the mainland. The detective chief inspector in charge of the investigation surveyed the area, making sure to leave the crime scene undisturbed, and therefore as uncontaminated as possible, for as long as it would take the forensic team to arrive from Glasgow. In the meantime, her team spoke to the public, to the fair organisers, and to Edwina and Tom who, on orders from Eilidh, had kept the castle open for the Masons and their staff. They questioned Mrs Mason, who had been called back from her hotel in Tobermory. But despite being polite at all times, the detectives wouldn't share anything with the increasingly impatient Etta. And in the face of a barely disguised glare from the DCI, Georgia Findlay, she decided it was maybe time to cease and desist.

The real sleuthing began only when the two women and one dog returned to their lodgings, once the police had told them and the public they were free to go. This was some time later, after the police had investigated who'd had access to the castle, reconstructed the last movements of the victim, compiled a list of people they had to talk to. But finally, the moment came when the trio could leave, with the instruction to make sure they were available for further questioning when required.

"I'm so tired," said Dora, pausing in front of the turret door that led to their accommodation. "I really hope we won't be scared by the ghost tonight."

"You can be sure that with all the police around, he won't come near."

"So, you're totally convinced it wasn't a ghostly affair?"

"Completely convinced. Didn't you hear Gary Mason talking about partnering with an *Italian* group?"

"Yes, I did… Wait a minute, you don't think…? Actually, you *do* think that the locals thought we were the Italian partners."

"I assume so."

"And they wanted to scare us so much that we'd pull out of the deal and scupper Eilidh's plan to sell the castle to Gary."

Etta nodded.

By this time, they had entered their reading room. It was cold, so they laid and lit a fire.

"It will take a while to warm this room up," said Dora. "We might as well go to the kitchen to prepare something hot and light to eat. We've had enough rich food today, but a vegetable soup will do us good."

There was so much to do to attend to the fire downstairs and prepare the soup upstairs that it wasn't until they sat down for their dinner that they had the opportunity to carry on discussing the day's events.

"Oh," said Dora, taking her mobile phone from her pocket,

"there's a message from Eilidh. She apologises for all the inconvenience and says she will be here in the morning. She's on a night coach to Glasgow right now. I wonder, if she had been here, whether the murder would have happened at all."

"Why do you say that?" asked Etta, her spoonful of leeks and carrots suspended in the air.

"Well, we heard passionately opposed views on the sale of the castle today. I wonder if she could have acted as a mediator."

"I think," Etta said, an expression of pleasure on her face, although it was difficult to say whether it was a result of the hot soup or the theorising, "that she was actually the catalyst for the murder. Regardless of where she was when the crime was committed, once she'd made up her mind to sell to Gary Mason, she'd put the chain of events in motion…"

"Would someone really kill to prevent a public property becoming private? It sounds rather a big leap from noble and rightful intentions to something awful and vile."

"I'm quite convinced that all fanaticism leads to evil, no matter how rightful someone's initial standing point might be. If you're not even attempting to see things from another point of view, if you're absolutely convinced you're in the right and everyone else is wrong, then you're likely to cause more harm than good, no matter what."

"For the first time," Dora murmured, "it seems to me that being in constant doubt for my whole life has not been such a bad thing."

"I doubt, therefore I live." Etta smiled. "But let's go back over what happened. When was Gary killed? He certainly had quite a few people wanting to talk to him after his presentation…"

"But we know he and his wife were at the Mull Forest Café for lunch. They left just before 2pm."

"Then we know that Sandra discovered him… what was it, five to three when we heard her screaming?"

Dora nodded. Yes, that had been the exact time they had passed in front of the castle.

"I heard more than one person saying they saw Gary accompanying his wife to the car park just after two, and then he headed alone towards the castle."

"That's a pity," said Etta.

"What's a pity and why?"

"Close family members are the most likely suspects in a murder inquiry, but it seems Mrs Mason has a rather solid alibi."

Dora nodded excitedly in agreement, her fringe bouncing up and down.

13

TALKING ABOUT MURDER

"I wonder," Etta said, "when the pathologist places the time of death, whether that tough buttoned-up policewoman will share any details."

"I really hope she won't," said Dora, smiling. "I mean, it wouldn't do for a police officer to share such findings with the public, particularly with two people directly involved."

Etta waved her argument away impatiently. "I wonder if Sandra found him dead, or…" her voice lowered to a murmur, her eyes sparkled with a strange light.

"But she was in shock!" said Dora, always quick to come to another person's defence.

"It doesn't take much effort to look shocked, and pretending to have found the body would also eliminate the trouble of having to leave the room unseen! But I agree, we should keep our minds open to all eventualities."

"Who else is a suspect?" Despite the gravity of the situation, Dora felt a little excited. It's very difficult to remain unmoved when a murder takes place, and not being new to the sleuthing game, she knew the rules as well as Etta did. She took a notepad and pen from her bag and started to compile a list.

"First of all, Grayson, Sandra's husband," Etta said.

"But he's in a wheelchair…"

"Which would offer him the perfect protection from suspicion, but who knows what he's really capable of?"

"If only he could stand up and walk over to fetch the mace from the statue. But then, if he were the murderer, surely he'd make sure his wife had the perfect alibi."

"Maybe she has. Imagine if the pathologist places the man's death at just after he left his wife, while everyone could see Sandra running her stall. She'd have a plethora of witnesses swearing she didn't move from there for at least 30 minutes after Gary had died."

"But then, if Grayson was the murderer, and they were working together, why was it she who had to discover the body?"

"Maybe to clear the crime scene. Maybe there was something she had to remove…"

"Like what?"

"Do you remember how she tried to touch the mace?"

"What significance does that have?"

"Maybe she wanted to leave her fingerprints on it, so when the police also find her husband's, she could say that earlier, he had wanted to see the mace up close, so she had handed it to him, and then replaced it."

Dora looked at her friend in total amazement. "I would never have thought of that. But I just wonder, if she had nothing to do with the murder, why did she enter the castle at all? No one was supposed to go inside, except Mason, who was already acting as if he owned the property, and probably his staff used the castle to store things for their presentation."

"That's a very good point. About Sandra, I mean. As for Mason's staff, we heard witnesses saying they went to lunch in Tobermory before Gary and his wife returned from the café. None of them was on the premises at the time of the murder, or if they were, the police will find out soon. Given the chance, we should ask Sandra what she was doing at the murder scene in the first place."

"How about Edwina?"

"She's my favourite suspect," confessed Etta with a large grin. "She acts like she has a divine right to the place, and when I mentioned fanaticism, she's the one who came to mind."

"And today, she had a fierce disagreement with the victim."

"She actually threatened him," Etta agreed.

"Which makes me think she might be innocent," Dora said, feeling as clever as her friend. "She's smart. She would never have drawn suspicion on to herself if she had murder in mind."

"Unless she wanted us to think just that."

"What?" Dora asked.

"That we'd think she'd have never threatened him publicly if she wanted to murder him, thus we'd conclude it wasn't her."

"Like a double bluff," but Dora didn't sound completely convinced.

"Well, I'm sure the woman is diabolical enough to do just that. We will need to find out where she was between two o'clock and five to three. I'm sure we can ask around about that. I guess she was supposed to be with the rest of that silly lot running the petition, so all we need to do is casually ask them how preparations for their 3pm presentation had been going and who was helping. The truth will emerge quite naturally."

"What about Josh McIntosh?"

"Straight into the suspects lot!"

"Debbie?"

"Her gaiety is so extreme, her energy so over the top, she could be borderline mentally unstable. I'm sure she's got all the traits of a potential serial killer."

This was too much, even for Dora.

"What are you saying? And how would you know?"

Etta suddenly felt she might have gone too far. But backtracking was too humiliating to contemplate.

"Well, I might have exaggerated a little, but I've learned to trust my gut over the years."

"OK, I will put her name on the list, but only on the grounds that they're *all* suspects until proven otherwise. Who else do we have?"

"There's Letitia," Etta answered promptly.

"But that woman is so sweet. Also she seems a bit... how can I say this? Like she has learning difficulties. She wouldn't be able to carry out such a cunning crime."

"There's nothing cunning about it. She saw Gary going inside the castle alone, she followed him, she saw the mace, she hit him. Full stop."

"I'm not convinced. She's such a dear."

"All the more reason to suspect her, then. But I want to play fair and give you one more option: someone else might have put the idea into her mind. Obsessed with it, she manipulated Letitia. *She's* the real instigator of the crime, and Letitia is just a pawn in her game."

"She?" asked Dora.

"I can't help feeling that Edwina is still the most likely suspect."

"I see," said Dora. "So, what's our plan for tomorrow?"

"Simple. We speak to people and try once more to get information from the police. Let's approach a different officer this time – there's bound to be a weak link in DCI Findlay's team. All we need from them is the presumed time of death, then we can run the investigations better than they can."

"Without forensics?" Dora wasn't able to hide her scepticism at Etta's bragging, which of course elicited a lecture from Madame Murder. Etta pushed her glasses up her nose and sighed deeply at having to explain, yet again, what was patently obvious.

"With all their tests and examinations, it will take ages for them to come to the very surprising conclusions that a) the victim was killed by another human, b) the victim was hit by a rare ancient weapon, c) the rare weapon was a mace and d) it came from the suit of armour next to the mantelpiece."

Dora burst into hearty laughter.

"In the meantime," Madame continued, "we will have spoken to people who – guess what? – will open up so much more to two harmless, sympathetic ladies than they would to the police."

Dora frowned at the word sympathetic, though didn't mention that perhaps only one of them was deserving of the description. "They won't tell the truth to the police, you mean?"

"That's not what I mean. Of course, killer aside, all the others will tell the truth to the police, but they will answer only the questions they are asked. However, we'll get to hear the speculations, things about the past and the present that may not seem to have any relevance to the case, so people won't feel they're worth reporting to the police. By untangling the web of relationships, we'll discover the real characters of people, their motivations, their aspirations. And this will lead us to the killer before the forensic scientists have even completed their list of tests to be run."

"That is pure bragging, Napoleon style."

The dog put his head up proudly on hearing his full name. Then, seeing that nothing interesting was going on, he shrugged. Who knows what the bipeds were talking about? But he was gratified to hear that he was clearly at the centre of their animated discussion, as he should be. Maybe they were hoping he would help them, knowing their tendency to run into trouble. He would oblige, faithful to his canine duties. But tomorrow. Right now, he already had a case to take care of: that of digestion and long nap.

As for Etta, for once, she took the time to ponder over Dora's words. Was she bragging? Yes, she was *excited* – very much Napoleon style – to be on the hunt again. And there was a specific reason for that excitement, even if she wouldn't admit to it, not even under the pain of torture.

It was right then that the *specific reason* dared to call her mobile phone.

14

HAPPINESS AND DESPAIR

Dora saw the changing shade of Etta's complexion as the woman stretched her hand over to the phone. She had no doubt the caller was *not* Etta's daughter, Maddalena. By the reddish colour expanding from her friend's cheeks to cover her whole face and the clumsiness with which she picked up her mobile, as if it was an alien object, Dora knew it had to be Rufus McCall. Despite Etta's furious denial that she had any sort of romantic feelings towards the man, Dora suspected otherwise.

Discreet as she was, she quickly piled all the dishes together and got ready to take them upstairs. Etta hesitated before taking the call.

"I'll come and help."

"No, dear," Dora objected promptly. "It's my turn. You can take care of the dishes tomorrow."

"Oh, thank you!"

"Come, Leon," and as Dora turned to make sure that the Basset was following, she saw Etta's face was all smiles as she collapsed into the armchair and answered her phone, her eyes expressing thanks for the privacy her friend had afforded her. But more miraculous was Etta's tone of voice, as if all its

99

customary abruptness and edginess had been smoothed down the very moment she heard Rufus's voice.

What a telling transformation!

DORA PUT ALL THE DISHES IN THE SINK, USING THE HOT WATER FROM the kettle as that from the tap was never as hot as she wished, and started meticulously washing them. Leon had indeed followed her, despite knowing the fire in the kitchen would not be lit. The wise dog had sensed something wrong with the sweeter of his two bipeds, who had given him plenty of reasons to be worried recently, even more so than the troublemaker. And that said a lot! Now, he could feel a flood was about to be unleashed. And he was not wrong.

"My dear doggie," said Dora as she passed the soapy sponge over the same dish for the fifth time. "I'm so sorry to inform you that you happen to live with a very selfish human being. I should be happy, Etta has found a good man indeed. But all I can wonder is what will become of me?

"Etta complains about this castle, but it has such beautiful gardens, and the reading room is not that bad. I'm sure even our bedroom, with a few changes, could be turned into something delightful… Well," even Dora could not stretch that far, "less gloomy, anyway. But every night, I dream of my old flat in Pietrapertosa. That was certainly dark and gloomy, and small too. I dread the very thought of having to go back there.

"At the same time, I can't expect Etta and Rufus to put up with me staying in Etta's house in Castelmezzano. What a wonderful year I have spent there! The building is so refined, with its high ceilings and light streaming through the windows all day long. I have adored cooking there and taking you for long walks, dear Leon. I planted all the seeds I could find on Etta's terrace, and as if by magic, the plants have grown beautifully. Even in the cold winter months – do you remember, Leon? –

you'd curl up on the carpet, soft music playing and these two old hags chatting the evening away, munching a batch of freshly baked biscuits, laughing our hearts out. Sometimes we'd invite all of the local gossips to join us."

Dora turned off the tap and removed her rubber gloves, even though she wasn't so much as halfway through doing the dishes. Her eyes were too full of tears. She picked up a tissue and blew her nose so loudly that even the ghost of Lord McGullion would have trembled in fear.

"And the travelling!" she continued as she sat on one of the rickety chairs. "We've had such glorious adventures, we've seen places I have dreamed of visiting for most of my life. And I still have such a long list to go. But how can I expect Etta and Rufus to take me on holiday with them? That said, I hope at least once in a while we might get together to remember these fantastic times. Even one weekend away would make the rest of the monotonous year worth living.

"Mind you, once I go back to paying rent and bills all by myself to run an ugly little flat, I won't have any money left for travelling anyway. Certainly, I could join Don Peppino on the bus trips he organises for the elderly. Etta used to say of the people who take advantage of the priest's excursions, 'They're as old as the hills', but it will be better than nothing. We will visit Pompeii and all the Madonnas in Southern Italy, and if we're lucky, we might convince Don Peppino to take us to Rome and see something else besides the Vatican and the Sistine Chapel.

"I feel we've come to the end of an epoch, but at least I was lucky enough to have experienced our long trips, the pleasure of driving while never sure of where we'd end up. And we've met so many people. I will keep in touch with them all, as long as I'm able to write emails."

Dora fell silent for a few moments. The thought was so silly, of course she'd be able to write emails. But all of a sudden, Dora felt more old and fragile than she'd ever done before. She took a moment more to acknowledge that strange new feeling.

"I wonder if people age just because of loneliness and lack of projects, challenges and fun things to do, rather than because time is passing by. It must be the quality of the days, months, years that makes us feel younger or older. But right now, I can't seem to think of anything cheerful. As Etta says, this will pass, as all things pass, both the good and the bad. Only I'm feeling a little silly tonight.

"As for you yourself, my sweetest doggie, Etta loves you deeply. I've been thinking about this too, and even if it breaks my heart, I've no doubt. I can't be that selfish. You have to have the best the world can offer. You deserve that."

The poor hound was edging towards panic. What was all this about? How could the ever happy and cheerful Dora-biped be carrying all this sadness in her heart? What was happening to the world? He sat down in front of her, searching her eyes and tilting his head on one side as if asking to know more.

"Don't you worry, my darling doggie, I've made my mind up. I will let you go and you will stay with Etta. You deserve that large, happy house, and I would never constrain you in my ugly flat. And Rufus – you like him and I'm sure he loves you in return. And they will go on enjoying home-swapping adventures, and they'll take you along. Rufus will buy a better car than my old Fiat, so you will travel in something larger and more comfy. But I will ask Etta if, when you're in Castelmezzano, I can come and take you for a walk every now and then. Maybe once a week will do. It won't be too invasive and I will still be able to see you, my sweetheart."

Dora paused to blow her nose again, trumpeting even more loudly than earlier on. The flood was overwhelming everything in its path, and it simply wouldn't stop.

"So, you see what an awful, selfish person I am. People think that I'm the generous one and Etta the hard nose, but the truth is that instead of being happy my best friend has found love, I can only think of my stupid self and the lonely years ahead. But the thing is, the very idea of being parted from you, Leon, really breaks my heart…"

And so violent were the sobs, so abundant the tears, that Dora had to give up all her attempts to contain them. Leon pushed his nose, followed by his whole head on to her lap and felt those large, fat tears drenching his face as the woman hugged him with the sweetest kind of love.

LATER, STILL ON SATURDAY

EVENING

hatsApp Group:

"Emergency Message:
All activities must be suspended for the time being."

What a weird day!

I was furious this morning when I found out about Gary's presentation. How dare he! But so many people attended and the objections from the public weren't as strong as I'd expected. I wish people could understand what he's really up to, but most folks seem to be blind to the impact of such a project on the island economy and its quirky character. It would have devastating consequences.

After the presentation, quite a few people attending the fair came back to our stall and asked to remove their signatures from the petition. Despite Gary being a smarmy liar, people believed him. I knew then that we needed to take drastic action. I only wish I hadn't threatened him after his stupid presentation. It is likely to look bad for me – the police will certainly be told about it. But I will just remind them that if

I really had murder on my mind, I wouldn't have threatened him in public. Truth was, I was really mad at him, and I acted on impulse. At my age, I should have learned to control my temper, but sometimes my youthful hot-headedness still comes out...

Anyway, for good or for bad, but I believe for good, Gary Mason is out of the way. Maybe once the chaos of the murder investigation has passed, we can carry on with our plans, but we will need to work fast. I wonder if Eilidh will change her mind after this. And that's another problem – she's due home tomorrow, which has thrown things into disarray. Now, she will certainly meet those two Italian hags. If everything had gone according to plan, they would have been fleeing from the island in terror long before Eilidh returned.

I thought it'd be good to give them a little show tonight as well, but Mr T rightly said it'd be too risky with all the police around. Also, we have the shadow of a hope that, distracted by the murder, they will forget to mention the... haunting! The nastier of the two hags made no reference to last night's happenings when we enquired. Maybe they believed it was a figment of their imagination. But maybe that's just wishful thinking.

(Just a wee digression: Mr T has done a terrific job. The man is so resourceful, I just wish he didn't agree with my every word sometimes, especially when he clearly doesn't actually agree. Have more backbone, man! But maybe I am being too temperamental?)

When Eilidh arrives, we'll let her discover what has been going on – we have no choice on that – and give her time to simmer down a bit, because she WILL be fuming. Then, and only then, will I speak to her, possibly late in the day. She might have calmed down enough to be receptive by then. After all, the murder should be the main problem she needs to deal with. Yes, I will remind her to focus her energies where they're most needed.

I wish things hadn't gone this far. Stupid, stubborn Gary!

SUNDAY

15

THE AUSSIE

The next morning, the two women and one dog had just returned from a short walk in the drizzly weather and were standing in front of the fire in the reading room when a frenzied knocking at the door startled them.

"Who's there?" Etta called.

"It's me, Eilidh."

Etta went to open the door while Leon, safe in the knowledge there was no ghost but a human being on the other side, charged over with his most ferocious "Woo-woo-WOOOF!"

"Stop it, Leon," Etta said. "I would have adopted a Rottweiler if I had wanted a guard dog." She opened the door and a woman with strawberry-blonde hair and porcelain white skin, decorated with a light smattering of freckles over her nose and cheekbones, came in.

"You must be Leon," she said, going down on her knees so that the dog could study her. "I was told how brave you are."

"Very brave, as long as there's no real danger," said Etta. Leon gave her his dirtiest look. He didn't appreciate this woman's dry sense of humour, especially in front of such a keen – and good-looking – fan.

Once His Highness, the newly crowned Prince of Glengullion,

had received his due homage in the form of pats and scratches, the woman rose to her feet and stretched out her hand to shake Etta's, then changed her mind and hugged her, and then Dora.

"Oh my!" she exclaimed as her eyes scanned the reading room as if taking in all the details. "I don't know where to start, but it seems I've managed to get nothing right for your stay…"

"I don't think you can be held responsible for the murder," said Dora.

"Oh, that!" said Eilidh dismissively, as if she'd been referring to something far worse.

"What did you mean, then?" asked Etta, feeling a little suspicious of the woman's manner.

"Well," said Eilidh, sitting in one of the armchairs that Etta had learned the hard way not to trust – the springs were so far beyond salvation, there was a very real risk of never being able to get up again, "the murder is certainly an awful thing to have happened. And to lose Gary Mason, too, just when I was sure I'd finally got rid of this place. In fact, that is why I came back immediately. I mean, I had to really, with the police investigation going on. But I didn't expect," and she looked around once more, "*this*. I could hardly believe my ears when Edwina said I'd find you here in the turret flat. I don't know what the silly woman was thinking. But why oh why does my life end up in a mess almost all… actually, forget *almost*, I mean ALL the time?"

Etta and Dora looked into each other's eyes.

"*Can you follow what she's saying?*" one telegraphed silently to the other.

"*I haven't got a clue,*" the other telegraphed back as fast as lightning.

Eilidh, with a daughter soon turning 18, surely had to be in her forties. This lassie here – after talking to Rufus, Etta even found herself thinking in a Scottish accent – seemed if anything to be in her early thirties. As if reading her thoughts, Dora shrugged slightly. She didn't understand either.

"Ahh," the woman sighed. "How am I to explain? Not about the murder, though I talked to the police on the phone yesterday and I'm going to meet DCI Findlay later. I hope she can explain more then. No, I meant Edwina. Why on earth did she put you up here? Didn't you tell her that I'd sent you the pictures of your accommodation at Glengullion?"

"We did indeed, but she said we'd have to wait for you to come back and take up any issues with you."

"But that's just silly. How could she not know this is the wrong flat? She helped me prepare the correct one."

"I'm afraid we don't really understand what you're trying to say…"

"My bad. The people around here often tell me I have a tendency to speak too fast. Perhaps it's because I grew up in Australia. And I have a habit of jumping from one subject to another, which, to be clear, is not an Aussie habit. It's just me."

The women looked at Eilidh, wondering if she wasn't simply bonkers. If she were, she likely wouldn't be the first madwoman they had met since arriving on Mull.

"There's no point in waiting for Edwina. She will turn up when she's ready, I'm sure. In the meantime, please follow me. And don't forget to wear something warm, it's cold outside."

"It's not much warmer inside," Etta couldn't resist adding, even though Dora glared at her.

"Scottish castles are never warm, even with central heating. I can't imagine how you two put up with just a couple of old fireplaces."

"We didn't have much choice," said Etta.

Eilidh burst into laughter. "You're right. But as I said, come along with me and I'll explain what I can."

Outside, walking briskly away from the cold and gloomy accommodation, they almost stumbled into a tall man with back-combed hair. He was as graceful as an actor, his whole demeanour elegant, even though he was wearing a dark leather jacket that afforded him little or no protection against the pouring rain.

"Jeremy, you'll never guess what's happened," said Eilidh.

"What's happened *this time*, you mean," the man replied with a friendly grin, a dimple easy to spot on his almost beardless face.

"Yes, this time it's Edwina. Guess where she sent my guests."

"I've no idea. I thought you mentioned they would be staying in the Steadings..."

"The west wing turret! Three storeys, no lift, no heating."

"How could she think you'd put them there?" He shook his head, horrified, then looked at the two women under the umbrella. "But maybe, Eilidh, you should make some introductions..."

"Oh, I'm so sorry. And that reminds me: I didn't even ask who's who. But you must be Dora, is that right?" Dora nodded as Eilidh looked at her, her salt-and-pepper fringe bouncing. "We exchanged a number of emails," Eilidh explained, looking back at Jeremy. "And so, this is Etta, and the most important one is, of course, Leon. Have you ever seen a more charming dog than he is? This is Jeremy, my fiancé."

The man shook hands with both women, finding it hard to squeeze a few words in edgeways. Eilidh marched on, chatting over everyone, and the three people and one dog filed after her until she stopped on the left-hand side of the castle. Here, it seemed, a newer wing had been added to the original structure. It was just one floor with not a single turret to its name, but it boasted the same sandstone and crow-stepped gables as the rest of the castle. Eilidh opened the door into a bright and airy living room. Blond-wood floors led to large French windows with – good gracious! – no dark, gloomy tartan curtains. A little fireplace stood in the corner and, more importantly, there were two heaters.

Still talking, Eilidh led her Italian guests into two bedrooms. These were decorated with delicate wallpaper, one in pastel mauve, the other in blue. Even here were four-poster beds, but they had white iron frames and light chiffon curtains. Neither room had a fireplace, but both had modern and very welcome heaters. White wardrobes and chests of drawers and comfy little sofas, one in dark mauve, one in light blue, were the finishing touches to the cosy rooms.

Dora couldn't help clasping her hands and picking the mauve bedroom for herself.

"It's a little cold as the heaters are switched off when the rooms are unoccupied," Eilidh explained. "But give it time and it will definitely warm up."

"It's already warmer than the other flat," said Etta.

"Oh, I feel so embarrassed," said Eilidh, banging her head with her hand. "You had to endure all of that. Now, I need coffee! Let's go to the castle... actually, no. Jeremy, let's help the ladies move their luggage first."

Jeremy just had time to nod before Eilidh was on the move again. Leon directed proceedings until he, Etta and Dora were settled in their new flat.

"I don't know what Edwina was thinking, sending you to the oldest part of the castle!" Eilidh, it seemed, was completely baffled by this lapse on the part of her friend.

"My theory is," said Etta, immensely relieved at having moved into their real accommodation, while realising Edwina's 'lapse' rather confirmed her theory, "that as the two of us are Italians, the people here, Edwina included, thought we were Mr Mason's business partners. The ones that would invest in and manage the proposed spa and golf course."

"Ha!" The woman banged her head with the heel of her hand again, a smile flashing on to her face. "How silly! But that would explain a few things. Edwina clearly wanted to scare you off and thought that placing you in the turret apartment would have you fleeing the place within days..."

"And you'd withdraw your offer to partner in the purchase of the castle," Jeremy interrupted hastily.

"There's more, though," said Etta. "I'm afraid on our first night, we also had some unwelcome *visitors*."

"Visitors?" asked Jeremy.

"At night?" cried Eilidh.

"I assume they wanted us to believe a ghost haunted the castle…"

Jeremy and Eilidh exchanged a confused look, so both Etta and Dora told them in detail all that had occurred the night of their arrival.

"I think they wanted to make sure we disappeared before you came back, Eilidh. If the cold and discomforts weren't enough to get the job done, the supernatural would overcome any further resistance."

"That must be it. But now, please come along to the castle," unstoppable Eilidh was already moving towards the door. "While the flat warms up, we could all do with a strong coffee. And I'm sure I've got a jar of cookies for Leon too."

The suggestion sounded too good to refuse.

16

A WEIRD REQUEST

E ilidh led her companions to the main part of the castle. They had to use the front entrance as the one from the gardens was still cordoned off, the whole Weapons Hall closed to everyone except the scene of crime officers who were still hard at work. Uniformed police were patrolling the area.

"That is a bother as we use the Weapons Hall to receive people," said Eilidh. "And it has easy access to the garden. I guess we will have to sit in the more formal Crystal Room…"

"Is it heated?" Etta asked anxiously.

"Yes, I asked Edwina to turn the heating on last night, so it'd be a decent temperature by the time we arrived today," replied Jeremy.

The Crystal Room, as its name suggested, was a large, elegant white room. Above an imposing long table hung a huge chandelier with crystal pendants and multiple streams of beads that refracted the daylight as effectively as if the sun was shining. A white marble fireplace cosied the room with fake flames, while all around them, cabinets displayed an impressive variety of glasses and bowls. In one corner, two large white sofas with a light red pattern, along with lamps shaded by the same fabric as the sofas, helped to soften the formality of the room.

"I'm glad there's no suit of armour around," whispered Dora, sitting down slowly on the sofa next to Etta.

"It is hard to believe they're not moving around," said Eilidh, smiling at Dora while drawing her legs up to her chest, her trousers rising to reveal funny pink socks. "Or listening to every word we say."

"And it was a mace," Jeremy reminded her, "that killed poor Mr Mason."

"Well," said Eilidh, "I don't think the police are considering any supernatural hypotheses at present."

"Wait until you tell them about the legend."

"The legend?" asked Dora, who always loved a good story. Remembering Edwina's skimpy explanation of the tragic story behind the haunting picture in their former bedroom, and its aftermath, she wondered if the loquacious Eilidh would add a few more details.

"Yes. According to legend, two centuries back, Lord McGullion, my ancestor, set fire to an entire village in order to clear the room to build this castle. But once the castle was built, he didn't get to enjoy it for long, as a mace from a suit of armour fell on his head and he died on the spot."

"Which is pretty much what happened to poor Gary Mason," said Jeremy.

"It is really weird," muttered Etta.

"More so," Dora added, "if you think of the ghost who visited us on Friday night."

"But as Etta said," Jeremy responded, a certain amount of irony in his voice, "the Lord McGullion that bothered you is most likely the product of calculated human trickery."

"True, I tend to forget that. Still… well, I guess you never know."

"On the contrary," said Etta. "I know. Last night, after the murder, no one, ghost or otherwise, came to bother us. Possibly the *spectres* were too scared the police would look into any strange goings on."

Jeremy grinned. "Very likely..." he began, but Eilidh interrupted him.

"Don't be so sure and don't jump to conclusions. I told you that almost ever since I arrived in Auntie Katherine's castle, I have felt something eerie."

"Who's Auntie Katherine?"

"She was my father's sister-in-law, she married his younger brother. When Uncle Donald died, she inherited Glengullion. She too passed away last year and left the castle to me. But what was I telling you about?" Eilidh had a tendency to ask questions only to be the one who answered them. "Oh yes, the presence I perceive. It's a weird feeling that accompanies me almost constantly when I'm here, like someone is watching over me lovingly."

"Really?" asked Dora. "Maybe it's your auntie." She shuddered, remembering the feeling she'd had of being watched in the turret flat. That presence certainly hadn't been loving.

"I perceive it as a male presence, if that makes sense."

"It certainly isn't Lord McGullion," said Etta. "I can't see much tenderness in him at all, unless he's different when he knows you're blood of his blood."

"That's it! That's exactly how I feel, as if we're somehow close, as if he wants to take care of me..."

"Eilidh, please don't give me the creeps," said Jeremy, shaking his head. "The presence, if it's not just something made up by the old timers, is not a benign one."

"Old timers?" asked Etta.

Eilidh chuckled. "That's what Jeremy calls Edwina and her entourage. What they call themselves is almost as amusing – the Pensioners' Posse. So if you hear people referring to the PP, you'll know what they mean."

Etta and Dora exchanged glances. They had heard the initials PP spoken quite a few times, but had disregarded it as irrelevant. Call themselves sleuths! Mind you, Etta had something to say on that matter, but it could wait.

"The PP are the people who want to turn the castle into a retirement home?" she clarified.

"That's right."

"As well as Edwina, we've met Tom, Sandra and Grayson, Debbie…"

"You've met all the main players, then."

"Letitia?"

"Letitia, along with Edwina, was my aunt's best friend, but she is a little vacuous nowadays. Dementia, the doctors said, but the others try to take care of her…"

"You don't think they might be involved in the murder, do you?"

Jeremy and Eilidh exchanged a meaningful glance. "Eilidh," he said, "we should really face up to this, because that's the kind of question the police are going to ask you."

"Do you really think they might be behind something so awful?"

"Maybe you're right," said Jeremy, after giving the issue some thought. "In fact, I can't imagine them doing anything so violent. The welcome they gave to Etta and Dora – the ghost thing – could well be part of their modus operandi, but homicide? I hope that would be stretching things far too far, even for them."

The tension that had been present on Eilidh's face, despite her jokes and chatter, seemed to relax a little, making her features look softer and more natural.

"I'm glad you think like me, Jeremy." She stretched her hand over to his arm for a long caress and a squeeze of gratitude. "As mad as I am at them, I can't believe they would do anything that wicked. Not Edwina, nor Tom, nor any of them."

"But," Etta objected promptly, "they are the ones who desperately didn't want you to sell the castle to Mr Mason."

"Gary Mason is the… I beg your pardon, was the kind of guy who had enemies right, left and centre. He was the kind of man for whom the end justified the means."

"Still, you had no hesitation in doing business with him?"

"The point is that I wasn't doing business with him. That is, I wasn't going to be his business partner. I was just selling him a property that has taken up too much of my already meagre finances. He came to me with a very good offer…"

"Why not accept the one from Edwina and the others? Wouldn't that have been more morally satisfying?"

Jeremy came to Eilidh's rescue. "Theirs wasn't really an offer. They just suggested Eilidh should wait to monetise the property and become the main investor in a rather hazardous project. With no guarantee whatsoever it would make money, there was no safety net for her. Sure, they'd pay rent, help to raise funds for some of the restoration, play their part in running the place and maybe turn it into a tourist attraction, but the risk would all be on Eilidh."

"And there's Josh and the cows," said Eilidh with a sigh. "Let's not forget that."

"Yes, that's one more project without legs that would have fallen on to Eilidh's shoulders."

"Mind you, I dearly love the place. It's just been too much for me. Maybe if I had that magic business touch and the strength to turn it into something profitable… I'm not saying what Edwina and the others have in mind is entirely infeasible, but it would be too much for me. I have neither the stamina nor the motivation."

"Now, compare this with Gary's generous offer."

"He actually made two offers. I could either take a good pot of money, or become a partner holding a minority of shares. I'd be paid far less in terms of cash up front, but I'd benefit from the shares in the long term. As I said, I don't think I could have partnered with Gary for long, so I was hoping to close the deal for the first option, get my money and set myself up in London with Elizabeth, my daughter. She will start university there in September."

"I remember you telling me you had an 18-year-old

daughter," said Dora, "but how is that possible? You look so young yourself."

"Thank you. I had Elizabeth when I was a young woman, just 20, so I'm 38 now. One more dreadful mistake. Not my daughter – I'm proud of her. I mean her father." Eilidh sighed once more. In fact, she sighed so much, Etta and Dora weren't sure if it was to take a breath before another torrent of words or a real sigh.

"You look so much younger," said Etta, grateful that Dora had asked the question. She would have made who knows what kind of gaffe? Dora was good at asking even the most delicate questions.

"Oh, thank you. Everyone tells me I look young, though at times I feel more like 50 or even 60. Especially on days like yesterday when the police told me about the murder. And," she looked around guiltily, "how awful that Gary should pass away before we signed the wretched contract! If you want to know, I wish it had already been signed. Now, I guess, I will have to start the sales process all over again."

Jeremy stood up and ran his hands over Eilidh's shoulders, giving her a little hug from behind. "Come on, honey, we'll make it through this. We'll find someone else who will take care of old Glengullion. Maybe the Italian investors will move forward anyway…"

"I doubt it. They were only interested because of Gary. On the other hand, Edwina and her friends will certainly be waiting at the door." Eilidh's smile was tinged with irony.

"We'll find something better," said Jeremy.

"In the meantime, I'll fetch a bite to eat from the kitchen," and with that, Eilidh leaped up and disappeared from the room.

"So, what about you, Jeremy?" Etta asked as the man sat again. "Are you convinced selling up would be the best thing for Eilidh?"

"Yes, I don't have any doubts. I mean, I understand all the emotions behind her decision. Eilidh's lived in thoroughly modern Australia since childhood, and when she returned to

Mull, she found a fascinating ancient property. Rundown, yes, but still full of... you know, the charm of old things. She explored the possibilities for a whole year, but the holiday lets, very much like the cheese project with Josh, turned sour. Literally, I mean, in Josh's case, the cheese was that bad."

"It tasted fine yesterday," Etta said.

"Actually, it was delicious!" Dora added.

"That was yesterday," said Jeremy. "How about tomorrow? And the day after tomorrow?" His brows almost crossed as his forehead furrowed, suggesting he had responded to similar arguments a number of times. "Anyway, it wasn't only Josh. Following what her aunt had already started, Eilidh has continued restoring rooms to rent out as self-catering flats and B&B, but they each require tonnes of work, and the return hardly covers the costs of keeping the place running. If Eilidh were an heiress, had plenty of money on the side for living expenses and seeing her daughter through university, she might have tried harder. But I am afraid she will lose the little she has and plough years of her life into something meaningless. There's a time for dreaming and another to take back control of your life, even if it is less romantic."

Etta and Dora nodded, sharing exactly the same views. Well, Etta did at least.

"So, when Gary's proposal came along, you advised Eilidh to jump at it?"

"Not exactly," Jeremy said, his impish grin deepening the dimple on his left cheek. "My beloved doesn't much like to 'be advised', so we discussed the pros and cons, and I told her whatever she chose, I would support her. In all honesty, when Gary first approached her, I wasn't exactly enthusiastic. I didn't like the guy much and I was really worried when Eilidh mentioned the possibility of partnering with him. But to my relief, we agreed on this right away – either she'd sell him the entire thing, or she'd look for an offer elsewhere."

Eilidh came back with a dish of shortbread and some dog

biscuits for Leon. The four humans chatted amiably over their snacks, until Jeremy took a look at his watch.

"Eilidh, it's almost time for the police to interview you."

"Goodness, I feel dreadful, as if I were the villain. I hope they don't see how nervous I am, or I will be included in the list of suspects…"

Jeremy grinned. "I'm sorry to disappoint you on that score, but you have rather a strong alibi as many people saw you on the coach from London to Glasgow after the crime had taken place. Just tell them what you know, and you'll be fine."

"Still, I'm a mass of nerves…"

"We'd better leave you in peace, then," said Etta, getting up from the sofa.

"Once again, please accept my apologies for all that has happened," said Eilidh, also standing up.

"Don't you worry," said Dora.

"Feel free to give me a shout if anything's not working properly, including ghostly appearances or any other sort of trouble. Oh, how silly of me! I almost forgot." Already at the door, Eilidh stopped, snatching her hand away from the knob, and stepped back into the middle of the room. There, she clapped her hand theatrically to her forehead and kept it there, implying that it was even hard for someone as talkative as she was to find the right words. "I'm not sure how to put this… please forgive me if I sound weird or blunt. Did you mention the ghostly affair to the police?"

"No, we didn't, as a matter of fact," said Dora. "They merely asked us what we saw when we found the body, if we saw or heard anything that could be related to Mr Mason's death, and why we were here. We told them about the homeswapping scheme, but they weren't particularly interested in that either."

Etta didn't speak, but she kept gazing at Eilidh, curious to see what this rather unpredictable woman was leading up to.

"That's great, because I want to ask you a little favour. Please, don't mention the ghost and those strange incidents to the police."

Surprise filled the faces of all the others present, Jeremy included.

17

PARTING WAYS

Unsurprisingly, it was Etta who responded to Eilidh's weird request, and she did so in her customary blunt style.

"Are you asking us to withhold information from a murder investigation?"

"Um… that's not exactly what I had in mind."

"But that *is* exactly what you've asked the ladies to do," said Jeremy, firmly.

"Well, if those incidents were related to the murder, then you'd be right. But… let's put it this way. Allow me to talk to Edwina first. This morning, I was so very mad at her, I didn't really let her speak. If I meet with her in a calmer frame of mind, I'm sure she'll have a plausible explanation."

"I see your point," Etta spoke gravely this time. "But the police have a right to the whole picture. We can't know what is and isn't relevant to their investigation. And frankly, I doubt that Edwina would tell you if the… what did you call them? The Pensioners' Posse? Yes, I doubt she'd admit to it if they had anything to do with the murder."

"But I promise you, they're gentle and inoffensive people when you get to know them. It wasn't them, but I'm afraid that if the police see them as possible suspects, they won't look anywhere else. And the real killer will be free to roam around and carry out his wicked deeds undisturbed. I know they've already excluded all Mason's staff and his wife, as they were all absent from the castle at the time of the murder. I only hope they have checked their alibis properly."

"The police are not stupid!" Usually the first to criticise the local law-enforcement officers, Etta was quick to jump to their defence this time. After all the sleuthing she'd done, she felt she was the only one with a right to pick their actions apart.

"I know, I know," Eilidh stretched out her hands as if to implore her guest to stay calm. "All I'm asking is one, maybe two days of silence. Let's see if the police come up with a different solution."

Dora looked at Etta, as ever willing to comply with the strange request. Etta felt much more sceptical, and she sensed that Jeremy agreed with her reasoning more than Eilidh's.

Someone rang the doorbell, and Jeremy moved towards the window. "The police are here," he announced.

"Then we'd better go," said Etta.

"Did we agree?" whispered Eilidh. "Just a couple of days and let's see what happens…"

"Of course," said Dora.

Etta glared at her friend. Granted, she herself might have withheld information from the police on a couple of occasions in the past, but it had always been of her own free will. Never as a favour to anyone else.

The four people and one dog left the Crystal Room and went over to the entrance door, which Jeremy opened to reveal Detective Chief Inspector Georgia Findlay with another police officer. DCI Findlay greeted the two women.

"We had a cup of coffee together, after we helped them move into their flat," Eilidh explained.

"Why did they only move in today?" DCI Findlay enquired.

"The heating in the flat wasn't working properly before," Eilidh answered quickly.

"It looks like we might need to examine the entire property."

"Of course," said Eilidh, but from her expression, Etta guessed she was biting her tongue.

"Will you be in your flat later?" the DCI asked Etta and Dora.

"We were planning a walk to the lighthouse, if the sky clears, but we can do that another day if you need us here."

"No, no, off you go. We've got plenty of things to go over with Ms McGullion. I just wanted to make sure you two weren't... up to anything." Georgia Findlay's narrowed eyes and sarcastic voice meant even Etta didn't dare to ask how the investigations were proceeding and if the police had a better idea of the time of death.

"Of course not," said Dora, smiling reassuringly.

"Is there no end to how weird this place can be?" said Etta as soon as they were out of earshot. "Even when we think we've solved the mystery of the ghost, who actually happens to be the least spooky being around here."

"Do you mean you find Eilidh spooky?"

"No, although she does seem to have been infected by the weirdness. I was referring to all the strange things that are happening..."

"There's a woman," Dora frowned, trying to pull her thoughts together, "who wants to sell a castle that is part of the local heritage and for which many people around here seem to have a vision. Actually no, let's call it a wish. On the other hand, I can understand Eilidh's desire to live her life as she wants. So, rather than weird or spooky things, I just see very human conflicts, plain and simple."

"It'd be all very normal or, as you said, human if it weren't for the fact someone's been murdered. A very extreme way, in my view at least, to solve a *plain and simple* conflict. And the owner of the place – the one who stood to gain the most from the transaction with the victim – has explicitly asked us not to tell the police about all the stupid tricks and cruel treatment dished out to us, two innocent guests. I don't think we did the right thing to agree to what we agreed."

"But it's just for two days…"

"What if someone gets killed in the next two days?"

Dora stopped dead in her tracks and looked at Etta in horror. "Do you think someone else might be in danger?"

"Frankly, I don't know."

"But if they've killed Gary Mason, who was the cause of it all, what would the reason be to kill someone else?"

"That's it. Can't you see the contradiction?"

Dora shrugged.

"Either we think Gary Mason was killed because he threatened to turn Glengullion Castle into a luxury resort exclusively for the rich, in which case we've no reason to fear someone else might get killed, but we do have a good reason to let the police know about the ghost and all the theatre those old folks set up as they'd be the most likely suspects. Or we think Gary Mason was killed for a reason other than the sale of Glengullion, in which case we don't know if the murderer is satisfied or not. But even if the latter hypothesis is correct, wouldn't it be better to tell the police about the PP and their nasty tricks?"

"My head's spinning far too fast. Can't we try to understand a little more before we reveal what happened to us?"

"What do you mean?"

"I mean doing a little sleuthing of our own, as we suggested yesterday."

"Well…" Etta flushed suddenly, then spoke slowly, wringing her hands. "Well, I have to confess, Rufus was rather worried on the phone last night. Actually, he couldn't believe we were in the vicinity of yet another murder. He made me promise we wouldn't get involved this time, at least until he comes over a week tomorrow."

Dora was surprised. And Etta knew why. Since they had been sharing their travels, Etta had never agreed to anyone's request to stop looking into a murder. Far from it, such a request would simply make her all the more determined to get to the bottom of the crime. Was the power Rufus held over her so strong? Dora wanted to find out. Immediately.

"And are you planning to comply with his wishes?" she asked rather impertinently.

"For once, I think I might," answered Etta, a little uncertainly. After pondering for a while, she added, "We don't need to get ourselves into trouble wherever we go…"

"And this is after we made a list of suspects just last night, and discussed all aspects of the murder thoroughly?"

"Indeed," Etta confirmed, feeling somewhat guilty.

"That's very disappointing!"

"Miss Pepe, are you telling me you want to meddle in business that might cause you trouble?"

"I'd at least give it a thought," was Dora's surprisingly petulant answer.

"What do you plan to do?"

"I can't see the point in discussing it any further with you as you clearly don't want to get your hands dirty."

Etta felt challenged. Of course, she wanted to sleuth, but at the same time, she didn't want them to run unnecessary risks – something that had happened a few times in the past. But in the past, there hadn't been a Rufus McCall waiting for her. Not that she believed there was anything of the romantic kind between them. Still, wouldn't it be nice to meet up with him at least one more time before they left Scotland? And wouldn't it be better to be alive and kicking for the occasion? And how come ever sweet Dora was all of a sudden so eager to investigate this time? Why couldn't she just clasp her hands and stare in peaceful wonder at the picturesque property?

"Why don't we go to the lighthouse?" Etta suggested, sure a visit to a pretty landmark would plant the seeds of peace in her friend and suffocate these newfound adventurous, rebellious ideas.

"I'd rather go to Tobermory and see what we can learn from people there," said Dora, again rather insolently and totally out of character.

"But I'm sure Leon needs a good walk."

"You're perfectly right, dear," said Dora. "That is exactly what you can do. I'll see you later." And before Etta could even think of a reply, Dora had planted Leon's leash in her hands, which were limp with surprise, and was gone.

18

TO THE LIGHTHOUSE

E tta looked at Leon, and Leon looked back at Etta.
"I've no answer, if that's what you're after, but as we're
here, we may as well go and check out this lighthouse. I'm sure
that strange friend of ours will be begging to visit it once we tell
her about the *poetry* of it all." Etta emphasised the word 'poetry',
mocking Dora's way of enthusing about the things they'd seen
on their travels. Leon looked a little doubtful, but being the
gentledog he was, he followed his grumpy biped.

Actually, that isn't strictly true. He started to follow her, but
there were tantalising smells all round, so how was a dog
supposed to resist? He stopped and took a pee here, then trotted
happily ahead, paused, took a pee there and a diversion to the
right, zigzagging across the path and pulling Etta in all
directions.

"Stop it!" the woman cried imperiously. "Come here!" The
dog did as he was told for once. Occasionally, even Leon could
pretend to be obedient. "You're making me seasick with all this
pulling and pushing, right and left, stop and go. I'd better
remove your leash, but promise you will behave."

The dog looked her in the eyes, his expression dead serious,
as if saying, "I solemnly swear to be good, the whole good,

nothing but the good." This lasted until he heard the click of the leash unhooking from his collar. Once free, he immediately followed the accepted order of things: he'd say where they'd go, when and how. After all, aren't Bassets natural-born leaders?

Etta threw her arms up in despair, then concluded she didn't mind if they didn't get to the lighthouse. She could still tell Dora the place was enchanting. After all, it doesn't take much imagination to describe a lighthouse and the *breathtaking* sea views, and the *magical atmosphere* around it. She could even tell her about their climb up the stairs to the top. And it was definitely better for everyone if Leon tired himself out. That was when he turned into a truly obedient dog who was satisfied to doze all night, not to mention the fact that when he slept, he was adorable.

So, she followed the hound. Leon would go towards the forest on the path they had walked the day before, only to take a sudden turn towards the coastal path. He looked up at the sign that said 'To the lighthouse', paused as if taking in its full meaning, then turned 45° and, as if in slow motion, raised his right leg, extending his hip wide with the elasticity and grace of a ballerina. Finally, he let go an abundant stream of pee against the feet of the signpost. Turning 180°, he kicked the air with his back legs, growling like an angry bull, then happily trotted towards the lighthouse, not turning once to see if Etta was following. In his certainty, he was convinced that even a bad-tempered servant knew her duty.

Etta banged her head with her hand, remembering what Dora would say when Etta got mad with the dog. "Let him believe he's the one in charge, and he will abide by your wishes." Etta had always wondered whether Dora used this psychological trick on her as well as Leon, which was why she'd never followed the advice. Now, maybe it was time to set her touchiness aside and reconsider her tactics for the foreseeable future.

It was at this moment of decision that ahead of them, two

figures came into view, emerging from around a bend and moving towards them. Sandra was walking alongside Grayson, who was propelling himself skilfully along in his wheelchair.

"Good morning," Grayson said, scratching the ears of Leon, who'd trotted ahead to say hi. "Such a sweet, friendly dog."

"Sweet, my tooth," muttered Etta. But she couldn't help smiling, ruining the grumpy persona she had so carefully affected.

"You will have a lovely walk, there's a brilliant view up there."

"Have you been all the way to the lighthouse?"

"Almost, but the last part is a bit rough. There've been some rockfalls and I didn't want to run into trouble with my wheels."

"Is that Iona?" asked Etta, pointing to an island in front of them, proud to feel as well-informed as Dora always was.

Sandra gave a gentle laugh. "Nope, Iona is on the opposite side of the island, so you can't see it from here. That's the Isle of Coll, and over on this side, that's the mainland."

"I see," Etta was mortified, but grateful Dora wasn't there to laugh at her. Besides, if attack is the best form of defence, she was ready to embrace the concept. "Are you feeling better after yesterday's shock?"

Sandra flushed and shot a puzzled look at her husband before replying. "Much better, thank you. In fact, that's why we came out for a walk. I needed some fresh air after that terrible discovery yesterday."

"I can imagine," Etta was being uncharacteristically sympathetic. "But how unfortunate for you that you of all people had to be the one to find him. How come you were inside the castle?"

Again, Sandra met her husband's gaze. This time, he nodded at her as if to say, "Go ahead".

Almost as if her response had been scripted, the woman explained, "I was simply searching for the ladies'. The chemical toilets outside were awfully busy and I wondered if I could use those within the castle. I knew Eilidh wouldn't have minded. In the hall, I saw something in front of the mantelpiece and wondered if someone had dumped a bag there. But when I got closer," the woman gulped, "I realised it was a man. Then, I thought he must have been taken suddenly ill, which is why I bent over him and recognised it was Gary. I touched him and knew straight away he was dead, but he wasn't cold yet. I thought he might have had a heart attack, then saw the blood and cried out.

"I confess, a stupid thought crossed my mind when I first realised it was Gary. I wondered if our hostility had caused him to fall ill. In that moment, I was scared, so I cried out not only to call for help, but also from fear. You know the rest."

"So, the entrance door was open and anyone could get in?"

"Well, a few of us know a little trick with the French doors. If you pull the handle all the way up, well beyond 90°, and then pull it down completely, the door opens. Unless it's been properly locked, that is. But in the morning, it's always open. It's convenient for the owners and guests alike to have easy access without having to carry a bunch of keys."

"Only this time, the owner of the castle was far away from Mull. How come the door was unlocked?"

"That's simple enough to explain," said Grayson. "Gary Mason and his team were using the castle to store all the equipment they'd need during the presentation. It would have been too awkward to give a key to everyone who needed one so they could keep unlocking and locking the door."

Etta nodded, but her brain was taking notes. *How well informed they are about Gary Mason and his team's movements, and about the murder location. And if Sandra and Grayson know the trick to open the French doors into the Weapons Hall, I assume everyone in the PP knows too…*

Her musings were interrupted by Grayson asking her how she'd slept last night, after all the distress and fear of the previous day.

"Oh, last night I slept just fine, thank you," replied Etta, putting her hand on to her heart and smiling her most sickly smile. "It seems that when the police are around, no one dares to disturb you, human or otherwise. And this morning, Eilidh helped us move into our proper accommodation. Apparently, Edwina totally misunderstood her instructions. I'm sure we'll sleep undisturbed from now on in our comfortable lodgings."

It was a very small glance that wife and husband exchanged, but it was enough for Etta to see. It clearly belonged in the "I told you so" category.

"By the way, what will you do now that Gary Mason has passed away?" Grayson asked.

"Are you asking me?" said Etta, looking right and left as if he might be speaking to another person. The couple both nodded. "We're Eilidh's guests. We didn't know Gary Mason at all, so why do you think the fact he was murdered would somehow have an impact on my and my friend's plans?"

At that, husband and wife exchanged a puzzled look, and Etta smiled inwardly. Maybe, for the first time, it was dawning on them that she and Dora, despite being Italians, had nothing to do with Gary Mason's plans.

19

TO TOBERMORY

Dora had driven her Fiat 500 slowly, slowly to Tobermory pier. But despite Etta's constant complaints that Dora was too prone to distractions to drive, she made it. And a good job too, as once she was back to living alone in her cramped flat in Pietrapertosa, she'd need to be as independent as she could.

She parked the car at the entrance to the town, grateful the parking spaces were large and accommodating enough not to require a great deal of manoeuvring. Before locking the car, she pulled down her seat, used as she was to helping the dog out. Only this time, there was no dog, of course. And she'd better get used to that, too.

"Wallowing in self-pity won't help, old bean," she reprimanded herself. "Rather, keep on keeping on." That was the first lesson she'd learned after her father, a keen gambler, had passed away and she'd found herself facing a queue of creditors asking for their money back. She'd been obliged to sell everything she owned, including her beloved family home, and seen all that had been certain in her life slide into uncertainty. "Keep on keeping on," had become her mantra, one she had taken to repeating every afternoon. It had inspired her to take on tutoring work in the evenings and even accept a job in a restaurant kitchen on Sundays. Life had been like climbing Everest, the summit seeming unreachable whenever she looked at how far she had to go. So she decided to concentrate on one step at a time.

A year later, she'd managed to pay all the creditors back, and had moved into a small flat. It was an ugly place to live, that's true, but at least she was free to walk the streets of her village again without the fear someone would swoop down on her to ask where their money was. That had been achieved through the power of her small daily steps towards regaining her honour and her freedom.

Two years later, she'd given up her Sundays at the restaurant and kept only the students she enjoyed teaching the most. She could finally join voluntary groups and do some of what she wanted with her newfound free time. She'd been proud of that.

Now, she had to face the harsh reality of leaving her present lifestyle behind. It had been so easy to adapt to the good things in life, the companionship of a dear friend, the love of a noble hound; it would not be easy to adapt back again, but it would be easier than when her father passed. At least no one would be following her around, demanding their money back.

And you never know what's around the next corner, she told herself. *Etta will always be my dearest friend even if we don't live or travel together. Keep on keeping on, Dora. But, it's time to focus. What exactly do I intend to achieve here in Tobermory? Hmmm… the bookshop. It's so easy to speak to shopkeepers, and the bookshop I saw when I arrived with Etta on Friday looked so charming.*

Dora looked at the pier, and then at the town. The drizzle had passed and the day was now sunny, so the colourful facades of Tobermory glowed softly in the sparkling light. She stopped to take it all in, determined to live this last trip to the fullest, closing her eyes to drink in all the smells, the chatter of voices, the cries of the seagulls, the fresh breeze caressing her cheeks.

It just feels too good to spoil it with the fear of the bad days to come. I might as well enjoy this good spell as long as it lasts.

She lingered by the windows of the arts and crafts shops, the souvenirs, the goodies from the bakery – what a temptation at all times! Then she stopped in front of the red and grey bookstore. One whole window was dedicated to books about life on the Scottish islands, from cookery to hiking, from poetry to biographies. The other window was focused on children's literature. Yes! She'd surely find what she was looking for there.

The shop's doors, on this summer Sunday, were open.

"Good morning," a cheerful woman welcomed her.

"Hello," Dora replied. "May I have a look around before making my requests?"

"You're most welcome to do so." The woman smiled, waving a hand around at the entire shop as if saying, "This is all for you." What a treasure a bookshop is, as if the readers are the real owners and the owners just the keepers of something that inherently belongs to anyone who loves books.

I need to buy a small notebook, Dora told herself, *for all the happy thoughts that come to mind during the day. Then I can read them in moments when I feel down, like I did last night.* And the very first thought she'd write down would be that readers are shareholders in a bookshop like the one in Tobermory. Such a thought would never fail to make her happy.

As if by magic, a selection of colourful notebooks materialised in front of her. She picked one with a funny illustration of a sheep on the cover and the words: "BAAA Happy!" Exactly what she was looking for.

Then, she immersed herself in the section dedicated to books about the island, finally emerging with a copy of *Island Wife: Living on the Edge of the Wild,* an autobiography of a woman who had lived her life in the Outer Hebrides, raising five children, knocking a hotel into shape and learning to run it, and creating the first whale-watching business in the UK. Dora would never accomplish all those things herself, but she knew through reading, she could live the lives of others vicariously. Another book, *The Ninth Wave: Love and Food on the Isle of Mull* by Carla

ADRIANA LICIO

Lamont, a chef living and working on the very island Dora was visiting, simply fell into in her hands. It was a cookery book, but there was also room for a few autobiographical bits and pieces from a woman who'd left Canada, and fallen in love with both Mull and a local fisherman. Together, they had created their own restaurant and love nest out of four cold stone walls. Twenty years later, she and her husband were still there, living the dream and having fun.

Her arms full of treasures, Dora finally returned to the shopkeeper and asked for her customary book.

"I collect *Pippi Longstocking* editions from every country I visit," she explained, "and despite having already spent some time in Scotland, I wanted to be in a very special bookshop like this one before buying my Scottish copy."

"You're in exactly the right place," said the woman. "You see, Astrid Lindgren is one of my favourite children's authors, so I try to stock as many of her books as I can. As for Pippi, I've got a very nice edition, illustrated by Ingrid Vang Nyman."

"The first illustrator of Pippi?"

"Yes, the very same. She's a Danish illustrator," said the woman, handing Dora the book. Dora browsed through the pages, smiled quite a few times.

"I will take it, along with these two and the notepad," and she laid her selections on the counter. "I was also looking for a book on Glengullion Castle and its history… or legends."

The shopkeeper took the books – quite a heavy lot – from Dora and shook her head.

"I'm afraid such a book hasn't been written yet, which is a pity as Glengullion is a place full of history. Not always that pleasant, though."

"Spooky tales are always entertaining. I mean, even the darkest deeds seem to acquire a certain charm after a few centuries have gone by."

The woman gave the issue some serious thought. "That's very true, but it's slightly different when the legends still seem to be far too alive to have that cosy feeling of detachment the passage of time normally brings."

Dora looked at her, puzzled. "I'm not sure I understand."

"Well, just outside of Tobermory, there's a house that is said to be haunted. People swear that from time to time after midnight, they've seen strange lights or heard laughter or cries coming from inside. But if you dig a little deeper, you'll tend to learn that those people had just come out of their favourite pub when they saw what they claim they saw. So while the place is definitely rundown and spooky, at the same time, the stories about it are only true as long as you want them to be."

"Like when Pippi launched an adult into a tree?"

"Exactly! It's a tacit agreement to suspend belief."

"While at Glengullion…" Dora spoke softly, but more assertively than her interlocutor might have expected from such a sweet old lady.

"While at Glengullion…" the shopkeeper picked up from where Dora had paused. "Um, how should I put this? Do you know about the legend and the curse upon Lord McGullion?" When Dora nodded, the woman continued, "Well, strange things keep happening. *Real* things."

"Like the murder yesterday afternoon?"

"Oh, you've already heard about it. That's a shame."

"But surely you don't think the murder is related to any legend of old… do you?"

"Well," the shopkeeper's eyes wandered around as if searching for the best words, "the truth is that I don't know. I mean, I know a man has been brutally murdered. Also, the killer used a mace, just like in the legend of Lord McGullion."

"You mean the culprit might have been a ghost?"

"No, no, certainly not a ghost. Still, isn't it strange that the curse is still in operation, even if it's using human hands?"

"You mean the murderer was somehow compelled to kill?"

"Something like that, yes."

"But you could just as easily turn it around and say that the murderer took local folklore into consideration when planning his crime…"

"I see the point you're making. But if you take the historical perspective, it's accident after accident after accident."

"I beg your pardon, I don't really understand."

"Well, if you've heard a little of the legend, you might have heard that Lord McGullion was a man as ambitious as he was cruel who didn't hesitate to burn the village settlements to the ground to make space for his castle. When an old woman went to him to complain about what he had done and beg for some kind of recompense for the poor villagers, he laughed in her face and told his servants to throw her out. But before they could do so, she stood in front of him and cursed the castle and the McGullions. She said neither he nor any of the firstborn among his descendants would ever be able to enjoy the castle for long. Thus, they would all suffer through the centuries for the pain he'd caused."

"How awful!"

"The woman, I hasten to add, wasn't just a commoner. She was the wisewoman and healer of the village, but many believed her to be a witch."

"What about the curse? Did it work?"

"So it seems. Not long after Lord McGullion died within a month of the castle being completed, his firstborn died there in a fire. After that, it became customary for the property to be left to the second born."

"And did it work?"

"Apparently it did. That is, until Eilidh's grandfather decided to ignore the superstition…"

Dora was all ears. "What happened?"

"Eilidh's father, Duncan McGullion, was the firstborn in the family. He was a fair man, he studied hard, he was responsible, so his father decided to reward him. For the first time in generations, it was the firstborn, Duncan, and not Donald, his younger brother, who inherited the castle.

"All seemed to go well to start with. Duncan did some restoration work on the castle, then a couple of years after he married Eilidh's mother, the family could finally move into the property. But one night – maybe by accident, maybe, as some say, because madness seized him – he set the castle on fire."

"Really?"

"Really! He died in the flames. Or at least, he disappeared. No one has seen hide nor hair of him since. At the time, Eilidh was just a baby and her mother decided to go back to her native Australia, passing the castle on to Donald as the tradition had dictated in the first place. The castle, which was only badly damaged in the west wing, was repaired and the new owners, Donald and Katherine, moved in.

"But not for long. The couple was never blessed with children, Eilidh's uncle's health deteriorated, and he and his wife moved to the South of France. Only after his death did his widow, Katherine, come back to Scotland. She was working on a restoration process when death took her. In her will, she left it all to Eilidh."

"This is all very interesting, but it has nothing to do with Gary Mason's death. Surely he's not an heir of Lord McGullion?"

"Good point," said the bookshop owner. "It's just the way he died, it is so reminiscent of the past."

"True," Dora said, paying for her books and saying goodbye. But she felt dismayed as doubt crept into her mind. Could Gary's death have been an omen? Might Eilidh, the firstborn of the next generation of McGullion's, be in danger too? Should she mention this to Etta?

No, it was just a superstition.

Wasn't it?

20

ROCKFALL

"Talking about Iona," Sandra said suddenly, "we're heading over there tomorrow, which promises to be a very fine day. Why don't you and your friend come along?"

"Does that mean a ferry ride?" Etta asked, horrified.

"I'm afraid so," replied Grayson, smiling.

"It's barely ten minutes," added Sandra.

"Ten minutes… and you're sure the weather will be fine?"

"That's what the weather forecaster promised."

"Is there anything there worth seeing?" Etta decided to stop pretending she knew anything about Mull and the surrounding area after her previous gaffe.

"Just the ruins of an abbey," said Grayson with a wink.

"It's a whole abbey," Sandra protested, gently smacking her husband's arm as if he was a naughty boy, "with pretty cloisters and a church. It's not just ruins. Besides, it's a place rich with spirituality, whether you're a believer or not."

Just the kind of place Dora is determined to see, thought Etta, her grey cells coming to a string of conclusions at the speed of light. *We might as well go with those two. I'll be able to keep an eye on Dora while letting her believe she's carrying on her sleuthing with this weird couple. And as I'm sure she's determined to go to Iona, better to do so on what promises to be a fine day. If I leave it up to her, we'll be riding the wild waters when the sea is at its most angry.*

"Yes," she said after only a fraction of a second's pause. "I believe my friend will be delighted at the idea, but I will confirm it with you as soon as I've asked her. May I take a contact number? And where should we meet?"

"We could come and pick you up at 8.30 from the castle," Sandra said, taking Etta's phone from her and tapping in her number. "It's almost two hours' drive to Fionnphort, from where we catch the ferry to Iona. Once there, we could take a little hike around the island and eat a packed lunch on the way. I know the perfect place for a picnic."

"So, we will just wait for your final confirmation this evening," Grayson added.

"Sounds perfect to me," said Etta, wondering if spending a day with not just one, but two murder suspects was a) a good idea and b) the best way to keep her promise to Rufus to stay out of trouble.

But for people like me, living on the edge is our daily bread, she thought, all of a sudden proud of her attitude to life, and this fine response should Mr McCall ever find out.

The four parted, and Etta and Leon carried on along the pretty coastal path perched above the rocks that led to the lighthouse. After a while, they found the rockfalls that Grayson had mentioned. They were nothing too dramatic, but she understood his choice not to go ahead in his wheelchair. For her and the Basset, the way was still fairly easy.

Finally, around one more hilly bend, the view opened on to the lighthouse. A whitewashed building, it perched on a group of rocks overlooking the sea, an infinite sky and the island of Coll in the distance adding more depth to the picture. In an impromptu imitation of Dora, Etta clasped her hands. The fresh ocean wind embraced her figure and coloured her cheeks an even deeper red than usual, but the woman stood there as if petrified, unaware of anything but the view in front of her. That was, until Leon decided enough was enough and barked to wake her from her trance.

"Isn't this stunning, Leon?"

"WoRRRF," even the pragmatic hound had to agree.

At the bottom of the building, a sign said that it was still a working lighthouse, but it hadn't been manned since 1960. What a pity that progress should have condemned such an occupation to history. A secondary path led to a cottage, which Etta assumed was still on Glengullion Castle land. She and Leon moved closer to have a look, but it seemed the place was inhabited. There was also a walled kitchen garden, sheltered from the wild winds, and this too looked well-tended.

The path kept going, until it came to a weather-beaten sign to Smugglers' Cottage. That was too difficult to resist. It took them a little out of their way, but Etta knew she'd find it easier to carry on walking than twiddle her thumbs, waiting for her friend back at the castle.

It took a good few minutes to get there. This second cottage seemed to have been left to fend for itself, although there were a few signs that the place was not completely rundown, that some order was kept in the garden. Etta tried to peer in through the windows, but the curtains didn't help. Maybe it was destined to be the next part of the reconstruction agenda, except there wouldn't be such an agenda any longer. Who knew who'd take Gary's place and what ideas they'd have in mind?

"Maybe it's time to return and see if Dora has managed to drive to Tobermory and back in one piece. Maybe I shouldn't have allowed her to go alone, after all. What if she falls into one of her trances while driving on those one-lane roads over the cliffs? How could I have been so stupid?"

Leon stared at Etta in disbelief. One of those trances, just like Etta had fallen into not even an hour earlier? But then, tuning into the urgency behind her words, or maybe just feeling hungry, the Basset started home at a good trot. Etta did not try to stop him; actually, she strived to keep up with him.

They had just rounded the bend after which the lighthouse would disappear from view when Leon not only put on the brakes and stopped in the middle of the path, he also sat. So sudden was his halt that Etta almost stumbled over him.

"What now?" she hollered as soon as she was sure she could maintain her precarious balance and not end up flat on her face on the ground. "Have you all of a sudden become a hopeless romantic who wants to enjoy a last view of the lighthouse?"

Truth was, she felt quite apprehensive. When Leon sat, it was usually nigh on impossible to persuade him to get up and move again. It seemed his bum could glue itself to the ground whether it were asphalt, concrete or gravel, and no human force, threat or treat would budge him so much as a millimetre. This was the last thing Etta needed, especially when she was in a hurry.

Etta breathed deeply, which helped to calm the tantrum she felt threatening to seize her. As stubborn as she could be, she was well aware that the dog was simply more stubborn in proportion to his size. But not reacting in a moment of urgency was asking a tad too much of Etta.

A storm of harsh words made its way directly from her stomach to the back of her epiglottis. It was just filling her mouth, puffing her cheeks out prior to release, when a sudden swishing sound made her raise her eyes towards the top of the rocky wall beside the path. A matter of seconds later, a torrent of rocks and pebbles rolled downhill just a couple of metres ahead of them, the swishing sound turning into roaring thunder.

"Goodness!" cried Etta, jumping back to stand beside the dog. A cloud of dust rose in the air as both biped and quadruped looked up. Etta could have sworn she saw a shadow moving, as if someone were standing up and disappearing into the forest above.

It was Etta's turn to sit down. Her legs turning to jelly, she sank on to a stone a few steps away.

"Leon, you just saved both our lives!"

The hound walked over to her, tail wagging, his head pointing to the way back home.

"You're right, it's not the time for lengthy discussions. I'll thank you later. Now, we'd better go home as quickly as we can, but you, dear dog, keep your ears open…"

21

SEIZE THE DAY

The shopkeeper's story had made Dora gasp. Fate could indeed be cruel to certain individuals. Her mind full of curses, doom, fire and human wickedness, she felt she needed a little walk to steady her nerves and bring her gently back to the present.

Despite her bag being heavy with books, Dora couldn't resist the temptation to visit a part of the small town she'd been attracted to from day one. A large Victorian red-brick house, now converted into a hotel, overlooked the pier from the top of a hill.

"I would gladly have stayed here. If we hadn't managed a home swap, I mean," said Dora to herself once she was standing outside the building. She peered along the narrow streets at lovely detached houses, well-kept gardens, the War Memorial, and started to wonder what it would be like if she lived in Mull. The words of the lady in the chocolate shop ran through her mind: "*Winters are for us. It's the islanders' time*." Such a lovely thought. At times when she was at home, she felt like people spent too much of their life running around and overworking themselves, never pausing to draw breath. Things weren't like that in the past.

No, Dora was not inclined towards feeling nostalgic for a

distant past. On the contrary, she was very grateful for the present and all the comforts it had brought. But maybe there were things that could be improved upon. Maybe she should create something like the PP and work with both the young and the elderly to bring back the sense of a tightly knit community. If she could no longer afford to travel, maybe there were still things she could do, provided she found the right people to help her. The smallest ball is, paradoxically, the hardest to roll as it seems to be making little or no impact.

She turned into one more narrow street and found herself facing yet another Victorian building. This too was a pretty hotel with a nice garden boasting the luscious grass typical of Scottish landscapes, but Dora felt a sudden chill, as if she was being watched. She scanned the tables under the purple parasols in the hotel's garden and recognised Debbie's shining eyes and Tom's large teeth and short white hair.

"Hey, there's our Italian friend," called Debbie. "You look tired, why not come over and have a cup of tea? Actually, you'd probably prefer a cappuccino. Would you like a cappuccino?"

And before she knew it, Dora was sitting with them, dipping a chocolate chip cookie into her foamy cappuccino, served in a generously sized cup.

"Been shopping, have you?"

"That bookshop is too tempting," and so intense was Debbie's gaze that Dora felt compelled to show her and Tom her purchases. They were enormously pleased to see her Island of Mull books, and Tom insisted she and Etta had to visit the Ninth Wave, Carla Lamont's restaurant in the western part of the island.

"Possibly on a Steampunk Tuesday," suggested Debbie. "When they dress for the occasion."

"Carla," Tom explained, "loves fun and surprises, and not only in her kitchen, which she rules like an empress."

"That lobster clip in her pink hair is fabulous," said Debbie, chuckling. "And her husband used to be so quiet, but now he's become such an outgoing person. He's always been a good chap, but since he met Carla, he shines. Love can really change you."

At those last words, Tom sighed. Debbie went quiet, and Dora thought of Etta and Rufus.

"Have you been married?" Debbie asked Dora bluntly after a long pause.

"No, never," said Dora.

"You never met the right guy?"

"I met him, but I hesitated and didn't seize the moment."

"Did he marry someone else?"

"Nope, leukaemia struck and took my Giacomo away, and I've always regretted insisting we wait a while instead of living by his side for those two years we could have spent together."

"You didn't marry him because he was ill?"

"No, that's absolutely not what I mean! He was fine at the time he asked. But I was in a dire financial situation, as my beloved father had indulged in gambling to the point that he left me up to my ears in his debts. I was too proud to marry Giacomo then, in case it seemed like I was only doing so to get myself out of trouble."

"Did you think that way?"

"No! It was the gossips in town. Giacomo was a good man who came from humble origins. Not that my upbringing was rich by any means, but I had studied, I was a teacher. I knew because of the situation my father had left that people would say I'd agreed to marry someone of a lower social status just because he'd made a little money, he owned a house…"

"But that wasn't so?"

"He's the only man I've ever loved." Dora found with surprise that it was extremely easy to relate this painful part of her life to two complete strangers. Maybe it was because her situation was presently so precarious, but she could no longer keep it to herself. "But I was too proud and decided I wouldn't marry him until I was in a more secure financial position. Then people would no longer be able to say I had done so out of anything other than love…"

"Possibly they would have had something else to say by then!"

"True, it was a very stupid mistake on my part."

"Do you still regret it?"

"Deeply! Not because I'm an old spinster, but because you should always have the courage to live according to what you value, not according to what other people may think. Life is too short to be wasted on things or people that don't really matter."

"But you're still smiling and buying copies of *Pippi Longstocking*," said Tom.

"Well, again, you make your choices in life. It was a bitter moment when Giacomo passed away, but I could live the rest of my life saying I was the victim of bad luck, or I could learn my lesson and smile, looking out for beauty and good people wherever I go. Because all things pass. The future may be taken away from you in the blink of an eye, but no one can steal your past, the things you've done. Give me a beautiful view, a pleasant evening with friends and I'll make sure to save it – how does my friend Etta put it? In my brain's hard drive. What we've seized, what we've lived can never be undone."

"That's tremendous!" said Tom. "A terrific life lesson. I think I now know what I should do."

Debbie looked at him. "Yes, I'd say this lady was sent especially to speak to you."

Tom rose to his feet, said goodbye and moved into the restaurant. The two women later found out he'd paid for all their refreshments.

"I know I may seem crazy," said Debbie to Dora, "but I'm in a constant hurry, as if I was born with the urge to do everything I need to do in double quick time. Now, I know at least you will understand."

"I do," said Dora. "But there are many things I do not understand."

"Like what?"

"Like a ghost appearing to scare us on our first night when the police weren't around, then disappearing all of a sudden when they were. One, not to mention the police, might be led to suspect... strange things, come to weird conclusions."

"I see," said Debbie thoughtfully. Certain the woman really did see what she meant, Dora went on chatting as serenely as ever while her thoughts whirred in the background. She'd been jealous of Etta and thinking only of herself. How silly! She'd have to create a new life for herself, but creating can be satisfying, if a bit challenging.

"So, what's our friend Tom up to that caused him to run away so abruptly?"

Debbie laughed. "I think you might have made him realise he needs to be courageous instead of skirting around a certain issue of the heart."

"Then at least I've done one good thing this morning."

"Maybe two," said Debbie, winking at her. "Can I also assume that in your exciting life, you've never thought of investing in hotels, spas and similar?"

"I can confirm that."

"And your friend?"

"Neither of us, nor any close relative nor any of the people we know..."

"I told them so!"

"I beg your pardon?"

"Nothing, just talking to myself."

"As we're in the mood for confessions, why don't you tell me something about yourself?"

"There's nothing much to say, really," said Debbie, all of a sudden flushing and seeming a little shy. "I was a strange child, but Mum and Dad loved me as I was. Being a troublemaker at school was my way to hide that I found it so difficult to read and sit still. Maybe today I would have been diagnosed as having ADHD, but back then, it just got me punishments and more punishments. But Mum and Dad both encouraged me to persist.

"Twenty years later, I became a nurse, but I was still a troublemaker at the hospital. But at least one doctor liked me and said I was the most hardworking nurse he'd ever seen. And the patients used to say I was a little earthquake, but I'd always make them smile, and I never forgot or rejected their requests.

"I also managed to marry David, a very good and patient man. I'm a mess at home, I can't cook, I'd better stay away from an iron, but David says I'm still worth the price. Then we happened to visit Mull a few years before retirement and decided we had to live here. It took years to arrange, but we did it. Here, we met Katherine McGullion and Edwina, who suggested the castle would be such a cool place to live and form a community for the elderly. We embraced their project, and we hope we'll be able to call Glengullion Castle our home one day."

"That's certainly a worthy project, but is it worth the life of a person?"

"Of course not!" was the immediate reply.

"Where were you between half past one and three o'clock yesterday afternoon?"

"Are you sleuthing?"

"Just trying to understand…"

"Then you need to know the murder took place, according to the pathologist, around two fifteen, with a range of possibility of 15 minutes either side. Except Gary was seen entering the castle, after having walked his wife to her car, just after two, so you can cut down your question to where was I between two o'clock and two thirty. And the answer is I was overseeing the petition, and hundreds of local people saw me there."

"Wait!" cried Dora in surprise. "How do you know the time of the murder so accurately? The police wouldn't tell us anything until it was made official."

"As a nurse, I take care of the constable's Auntie Clementine. I go to her every morning to measure her blood pressure and make sure she takes her pills. Now, the first thing Clementine does when she wakes up in the morning is call her sister, the constable's mother, for a chat before breakfast."

"I guess this morning, they had a longer conversation than usual, after all yesterday's events."

"Very much so. And the constable is a pretty tough man, but his mother has always held the lion's share of the authority over him, even though he's an adult, even though he's in the police," Debbie winked at Dora.

"The poor man!"

"Mind you, it's information I wouldn't normally divulge, were it not for the fact that by this morning, every lad and lass in Tobermory had already heard it, because they're all related to someone in the know…"

"I see," said Dora. "As you've been so kind, would you mind telling me about the others? Where were Edwina and Tom, Sandra and Grayson?"

"They were all at the stand with me. But why don't you leave it at that? The police will take care of the rest."

"How about Letitia?"

Debbie looked a little lost, and when she answered, it was maybe a bit too defensively.

"She too was at the stand. She was with me at all times!"

"I see," said Dora. "I think it's time for me to go. I wouldn't want Etta to worry about me."

22

EAVESDROPPING

Only once she and Leon were in the safety of the castle gardens did Etta have time to think. All the way back, she'd been too busy looking out for any movement or sound around them, fearing another attack could come from anywhere.

She was facing the door of the cosy flat she would be sharing with Dora and Leon, but the sun now seemed determined to make up for the drizzle of earlier. Even though the new flat was far more inviting than the grim turret accommodation, she decided that sitting in the garden would be more beneficial to her thinking processes, not to mention that from there, she'd spot Dora as soon as she arrived. How impatient Etta was to tell her friend everything she had learned.

She forced herself to think about the rockfall on the way back from the lighthouse. Was it accidental? After all, she'd already found the signs of previous events. But if it wasn't accidental, who had threatened her life and why? Could Sandra and Grayson be responsible? Had they followed her every move from the upper path and decided when to strike? Did he really need to use a wheelchair? After all, they weren't from Mull, so who here could know for certain what limited his mobility? Had anyone seen his medical records?

Before taking a seat, Etta decided to have a look in the car park, just in case she spotted the Fiat. It took a mere glance to confirm that the strikingly yellow vehicle wasn't there; Dora was either still in Tobermory or on the way back. But the car park wasn't empty: Tom was there looking dejected, a pretty bouquet of flowers hanging from his hands. He'd opened his car door, but clearly thought twice about getting in. Instead, he walked to the left-hand side of the car park, threw the flowers in a bin, then returned to his car and left.

Etta was about to return to the garden when she noticed Eilidh coming out of the castle and walking away from the building, her demeanour determined. Etta turned to follow her direction of travel with her eyes and instantly knew what the woman had in mind. Coming along the same path Etta and Leon had walked, Edwina was making her way towards the castle, and Eilidh seemed impatient, to say the least, to intercept her.

Etta put a finger to her lips, an indication to Leon to stay quiet and hidden. Slowly, they followed Eilidh, using a conveniently placed box hedge to stay out of sight.

"Auntie Eddie!" Eilidh called loudly, making sure the woman had to stop.

"Good morning, dear," Edwina replied, her voice nowhere near as harsh and cold as it had been when she spoke to Etta and Dora.

"I've been calling you over and over again, why don't you pick up your stupid phone?" Eilidh snapped.

"I'm so sorry, Eilidh, but with so much going on – the fair, the PP petition to organise, then that man deciding to die in the very castle he wanted to destroy…"

Etta peered between the greenery of the hedge. The two women were now face to face as if they were about to declare a duel.

"The man didn't *decide* to die," Eilidh was enunciating her words angrily while clearly taking great care not to shout, but her arms were gesticulating wildly, filling the space around her. "He was brutally murdered!"

"I know, dear, and that's what is so awful – here at Glengullion and, worse, during the fair! I always knew he spelled trouble."

"You're looking at it all wrong! In case it isn't clear to you, someone deliberately killed that man. There's a murderer on the loose and the police are determined to find out who she or he is. Or even they."

"Yes, the police are pretty good at tracking down murderers nowadays, with all these new forensic techniques..."

Maybe Edwina couldn't see it, but Etta certainly recognised the mounting frustration Eilidh was trying to contain.

"Auntie Eddie, let me spell it out as frankly as I can. I know how you feel about Glengullion, but I'm determined to sell this place." She stopped Edwina from interrupting with a rapid gesture of her hand. "Anyway, this is not what I want to discuss, we've already done that. Now, all I want is your word that you and that group of eccentrics you call the Pensioners' Posse had nothing to do with the murder, or with this mysterious ghost that tried to scare my friends."

"Of course, Eilidh, we'd never dream of going round killing people with a mace!"

"You don't seem at all bothered by the fact Gary Mason was killed."

"On the contrary, I'm sorry that had to happen."

"Why does my life seem to be dedicated to putting up with the strangest people doing the strangest things? Auntie Edwina, I'm really worried. You don't *seem* in the least bit sorry for him."

"I can't feel sorry for that swindler. I didn't like him before he died, not after he tried to deceive you and make money off the back of turning this beautiful castle into a private haven for the rich and powerful."

"If the police heard you say that, they would send you straight to jail. I would be sorry to see that happen, but at least I would know I'd done my very best to talk sense into you. But as ever, you won't listen."

"Calm down, dear. The police can't send me to jail without evidence."

"So, you're saying there's no evidence to tie you to the murder? I'm so glad, that's exactly what I wanted to hear," Eilidh's voice was trembling with rage and sarcasm. "My aunt made sure she left no clues at the crime scene, that is good news indeed! I'm just glad Elizabeth isn't here to witness this, and you know what? The sale of the castle will carry on, no matter what tricks you and your posse get up to. Because I can't help but notice you have skirted neatly around denying being behind the ghostly visitation my Italian friends had to suffer on their first night, not to mention putting them in that awful accommodation. I don't want anything to do with this wretched place any longer, I wish I had sold it from Australia without even bothering to come over."

"Eilidh, calm down. You're red in the face, you're choking on your words. You need to make sure nothing bad happens to you, especially as you have young Lizzie to take care of."

"Thanks for the advice, but may I remind you that if there wasn't a bunch of fools playing idiotic tricks and sabotaging my plans, I'd be the happiest person on earth."

"With *Jeremy*, you mean?"

"What? I'd expect better of you, Auntie Edwina. How dare you sneer at Jeremy? What do you think is wrong with him?"

"He's a scrounger, it's as clear as day."

"*He's* a scrounger? While you, the woman who wants me to give the castle over to your posse, would be my benefactor, would you?"

"Exactly! I'm glad you see things my way."

"Don't be facetious, of course I don't. I wanted to try to speak to you, make you see sense once more, but it was a waste of time! Let me just tell you one thing: leave my Italian friends in peace. They've got nothing to do with any of this, they're just guests, not the Italians who were going to partner with Gary. Do you hear me? THEY'RE NOT THE INVESTORS, they just happen to come from the same country. As do a lot of people. Do I need to repeat myself again?"

Etta focused on Edwina's face. The woman looked slightly puzzled, as if this was something she had been made aware of only very recently, but still wasn't convinced about.

"I asked them not to mention anything about the so-called ghost to the police, but that's the last time I'll cover for you. And now I'm finished with you. I don't want to speak further on the subject, nor hear any arguments. I've got too much to do here, so please stay away for the next few days."

Eilidh turned on her heels and marched back towards the castle. Edwina stood where she was for a while, waiting until the young woman had disappeared, then turned around and marched decisively towards her car. She arrived at the car park just as Dora was getting out of the yolk yellow Fiat. Edwina who, it appeared, had turned back into the icy creature she'd been when they arrived nodded a curt greeting, got into her car and left.

When Dora walked towards Etta and Leon, a heavy bag hanging from her arms, the dog ran to her, all happiness. He preferred to keep his flock together; it cost him less effort and concern to have them both under his watch.

The two women looked at each other, smiles dawning on their faces.

"Oh, Dora, we missed you so much, and we've got plenty to tell you."

"That's good," and Dora looked pretty much back to her usual self. She slipped her only free arm under Etta's and they walked together towards the garden. "I've got plenty to tell you too."

SUNDAY
EVENING

Q uite a day!

Eilidh is furious with us, especially with me. She made such a scene, but really, she doesn't understand. I hope once she cools off, she will be able to see things from our point of view. Anyway, we have time. The only buyer who had come forward is no longer with us. The challenge will be getting through the transitional period without getting caught.

The red-headed devil and her puppet of a friend seem to have put two and two together and are hinting that it's no accident the disappearance of the ghost coincided with the arrival of the police. Don't you worry, dear, it's just a wee pause. We'll be back to keep you awake with things that go bump in the night.

By the way, just before I had my encounter with Eilidh, Mr T turned up with flowers and a big smile on his face. He's very sweet, but we're both way past the age for romance. And unfortunately, he's not really my type. He's always so nice to me, he will always be a good friend, but he can be no more, the dear man. How he even came to think along those lines is a mystery to me. I've always kept my distance, never encouraged him, so he must be delusional.

I wish at times he could be just a little tougher. Take risks, do things his own way. He always depends on me, agreeing with every word I *say, being too respectful. It's quite annoying, actually. So as much as I felt bad for doing it, I refused the flowers, told him to stop being so silly and concentrate on getting ready to do everything we need to do. His face was as disappointed as that of a child who craves constant approval, but I can't be anything other than who I am. And there's already L, the other 'child', to take care of.*

Anyway, what's done is done. I told Mr T to come to the next PP meeting in a couple of days, but I don't want to see him in the meantime. Maybe that was harsher treatment than he deserved. I wish I didn't have such a sharp tongue.

Enough ramblings for the day. There's work to do.

MONDAY

23

IONA

After a one-and-a-half hour drive, Etta, Dora and Leon were on the ferry to Iona, in the company of Sandra, Grayson and Letitia. Leon had had to travel in the rear of the estate car with Grayson's wheelchair. He had been able to pop his nose up over the headrest and check what his humans were doing from time to time, but he didn't much like the arrangement, used as he was to taking up the entire back seat for himself. Being downgraded to the luggage compartment was humiliating, so the day hadn't started well.

Sandra parked the car in Fionnphort as only residential vehicles were allowed on Iona. The sea passage was a little rough, but even Etta had to agree that it took longer to get on and off the ferry than to cross the short stretch of water.

Letitia was happy and cheerful throughout the entire journey, telling her companions stories about her mother and extended family as if the events had happened the day before. Sandra encouraged her to indulge in her memories, quizzing her about the details: what did her mother look like? What exactly did she say on this or that occasion? She certainly gave no indication that she had heard the same stories time and time again.

"But," she whispered to Etta and Dora as Letitia was helping

ADRIANA LICIO

Grayson with his wheelchair, out of earshot, "the doctors have recommended that we try to stimulate her brain into more recent recollections and creating new emotional memories. Tomorrow, she probably won't remember she was on Iona with us, but she will know it was a happy day."

"She will forget everything else?" Etta asked, shocked. When she spoke to Letitia, she thought of her as a little dreamy, but she hadn't suspected the woman found it so hard to recall recent events.

"Well, I'll try to anchor some of her memories to certain details from the trip. Sensory details work very well, so while we were on the ferry, we listened to and tried to imitate seagull cries. Creating new memories is very important, although she doesn't always remember the things I think she will. But I will show her pictures of today and we'll discuss them on the ferry ride back, and tomorrow."

"That's good of you," said Dora, impressed.

"She's a good friend, no matter how her memory and mind may decide to work. But more to the point, this is exactly the premise behind the PP project. Do you know about the Pensioners' Posse, by the way?"

When Etta and Dora both nodded, the woman continued. "Being surrounded by a community of supportive friends has an altogether different value to a professional-as-you-like nursing home. We want to feel useful because we *are* useful."

"You're not as old as Edwina and the others," Etta noticed.

"Despite the group's name, age isn't the point. I'd be delighted to live in a place with other people around me and have plenty to do, projects to discuss, things to create and strive for. Since we got involved with the PP, Grayson has felt so much happier. He had spiralled into a negative cycle a few years ago, maybe not quite clinical depression, but he was very close to it. Now, he feels stimulated. He has expertise that is useful to the group, such as his management and organisational skills. And I see a gleam of joy in his eyes whenever Edwina, Tom or Josh call him up for advice. Even now," she turned towards the two behind them, Letitia smiling and pushing the wheelchair while chatting non-stop to Grayson, "you wouldn't know who's helping whom. And feeling useful is a basic human need. We're not simply social animals; we need to help others to feel fulfilled."

"I see how it must have come as an awful blow when Eilidh announced she was selling Glengullion to Gary Mason," said Dora. Etta looked at her friend in surprise. That was exactly the point *she* was going to make, only she had still been debating over remaining loyal to the promise she'd made to Rufus. But hadn't someone tried to crush her and Leon under a rockfall only yesterday? Was the suppression of self-preservation instincts included in the deal? Surely not.

She had spent the whole night debating the issue in her head, and now here was Dora, quizzing suspects exactly as Etta herself loved to do.

"Indeed it was, because in the past year, we've made all sorts of plans to leave Manchester and come to live on Mull permanently. The Mull Forest Café, which is owned by members of the PP, gave us so much encouragement. After many failed attempts, here was proof that our members could make a success of a business."

"What about Josh McIntosh and his cheese?"

"Have you had a chance to try it?"

"Yes, so tasty…"

"That only came about after a number of failures. But now he's identified the right cow breed, the right pastures, the right process for making excellent cheese, he's ready to scale up and increase production, generating the funds for larger stables. Over the next couple of years, he plans to hire people to help him with the cows and the cheese production, and export his product to the mainland. He won't produce for supermarkets, but for gastropubs and fine-dining restaurants, not to mention direct sales via the internet. As you can see, my husband has taught the

ADRIANA LICIO

PP – and me – loads, as I wouldn't call myself a business expert by any means. But Grayson, he loves it." As she laughed, her round black-framed glasses danced on her nose.

Passing drystone walls surrounding green fields and farms, they reached the Abbey, a Gothic building made in stone. This centre of worship, Grayson explained, had been founded in 563AD by St Columba. As an aristocrat, the Saint had won wars back in Ireland, but he felt sick to the stomach of bloodshed and came to Iona in search of peace for his soul, nourishment for his spirit. The island gave him all he needed.

"The St Columba monastery," Grayson went on in his keen voice, "went through times of decline and resurgence. It was remodelled throughout the centuries, and what we see today is basically the Benedictine monastery from the Middle Ages, but with additional restoration works that took place in the twentieth century. The Iona Abbey is now an ecumenical centre, but anybody from any religion, or no religion at all, can enjoy what this place offers."

Etta looked at him quizzically, then took courage and asked her simpleton question. "But what exactly does it offer? Besides being a tourist attraction, I mean."

"The chance to wonder about the great questions of life. What is life's purpose? How did we come about? Is there anything waiting for us after death? All those questions we tend to forget in the daily trudge."

"This is the *real* place for reset," said Sandra, mocking the title of Mason's presentation.

"Let's go and see the cloister," said Letitia impatiently, looking at the door in front of them.

"What cloister?" asked Grayson, feigning ignorance.

"There's a beautiful cloister inside. You're sheltered from the wind and can enjoy the silence."

"So, we're just going to have a look at the cloister, and then we'll leave?" Grayson was still playing dumb.

"Of course not!" cried Letitia almost in horror. "From the

cloister, we can get inside a tall church all made in stone, with many arches and pretty windows. There's a room – a mysterious room – at the back."

"So, you've been here before?" asked Dora.

"Many times. I used to come to Iona with my mother and father, and my sisters."

"And have you come here more recently?" asked Sandra. "Maybe with a friend?"

"Oh yes," Letitia laughed. "One day, I came with Edwina. The weather was so bad, there was a gale howling and we feared we would never be able to leave the island and go back to Mull. But we had a few laughs as the wind took my hat and we had to run to catch it," and again, she giggled cheerfully.

"Are you good friends with Edwina?" Etta asked.

"Oh," Letitia said, a seraphic smile on her face, "she's more than a friend. She loves me like a sister, which is a good thing as my two sisters have both passed away."

"I'm so sorry to hear that. Don't you have any nephews or nieces?"

"Of course, I've got three. Three beautiful little children." Under Sandra's invitation, she told Etta and Dora the names of her sisters' offspring, but she insisted on describing them as children.

"In fact, they're all grown-up now," Sandra explained as she entered the serene cloister with Etta, Dora and Leon. Letitia and Grayson had once again gone ahead. "And she hardly sees them. They don't come over to visit, so the only memory she has of them is when they were children."

Passing through the enchanting and peaceful cloister, they walked into the church. Just as Letitia had said, it was beautiful and calm, the perfect place for getting lost in one's own thoughts. Constructed in the local stone, the church interior was welcoming and intimate, while also being wonderfully gothic and empty.

"That's so we can fill it with our prayers and wishes," Dora said in her most Dora-ish style.

Then Letitia guided them all to the secret room at the back of the church. Maybe it was intended as a place for deep meditation as it was completely isolated, only a slit window showing a glimpse of the fields outside and the sea in the distance.

"You can see things from here," she said. "You can see things, but not be seen!"

24

HOME TRUTHS

E ilidh was walking along the path from Glengullion to the lighthouse. She'd felt badly in need of exercise, some fresh air and, most of all, time to think. The two Italian ladies were out for the day, Jeremy had gone into town, the police had declared they didn't need her for the moment, which made a refreshing change. Edwina – her aunt's best friend and the woman who'd given Eilidh so much reason to worry – was away, busy as ever, hopefully not causing trouble.

Was that likely? Eilidh shook her head. Nope. Recently, it seemed Edwina's only purpose in life was to create as much trouble as possible for this poor Aussie. Nothing more, nothing less.

Was she, Eilidh, doing the right thing in protecting the old woman? She'd asked Etta and Dora to keep quiet about the PP's dastardly ghostly tricks because she'd felt sure there was no way Edwina could have been involved in anything more than the stupid prank. But her demeanour, her whole attitude every time Eilidh tried to reason with her... well, it had all combined to make Eilidh uncertain and doubtful.

Worse than that, even Jeremy, usually so supportive and understanding, had said how stupid she was being to withhold information from the police. If Edwina and her friends were innocent of the murder, the police would find the real killer. DCI Findlay was far too professional to arrest the first suspect she came across. This isn't a silly movie, he had said, the police know what they're doing.

I wonder, Eilidh thought, not for the first time, *if I am behaving like a child… at 38! How daft of me. But what should I tell the police now? Oops, I forgot one little detail: there was a ghost disturbing my guests the night before the murder. But I don't think it's a real ghost. Actually, I suspect it was a trick played by my aunt's friend, Edwina.* She stopped in her tracks. *Yes, Chief Inspector, the very same woman who publicly threatened Gary Mason… when was it? I believe merely a couple of hours before he was killed. You don't think there might be a connection, do you?*

She banged her head with her hand in a characteristic gesture. "Why me?" she asked out loud. "Why can't my life proceed in a slightly more normal way? I inherit a property, I decide to sell, a buyer turns up, I move to London, happy ever after. Isn't that what would happen to 99.9% of people in the same situation?"

She sighed, looked at the ocean glittering under the sun, breathed in the fresh air and let it go slowly, enjoying the scent of the breeze as it filled her nostrils first, her lungs next. She stretched her arms to make room for more air and repeated the process.

"Oh, dear Mull, you can be so inspiring when you want to. I will miss you, but I just wish things between us were a little easier. But I know exactly what I should do. My life is not here, but Jeremy is from Mull, so we'll come back for holidays, and without all this weight on my shoulders," and she pointed to the castle. "I'll be happy at the thought of returning, free of the trappings of the former Lady of Glengullion…"

"No pain, no gain!" said a voice behind her, startling her.

"Josh, you gave me the fright of my life!" She breathed out to discharge the adrenaline. "How long have you been listening?"

"Ten minutes or so."

"Without making your presence known?" She could hardly believe anyone would be so rude and sneaky.

"Just trying to understand your perspective on things, but frankly, it seems to me you're taking the easier route. No great project ahead for you, My Lady."

Eilidh felt rage embracing her, but an impish look in Josh's eyes made her realise an outburst was exactly what the provocative scruff was after. Making a big effort to rein in her fiery temper, she opted instead for a good dose of British sarcasm to cure him of his nosy ways.

"What kind of mother would *possibly* want the money to support and spend time with her only daughter and living relative when she could remain on a remote Scottish island and throw what little she has at a crazy project that only benefits a bunch of old people whose marbles are long gone? Oh, and some cows. Silly me. Let's not forget the cows."

"That's not the way you should look at things..."

"So, Mr Know-it-all, please enlighten me. How should I look at them?"

"Whether you want to be or not, you're a member of this community of people, here on the island of Mull. You've been blessed with responsibility for not only a material inheritance – a castle, no less – but also the aspirations, the traditions, the projects of the people who live on this land, who want it to flourish and stay theirs. A collective theirs, rather than it becoming an anonymous place reserved for the super-rich who would never dream of integrating into island life."

"Aren't you forgetting something?"

"What?"

"For a year, I tried to make things work, but they just didn't."

"Oh, come on! You weren't even here most of the time, so you didn't try that hard. You were expecting things to work out without any real effort on your part."

"Do you want to see how much money I poured into the B&B and holiday let idea?"

"And the rooms remain unoccupied. Apart from those two Italian ladies, the whole castle is empty and we're in the height of the summer season."

"The holiday lets are empty *this season* because I finally gave up. I tried, but things didn't work out."

"Why did you *try* at all?"

"Because I was stupid! I arrived here and was taken by the beauty of it all. Apparently, even the pragmatism required to be a mother hasn't cured me of romanticism. I was brought up in Australia, lived in a fair-sized modern city and spent only a few days each year touching on the wilderness while on holiday. And that was it. When I arrived here and saw the cute town, the quaint island, the fairy-tale castle and heard the stories, I was enthralled and I fell into the trap. When the PP came to me with their apparently sound business proposals, I listened. Mind you," she silenced him as it was clear he was about to make an objection, "I don't blame anyone but myself for not seeing that those proposals were *not* sound. I'm sure they – you – everyone who made them – were all well-meaning. I was the one who should have recognised the impossibility of it all along. But, you know what?"

"What?"

"Yesterday's gone. *Today*'s the best day to make a change! Which I did, which I'll do. There's still time for me to make amends for my mistakes…"

"You're reading it all wrong. You were right when you fell in love with this place, before Gary and Jeremy brainwashed you out of your dreams. And you *never* tried hard to make the castle work for you, because if you really want something, you don't give up at the first obstacle."

"If you're so determined to carry on with your project, come up with a sound financial offer. I'm looking for buyers."

"My financial position, at present, is not as healthy as yours.

There's been no inheritance dropping into my lap. Instead of putting up your defences, try giving back to the community. I told Katherine she should leave the castle to Edwina, not to a stranger on the other side of the globe."

"You told my auntie *what*? How dare you! May I remind you she was MY aunt? Did you really try to influence her? What are you guys up to?"

As Josh opened his mouth to respond, Bree came galloping towards the pair of them. She barked, but before Josh could reach her, she turned and ran forwards a few metres. Then she looked back at the two humans.

"She wants us to follow her," said Eilidh, who'd loved the border collie from the first moment she set eyes on her. Bree's bark took on a tone that brooked no argument. She ran in a circle around them, then sprinted ahead, stopping to glance back, breathing heavily.

"Something's wrong," said Josh.

"Let's go, girl," said Eilidh, pushing forward. What had happened now? Images of the dog leading them to a dead body filled her mind. What was going on at Glengullion?

25

GAELIC PATTERNS

Once they were back outside in the grounds of Iona Abbey, Sandra suggested that they take advantage of the beautiful weather and walk all the way to Dun I, the main hill of the island.

"There are great views from there over all the landmarks and beaches."

Exiting the Abbey grounds, they came to a whitewashed cottage which sold arts and crafts. Dora, unsurprisingly, was attracted by the pottery exhibited in one of the windows. On entering, they were welcomed by a woman in her thirties, with short brown hair and long dreamy eyebrows, a determined chin and a cute dimple on her cheek.

"Good morning..." the woman began, then her eyes fell upon Sandra and Grayson, "Och, it's you guys. How are you doing?"

"We're fine, thank you. We're taking Letitia and our new friends on a tour of the island. Etta, Dora, this lady is Jenny, Jeremy's sister," Sandra explained. "And Jenny, this handsome chap is Napoleon," she added, being sure not to overlook the noble hound, who huffed in approval at his introduction.

"I thought your face had a familiar quality," Etta said,

matching the woman's features with Jeremy's: the same dark eyes surrounded by thick eyelashes and those long eyebrows.

"Because of the unfortunate incident at Glengullion," Sandra explained, "Jeremy and Eilidh came back to Mull earlier than they had planned. But I guess you already know this."

"As a matter of fact, I didn't know. Jeremy and I don't really stay in touch much these days," Jenny replied, anger flashing on to her face.

"I thought you were close," Sandra said in surprise.

"People change when their life moves in a new direction. Jeremy has changed a lot since…"

"You don't mean because of Eilidh?"

"Let's just say that if she hadn't come into the picture, maybe things would have remained as they had been between us."

Sandra looked puzzled. A bit reluctantly, Jenny explained more. Perhaps she felt she had already said too much.

"I'm not a clingy sister, jealous of her brother's new life. But we had planned to open this gallery together. He was meant to help me run it, but just when things started taking off and I became rushed off my feet, he suddenly pulled away."

"Do you need help? A shop assistant, maybe?"

"I'm pivoting, setting up a cooperative of artists so that each of us comes to Iona to run the shop one or two days a week. This way, we all have plenty of time for creative work, but it's good to meet people in the shop and listen to their comments, or explain the story behind the items on sale."

"Have you already found artists willing to take their turn?"

"At least one, Albert. He's the artist behind those paintings you're looking at, who comes over on Saturdays and Tuesdays at present. I hope to have a couple more joining by the end of the month. It was a sudden pivot, but I think I've got things under control now."

Etta and her companions looked at the beautiful paintings Jenny had indicated. Large strokes in a multitude of greens, blues and greys with flecks of other colours depicted the ocean waves, the fields, the ever-changing sky. Some paintings featured the few cottages that made up the village, and beyond them the reassuring presence of the Abbey. Even in a painting, you could feel the peace and serenity that emanated from it.

"And it seems you have plenty of customers," said Grayson, looking round at the tourists browsing in the shop.

"I confess, I was devastated when Jeremy announced he was leaving Mull and our project. But sales have been encouraging. It was a good idea to set up the gallery so close to the Abbey grounds. People arrive here keen to explore the island's tradition, so they are happy to speak to us and – of course – buy things to remind them of their visit. Most of the time, they only buy small things, but occasionally one will fall in love with our larger creations. I'm positive we will make a success of this venture."

"How about finances? You know I was a chartered accountant, so I'm happy to help. If you need me, just ask."

"Thanks, Grayson. We already have our own accountant, but I'll keep your offer in mind as we might need some more strategic thinking. Thank you! But how are things at Glengullion? I know Eilidh wanted to sell to Gary Mason, which must have been a blow for Tom and the rest of you."

"Yes, it has been a blow for all of us, and Tom has invested so much energy into the PP project. We're not too sure what will happen now. After Gary Mason's death, I mean."

Despite her good intentions not to pry, Etta couldn't resist a small – 'inconsequential' she described it to herself – question.

"So, Jenny, you know Tom?"

"That's right," answered Jenny, rearranging a display of colourful pochettes that the customers had left in a mess. "I know him from amateur dramatics at Tobermory's theatre, where we've had so much fun. I was in charge of the costumes and make-up, while Tom…"

"Jenny, could you tell me more about those sculptures over there?" Sandra interrupted clumsily, slipping her arm through

Jenny's and almost dragging her towards the far side of the shop.

You're a bit too late, lady, thought Etta, *the cat is out of the bag. So, Tom is an actor with theatre experience, which clarifies quite a few 'ghostly' things.*

She looked up at Dora, who nodded. She'd made the connection too.

At this point, Etta became unusually enchanted by the work of the silversmiths, ranging from beautiful jewellery to whisky tumblers, all incorporating ancient Gaelic symbols. After much deliberation, she selected a silver brooch. It was a bit too similar to the one she'd seen Edwina wearing, but you can't aim for perfection in an imperfect world.

"That's the Celtic knot of peace," Jenny explained, having finished with Sandra. "It symbolises the harmony that you can achieve when body, mind and spirit are aligned."

"Fancy that," murmured Etta almost to herself, her mind running to how her daughter in Granada mentioned doing yoga out on her balcony and greeting the sun first thing in the morning, along with other woo-woo connect-with-the-universe things. "Maddalena will love that when I tell her."

"It looks like the one Edwina always wears." So Dora had noticed too.

"That's the only thing I don't like about it."

"If that would be your only reason not to buy it, it's not a good reason at all."

Etta accepted the sound advice and bought her brooch.

As for Dora, she was as ever attracted by the pottery, but in the end decided on two tea towels, which far less voluminous and fragile, displaying red woodpeckers. These were made, Jenny explained, by a textile artist who was also responsible for a collection of cheerful tote and zip bags featuring the island's animals.

"And what creations are yours, Jenny?" asked Dora.

"Those," Jenny said, pointing to a few paintings in one

corner. Etta had bypassed them, her eyes, captured by all sort of beauties, not lingering long. Now, Dora returned to that corner, Etta followed and they both forced a few compliments out of their mouths. Jenny thanked them graciously, then the group left the gallery to continue their walk.

Once they were outside the shop, Grayson said, "What a good idea to have the artists share the running of the place. That also means they can offer a far wider range of products than a single artist could, so each visitor can find exactly what they want. And with a bunch of people rotating the duties, no one has all the trouble of running the shop day in, day out."

"Are you mentioning this," Sandra asked shrewdly, "simply for speculation's sake?"

"Of course not. It's an interesting model we could use for Glengullion too."

"You're right, especially now we're free to make plans again." Shaking her head as if to distance herself from such thoughts, Sandra addressed Dora and Etta. "Did you like Jenny's paintings?"

"They're not bad," Etta said, unusually diplomatically. It was Dora who seemed to have trouble finding the right words.

"I confess, I passed them by without noticing them. They're rather… somehow…"

"Very ordinary," Sandra completed for her. "We all have our gift, and I've always felt Jenny's is organising. As an artist, she's not bad, but she won't ever wow you."

Dora nodded in agreement, clearly relieved that the woman had her strengths.

"And the world desperately needs organisers!" she said.

"I'll take that as a compliment to my poor unartistic self," replied Grayson, laughing.

The road passed through green pastures and fields, until they reached the Thirsty Monk Pub. The cottage-like building had a little porch outside and Grayson said he'd stay there while the others continued their hike.

"I could stay and keep you company," Dora offered.

"That's OK, I'm meeting a friend for a chat," Grayson said.

"A *male* friend," Sandra specified. "He's had his fill of women's talk for today, so we'd better leave him in peace so he can recover for the return trip."

"I never said that!" said Grayson.

"You didn't need to," Sandra winked at him. "How about you, Letitia? Do you feel like walking a little more?"

"Of course!" The woman was evidently enjoying the hike, and the company.

"I'm so glad," Sandra said, gently squeezing Letitia's shoulders between her hands. "I've got plenty of water and sunscreen." Pouring a good portion of cream into Letitia's hands, she guided the elderly woman to massage it on to her face, arms and hands. "Just in case it feels hot enough for short sleeves."

Once all preparations were done, Sandra kissed her husband goodbye and they left him at the pub to wait for his friend. As they walked away, Letitia asked to hold Leon's leash.

"We can let him run free a little further on," said Etta, "but in the meantime, you can certainly do that. But if he pulls, let him go. You wouldn't imagine how strong he can be."

26

AN EMOTIONAL RESCUE

"Bree's going towards the beach," Josh said, turning on to a narrow path that led down to the sea. A part gravelly, part rocky beach stretched out below them, a number of boulders in the foreground barring the way.

The path down was not an easy one. Eilidh was wearing soft trainers that were skidding on the slippery stones.

"Give me your hand," Josh said. Eilidh hesitated. "You don't want to add to your troubles by twisting your ankle, do you?"

"Certainly not! As I've just told you – or rather, as you sneakily overheard – I've got more than enough on my plate right now." She stretched out her hand. He took it delicately but firmly and held her stable whenever she lost her footing. Certainly, his sturdy walking boots helped him keep his own balance, those and the fact he was used to walking in the terrain.

Once they were on the shore, they let go of each other's hands simultaneously, as if startled by the contact. Bree ran ahead and barked, calling for them. They hastened their pace at her worried expression. Then, suddenly assailed by doubt, Eilidh looked back. This part of the beach was very much hidden from the upper path. She hardly knew the area – did anyone even come here? Had she added to her list of mistakes by following Josh McIntosh? Border collies are very smart dogs who can be trained to do a million tricks, so had she fallen into the man's cunning trap?

Still walking briskly, she took her phone from her jeans pocket, meaning to send a message to Jeremy to let him know where she was, and with whom. But, almost inevitably, there was no signal.

The dog carried on galloping along the shore, barking whenever she thought they weren't going as fast as she needed them to. Josh turned, noticing Eilidh was falling behind.

"Are you tired?"

"Of course not, but I can't run as quickly as you. Go ahead." Pretending to follow, she looked back at the slippery boulders, the narrow path heading to the safety of home, realising she didn't stand a chance if she tried to run. He'd catch up with her immediately.

As she considered her limited options, the dog finally came to a stop close to a dark grey mass. Had something been left on the beach on purpose to catch her unawares? Or was it a body? But it was rather a short body – surely not a child? Or someone bitten in half by sharks?

Curiosity won and Eilidh marched on, her eyes staring at the strange mass. Then, it raised its head. Bree licked the creature and stopped barking, while two round puppy-dog eyes settled on Eilidh and Josh, a bushy moustache twitching slightly.

"A baby seal!" she cried at the same time as Josh.

"She's strayed on to the sand," he confirmed, "and is too weak to run away."

"Goodness!" exclaimed Eilidh, tenderness, compassion, desire to help filling her heart.

"Don't touch her," said Josh, his voice soft as he looked at the seal's body.

"But we have to help the poor little thing."

"I don't see any blood or an obvious wound," he said, examining the seal from a few steps away. "But it looks like she's been left alone. I don't think her mother knows where she is…"

"Poor dear, don't you worry, we're here to help," Eilidh whispered to the animal. Before she knew what she was doing, she was caressing the not-chubby-enough body.

Josh looked at her.

"I'm so sorry!" Eilidh pulled back, realising she had ignored his instructions.

"Don't worry. She's so thin, I don't think there is any chance her mother is still close, which was why I didn't want you to touch her and mask her scent. It seems she is lost and all alone. And she's so tired, she doesn't even have the energy to be scared. So go ahead, she seems to like you. In the meantime, I'll call the rescue team."

"There's no phone signal here."

"You're right," he said, checking his phone. "How did you kn…" then he stopped abruptly and gave her the hint of a cheeky grin. "I see. You were a little worried, out here on your own with me."

"No! I just thought it'd be good to alert someone in case of an emergency."

He shook his head, clearly not buying that.

"Would you stay here while I go back to where I can catch some signal?"

"Absolutely! We can't leave her here alone," said Eilidh. "And you'll be faster than me. But can't we just call the emergency services?"

"I'll walk back to the upper part of the path, where there's usually a signal, and call Mull's wildlife rescue team directly and explain where we are. We can't waste any more time, as I'm not sure how much longer she can survive."

Bree looked at Josh, undecided on what she should do.

"You stay here with Eilidh," he told the dog. "I'll be back soon."

"Thanks for keeping us company, Bree," Eilidh whispered. "You've been such a great girl."

The dog licked the seal's head. Despite the creature not exactly being small, Bree's maternal instinct told her this was a puppy. And more to the point, a puppy in need.

Eilidh caressed the seal. When the baby animal looked at the woman, her dark round eyes searching deeply into hers, Eilidh simply knew she trusted her. She knew Eilidh wasn't a threat. Again, a feeling of warmth, tenderness and love overwhelmed her.

"You'll be OK, baby girl, we'll take good care of you," she whispered, feeling as she'd done when, as a child, she'd rescued a young koala from a bush fire. Like this one, that had been a chance encounter. She must have only been around ten, but now she felt exactly as she had done then, as if the intervening time didn't exist. She was that same child, tenderness invading her heart, with the same wish to help.

The koala had survived thanks to a local rescue centre. "And it will be just the same for you," Eilidh whispered to the seal as Josh returned. Bree galloped towards him as soon as she spotted him from afar. She was so lively, and yet so calm when she approached the seal puppy.

"She's not scared of me," Eilidh told herself as her hands gently massaged the seal, as if wanting to hug and protect her and convince her to hang on in there.

"Well done," Josh said as he approached Eilidh and the seal, a rare smile dawning on his face.

He isn't a bad man, thought Eilidh, her eyes lingering on him in confusion. *If only he'd allow more smiles on his face.*

"Rescue is coming," he informed her. "We're lucky, Stephanie knows exactly where we are."

"Stephanie?"

"She's a young biologist who's been working on Mull for the past year, and the whole team has experience in rescuing seals."

It was a while before a boat approached and Josh waved his

arms to signal where they were. When the team came ashore, they looked at Eilidh, lying beside the seal, then at Bree who was not on a leash.

"Not standard procedure," said a blonde woman who'd introduced herself as Stephanie, kneeling down to examine the pup.

"She's behaved very sweetly, no attempt to bite or defend herself. Maybe she's just too weak." Then Josh pointed at Eilidh and added, "Or maybe she likes her."

"She's weak indeed, and in need of some serious hydration," Stephanie said. "But you're curious enough to look around," she added, speaking to the seal. "You'll get there, won't you?" Stephanie looked up at Josh again. "She's not bleeding from anywhere, so she was probably separated from her mum by the rough waters and stranded on the beach. Her mum couldn't find her and she's too young to provide food for herself."

After assessing the seal's condition, Stephanie, helped by the other rescuers, gently moved the pup on to a trolley, and then into the boat.

"She likes company," said Eilidh. "Don't leave her alone."

"Oh no, she won't be left alone. At the rescue centre, she will meet vets and helpers who are more than friendly, they're mummy-style friendly. And as soon as she feels better, there are other pups for her to play with."

"Thank you! So, do you think she'll make it?"

"She wouldn't have survived many more days out here on her own, but I think she's determined to live. Josh has my contact details, and I his, so I'll keep you informed. If you wish, in a couple of months' time, or whenever we feel she's ready, you could come and help us release her back into the sea."

"Really?" Eilidh asked. "Other seals have successfully made it back to nature?"

"She's not hurt, although she will need a proper check up by a vet who will run all the required tests. But yes, the centre manages to save most of the pups who arrive with no injuries or disease."

"Bree found her," said Eilidh.

"She's an awesome girl," Stephanie smiled at the dog. "She hasn't scared the seal, nor treated her as prey."

"Shepherd's instinct," Josh said, a twinkle in his eyes the tell-tale sign of how proud he was of his dog.

"Great job, all three of you." With one last grin, Stephanie jumped on board the boat and the rescue party left.

"Oh, those eyes and that funny moustached nose." Eilidh broke the ensuing silence. "Will you let me know about the seal's progress?"

"Of course I will," said Josh as they slowly made their way back. They walked in silence, each lost in their own thoughts.

"Where are you going now?" asked Eilidh finally, once they had reached the main path.

"I thought we'd accompany you home."

"Thanks, but you don't need to do that. Where were you heading when we met?" Eilidh looked to her right where the upper path to the lighthouse – and Josh's cottage – started.

"Home," said Josh, whistling to Bree and jerking his chin at the path. The border collie circled once around Eilidh, who gave her a good stroke, and then danced towards home. "See you," said Josh, his characteristic sombreness returning.

"See you and… thanks," said Eilidh, but he just shrugged as he walked away. "Such a wild man," she murmured, regretting not having allowed him to accompany her to the castle. Her rejection of his offer had broken a connection that had built between them, and now more than ever, she needed a local ally.

"No more thinking about cute seal pups," she told herself. "It's time to go back to trying to organise the sale of the castle and hope it's not just wishful thinking."

A buzz from her mobile alerted her to the fact she had phone signal again. She checked the display and saw a text message from Yasmine Mason, Gary's wife. Maybe all wasn't lost after all.

"I need to speak to you. I can't just give up on my husband's plans and vision."

"Yes!" Eilidh exclaimed in triumph as she tapped Yasmine's number.

27

THE WELL OF AGE

On the path to Dun I, the hill overlooking the island of Iona, Letitia and Leon got along very well indeed. The hound appreciated the way this Scottish lady admired him, never tried to boss him around or tell him to do anything he didn't want to. He could lead her by her leash without her resisting, as the badly behaved Etta would have done. Letitia had been well trained. She stopped whenever he had to smell and pee over important matters, she followed him in his explorations, and in return, he afforded her the courtesy she deserved. Instinct told him to refrain from pulling and tugging; instead, he guided the vulnerable biped gently. The two were in perfect harmony and, thanks to stops, chats and laughs, managed to keep pace with the other three women.

When they left the road and joined the path, Leon was unleashed. Letitia followed him fondly with her eyes as he trotted and galloped and snorted and bragged. She was a true fan, this gentle smiling lady.

As they climbed, the wind became stronger, but the sun kept shining. The women were sweating, but they didn't dare remove their fleeces. It was good they had Sandra with them as the path wasn't well signposted and it often split into a number of different branches. Etta now knew why both wife and husband had insisted they wear their hiking boots, as the terrain got more and more boggy and uneven the further they went. They slowed down when Letitia seemed a bit out of breath, but she was determined to catch up with Leon and encouraged them to carry on.

Once they reached the top, the view was stunning. They gazed at all the details of Mull's western coast.

"That's Staffa," Sandra said, indicating a little spot to the north.

"That's where the puffins are," Dora said with a huge smile and dreamy eyes. "We definitely want to visit there." Etta looked at her in horror. The dot of land looked extremely far away.

"There's Fingal's Cave," said Letitia. "We went there, didn't we?"

"And a fine trip it was," Sandra answered, "even if the sea was a little rough. Do you remember what happened to Tom?"

"He spilled his coffee," said Letitia after a moment's thought.

"That's correct, smart girl," said Sandra. "And you can see Canada over there!" she added, pointing west where the ocean opened up.

"Where? Where?" asked Letitia.

"It was just a silly joke of mine. Canada is much too far to be seen from here. But isn't it fun that we know exactly where such a distant country is?"

"It feels so close." Letitia smiled. "And some of my family went there."

"When was that?" asked Dora, always curious to listen to old stories.

"After the Second World War, I believe. My mother kept in touch with them and they came to visit quite a few times. They loved Scotland. But Canada is such a beautiful country too."

"Have you been there?"

"No. We were meant to go, but my father got sick just before we were due to fly. Mum said it was an excuse, he was so scared at the very idea of taking a plane, not to mention leaving the farm for almost two weeks. But I cried for days. I used to write to Lorelei, a distant cousin about my age, and we had planned everything we wanted to do together…"

"Such a shame!"

"Indeed it was. I never got to see Toronto, the big shopping malls and the modern flat they lived in. Lorelei sent me pictures and now I almost feel as if I've been there. Or maybe it's my brain playing silly tricks."

"Shall we sit down?" asked Etta, pointing to a mixture of heather and moss. "And have something to drink before heading back down?"

"I wouldn't sit there," warned Sandra. "It may be wet." But Etta had already sat and said it was fine. Only when she got up, her trousers were soaked and she admitted feeling rather cold in the posterior! Letitia laughed heartily and Sandra nodded.

"We will always remember this walk, with funny Leon jumping and hunting for rabbits, and Etta getting wet where the sun never shines."

"And almost seeing Canada," said Letitia.

"I'd rather you didn't remember my part," grumbled Etta.

"You're a funny lady, always grumbling," replied Letitia. Etta opened her mouth to respond, but Dora hushed her.

"I believe Sandra is trying to create a new memory for dear Letitia," she whispered into Etta's ear as the others walked ahead.

"That's all very fine, but I'd rather my wet bum wasn't a part of it."

"But funny accidents are so easy to remember, so… well done! You've made a brilliant contribution."

Etta shook her head vigorously in protest, then decided a change of subject would be a wiser move.

"This isn't the same way we came up," she called to the other two.

"That's correct. We're heading to Tobar na h-Aoise, the Well of Age in Gaelic. It's just a short detour."

"The Well of Age?" asked Dora. "What's that?"

"Let's get there first, and then you'll see."

Moments later, they stopped in front of a little pool. Dark waters were contained between granite boulders, and the lush grass was shining under the sun on the opposite side.

"The water is so cold," said Dora, who'd kneeled down to touch it.

"True, but as you've taken the trouble to get down there, you may as well rinse your face with it too."

"Why?"

"To restore your youth."

"I wish!" said Dora as she merrily splashed some of the water on her face.

"In that case, I wouldn't mind turning the clock back a few decades," said Etta, doing exactly as Dora was doing.

"My face definitely feels younger already," announced Dora, laughing as the blood ran to her cheeks to counter the sudden cold.

"It didn't work for my joints, I'm afraid," said Etta, struggling to get up again.

"Well, if it doesn't work age wise, you might find it marks the start of a new life."

"Really?" said Dora.

"Indeed. Pilgrims to the Abbey would worship in the church, then walk all the way up here and wash their faces in this pool to mark a new beginning in their lives."

"A new beginning?" And before Etta could stop it, an image of a certain man in a kilt with an irresistible velvety laugh filled her mind. She glanced at Dora to make sure her face hadn't given her away.

"Such perfect timing," whispered Dora, also falling into her most secret thoughts.

Sandra invited them to sit on the rocks. "They're drier than the grass, and if you have a raincoat in your rucksack, you can use it to make your seat a little more comfy."

As if under a spell, they sat in silence. Even Leon settled at their feet as the women contemplated the pool and the sea all around them, each in her own thoughts, but enveloped in a curious feeling of togetherness.

Etta shook herself from her stupor. Was she becoming sentimental? Was that what her new life entailed? Well, she'd see about that! Wasn't Sandra – this friendly companion at her side – firmly on her list of suspects?

As the thought crossed her mind, the others also seemed to come back to the here and now.

"It's time to go," said Sandra. "Do you all feel rested?"

The other three women nodded, while Leon sprang up on all fours, ready to fight anyone or anything that might get in their way, even the fiercest bull. Not to mention capturing at least a dozen rabbits.

They found Grayson busy talking to a couple of people in the pub. Sandra called him over, impatient to show him the photographs she had taken on their excursion, and Letitia was happy to fill him in on Etta's wet bum escapade, in her view the highlight of the whole day. Only when Sandra asked him if he noticed any difference between their appearance right now compared to before they'd left did Letitia have a moment of uncertainty, but her expression quickly cleared when Sandra mimed splashing water over her face.

For his part, Grayson didn't hesitate. "Sandra, you're pretty as ever, but this young lady is far more beautiful than I remember."

Letitia giggled at him.

I can't believe how much effort these people are putting in for this woman, and they don't even live on Mull, Etta thought. *But are they just helping Letitia, or are they creating a connection between them so they can manipulate the poor innocent soul at will? I won't share any*

ADRIANA LICIO

of that with Dora, or she'll get mad at me, but at least one of us has to keep our eyes and ears open.

The memory of the rockfall came to her mind, and with it the sudden realisation that when she'd looked for Dora in the car park on her return to the castle, she'd seen the estate car – the one Sandra had driven from Tobermory to Fionnphort. So, Sandra and Grayson had still been in the vicinity of the castle after the rockfall incident, but when she had met them on her way to the lighthouse a while earlier, it had seemed to Etta that they were planning to return to their accommodation in Tobermory.

Was Grayson's lack of mobility – if it was lacking at all – totally incapacitating? Was he completely unable to walk? And again, Etta's thoughts returned to the couple's deep connection with Letitia. Whose benefit was it really for?

That's the problem, Rufus, Etta thought, sighing. *When you've got a sleuthing instinct, it's so hard to let it go. It's like asking Leon to ignore the tantalising smells in a field full of rabbits.*

28

AFTERNOON TEA

On the drive back home, Dora felt grateful. It had been a splendid day and she was glad she had decided to make the most of this trip. Maybe even after Rufus joined them, Etta would agree not to cut it too short. Perhaps they would still be able to enjoy a few other swaps on their way home, or even stick to the original plan of a long trip around Europe. Who knew?

Once back in Castelmezzano, Dora would examine her options. Maybe she could find a decent little home to rent there that was within her price range; she didn't have to return to the dismal flat in Pietrapertosa. She would love to live close to Etta and Leon, although she'd never be invasive of their privacy. And, she thought with a smile, wouldn't Etta and Rufus want to visit Scotland every now and then? Maybe even Etta would brave taking a flight if Rufus was with her. In which case, wouldn't Etta be happy to have Dora to take care of Leon on those occasions?

Anyway, old bean, you should only worry about the things you can influence, Dora told herself amiably. *That which you can't control will happen as it is meant to happen and there's nothing you can do about it. Stop whining and enjoy life, this trip and... this sleuthing!*

"There you are," said Sandra as she drew to a halt in the castle car park. "Hope you've had a nice day."

"A most splendid one," said Dora.

"It was nice," said Etta.

"Worf!" said Leon, grateful to be out of the luggage compartment, a situation which had deeply wounded his pride. Being treated like a sack of potatoes – that was no way to behave towards a noble hound. His injured feelings were only soothed by Letitia hugging him goodbye and telling him what a wonderful dog he was. This lady certainly had more brains than most bipeds put together.

The five humans parted with promises to see more of each other and many expressions of thanks. Dora had noticed in this past year of travelling with Etta and Leon that walking together creates an unbreakable bond between people.

Maybe it's part of our ancestral tribal instinct, she thought with a smile, picturing herself and Etta in primitive times, wearing leopard skins and carrying heavy wooden clubs.

They had just turned the corner to head for their apartment when they heard a car arriving.

"That's Eilidh," said Etta, looking back.

"Let's wait for her, maybe she's got some news."

Eilidh left the car and joined them with an excited grin painted all over her face.

"So good to see you, ladies," she said. "Come on, let's have tea, I've got loads to tell you!"

Etta looked like she was about to mutter something about their long trip and those terrible 10 minutes crossing a wild sea, but Dora read her mind and nudged her in the stomach.

"Thank you," Etta coughed out a breath. "Of course, what a great idea."

"Are you sure you're not too tired after our daytrip?" Dora asked, smirking at her friend.

"Not at all," Etta returned a sickly sweet smile. "You know how much I love ferry rides, dear."

"A pity it was so short. We didn't even have time to get up on deck before we arrived."

"Certain experiences transcend time," Etta hissed at her friend, sickly smile still in place as Eilidh showed them into the garden, bemused at their banter.

"The sun is still out, so please do take a seat here. I'll nip inside and prepare tea, and see if I can get hold of Jeremy. His car's in the car park."

After 10 minutes or so, the couple reappeared together. Eilidh was carrying a three-tier stand filled with sandwiches, scones, crumpets and cakes, while Jeremy had a stack of plates and napkins in one hand, a tray with a selection of marmalades and jams and pots filled with clotted cream in the other.

"We decided the occasion deserved a high tea," said Eilidh.

"It's magnificent," said Dora.

"I won't be a moment," said Jeremy, heading back into the castle hall and returning a few minutes later with a teapot and cups. "Just let it brew."

"So, what's new?" Etta asked, impatient as ever to get to the point. "Have the police found the killer?"

"Well, no, actually, it's not that." Eilidh looked embarrassed. "I must sound awfully selfish… the thing is, I received a message early this afternoon. Yasmine wanted to see me…"

"Yasmine?"

"Yasmine Mason, Gary's wife… um, widow." Eilidh looked uncertainly at Jeremy, who nodded his head in support. "I went to her hotel in Tobermory and she told me she has thought about the whole issue. She doesn't want to give up on her husband's plans and dreams, so she is willing to carry on with the purchase of Glengullion…"

"That's good news," Etta said encouragingly. But Dora wasn't so sure. She couldn't help warming to the idea of the PP running the place.

"Yasmine's going to Glasgow for a few days," Eilidh explained, the unfortunate cucumber sandwich she was holding gradually coming apart as she waved it in the air, gesticulating with her hand. "The police have granted her permission, of course, as she needs to follow up on business matters for Gary. But she will return to Mull at the weekend, and she won't stay at the hotel. She will be staying here at Glengullion to show the Italian investors and the people in Mull that she means business."

Jeremy didn't look overly enthusiastic at the prospect, but Etta spoke before he could.

"Stay here? After Gary was murdered in the castle? I don't think that's a great idea."

"I agree with Etta," said Jeremy.

"Why?"

"My dear Eilidh, we still don't know why someone killed Gary Mason, but it could well be to do with the proposed purchase of the castle. Once Yasmine makes her plans to carry on with the purchase public, the killer might have the same motive to get rid of her too."

Jeremy nodded, his face solemn and worried.

"If they wanted to kill Yasmine," Eilidh protested, "they could just as easily do it at the hotel. And there'll be no fair, so far less people around. She would probably be safer here than in the middle of Tobermory."

"That might be true," Jeremy allowed. "But is it necessary?"

"Also," Eilidh said as if he hadn't spoken, "I don't think Gary was killed because he wanted to buy Glengullion. That's too obvious and the people around here are not as stupid as that, I'm sure. Yasmine shares my feelings: we believe someone has acted upon an old grudge they've held against him for years. Glasgow isn't too far away and Gary had plenty of enemies there. Any one of them could have followed him here – it was no secret he was planning to come over – and seized the opportunity, as simple as that."

"Have the police confirmed your theory?" Etta asked, her sceptical expression showing how unconvinced she was.

"Well," Eilidh admitted, "not in so many words."

"And they still don't know about the ghost incidents, either," said Etta. "And that's not all. If it hadn't been for the keen senses of Leon here, he and I would now be lying flattened beneath a rockfall."

"My goodness!" cried Jeremy. "I didn't realise things had turned so threatening…"

"There are always rockfalls on that path," Eilidh cut him short. "All the time, especially after the torrential rains we've had in the past few days. And even if it wasn't accidental, I don't believe Edwina and the others would do anything so nasty. The ghost thing and scaring my guests isn't really comparable with putting lives at risk."

"How can you be so sure?" Even Jeremy, for all his patience, seemed to be getting tired and frustrated with his fiancée's stubbornness. "That woman was going to inherit it all, and then your name came up."

"What woman?" Etta jumped in.

"Edwina."

"Jeremy, please! That's village gossip and nothing more."

"Nothing more? How can you say that after Gary Mason was killed in *your* property?" Jeremy was red in the face as he waved towards the castle.

"Jeremy, that's enough!"

"As usual, you don't want to listen to what I have to say, so I'd be better off leaving. Because I can't keep my mouth shut any longer. Having Yasmine stay here is a stupid, senseless plan."

With that, he got up and left. They heard a screech of tyres as he drove his car away at speed shortly afterwards.

"How silly men can be. I'm sorry you had to witness such a scene," murmured Eilidh, though the red tinge to her cheeks and the brightness of her eyes hinted more at contained rage than embarrassment.

"But he's not wrong, dear," said Dora soothingly. "It might not be the best idea to allow Yasmine to stay here."

"It's the *worst* idea ever," stated Etta emphatically.

"Jeremy wants the place sold just as much as I do, but he's full of irrational fears, while my greatest worry is that if I miss this chance, I will never sell. Where else would I find someone financially strong enough to come up with such an offer? It's a once-in-a-lifetime chance, I don't want to miss it. And Yasmine believes if we don't act fast, we will lose the Italian investors, without whom she wouldn't go ahead. We need to show them right now, this place is perfect. The location's amazing, the community is splendid and Gary's death had nothing to do with the island."

"By the way, what did Jeremy mean about Edwina being supposed to inherit the castle?" asked Etta. Dora winked at her, silently teasing, *"You see, you can't help sleuthing,"* to which Etta waved her away with an irritable gesture that indicated, *"This is just an innocent question."* Dora smiled and telegraphed back, *"Of course it isn't."*

"My auntie and Edwina were very good friends who worked on the PP project together. As you've seen, they haven't achieved any great results, with the possible exception of the Mull Forest Café, which was crowdfunded and has done really well ever since. So people thought Auntie Katherine would leave everything to Edwina, but when the will was read and they discovered she'd left it all to her only natural heir, some of the locals were surprised."

"Bitter and disappointed," Etta suggested, "would be better words, maybe?"

"I don't think so. No… that is… maybe. They couldn't have been 100% sure who would inherit, but frankly, if my aunt intended to leave everything to Edwina, I don't think she would have changed her mind all of a sudden. Actually, I'm sure she would have made it quite clear to the people close to her."

"No one's ever mentioned another will?"

"No, there was only ever one will that she wrote as soon as she arrived here from France after Uncle Donald died. She later added a minor donation to the PP, but the bulk of the inheritance was always intended for me."

"You have to admit it's a little weird, though, if your aunt had devoted so much time to the PP that she left them so little. Maybe, she planned to leave them more, to change the will, but as so often happens, she kept putting it off until it was too late."

"Such is life!" said Eilidh a little bitterly. "Do you think I should part with the castle just because my aunt might have changed her mind? You see, beyond the castle itself, there wasn't much else. There was just enough money to pay inheritance taxes and for me to invest in the property for this last year, but those efforts didn't achieve anything. That was it. Maybe Auntie felt she wanted to keep the castle in the family – Scottish people often feel huge loyalty to their clan. Or maybe she felt the PP project wasn't going anywhere, which it plainly isn't."

"She didn't leave you any instructions or a personal letter explaining…"

"Nothing of the sort," Eilidh shook her head. "Her solicitor merely contacted me after the reading of the will to ask me if I wanted to accept."

"And you said yes immediately?"

"Of course. Well, almost immediately. I asked first if there were any debts secured against the property, and the solicitor said no and explained it was an important local landmark. He did, however, warn me it was rundown and badly in need of repairs and modernisation, but he asserted that I would be free to sell it at any time or keep it if that was my choice. He added that the money to cover the taxes was provided, which I was grateful for as it never occurred to me I'd have to pay so much to inherit what is rightly mine. But that was all he said."

Dora poured a second cup of tea for them all, handed Leon a little piece of crumpet and, when Etta wasn't looking, a morsel of prawn and mayo sandwich, knowing how much the hound adored it. The pause in the conversation reminded Dora there was one question in her mind.

"We were on Iona this morning," she said.

"Isn't it an amazing place?"

"Indeed, we've never experienced such a feeling of serenity and peace," and Dora chirped on for a while about the Abbey and the Well of Age. "We also met Jenny, Jeremy's sister, who told us about the artists' gallery she is running. She happened to mention that Jeremy pulled out of the project."

"Jenny is such an excellent manager, I wish she'd taken over Glengullion," Eilidh laughed at her own joke. "She's not like me, so… so… woo-woo. She's the practical type, but she's also a bit headstrong, and Jeremy realised that as much they love each other, they couldn't ever work together."

"Love each other?" Etta's eyebrows shot up to her hairline. She obviously wouldn't have called Jenny's contempt towards her brother an example of love.

"Well, you know, brothers and sisters always fight and get mad at each other. Anyway, I'm positive as soon as we move to London, putting enough miles between them, the two will be back on good terms. Jenny will see that in the end, it was for the best that Jeremy walked away from the gallery project."

"And you were together in London, planning your future when the murder happened?" said Dora.

"Not exactly. That is to say, I was in London with my daughter. Jeremy was in Oban, attending to some business there. When we heard what had happened, he drove to Glasgow and spent the night there, so he could meet me from the overnight coach in the morning and drive us to catch an early ferry to Mull. Public transport isn't great, especially on a Sunday."

"What time did the police inform you of what had happened?"

"Late in the afternoon, though I can't remember exactly when…" Then in one of her characteristic bursts of clarity, Eilidh caught up with her own thoughts. "Actually, I can, because I rang Jeremy a few times around half past four, soon after they'd told me what had happened, but he didn't answer. He'd forgotten to take his phone out of the car and he called me back after five."

"When did you leave London?"

"By the time Jeremy called me back, my only option was to get the night coach to Glasgow. He said he'd be at Buchanan bus station to pick me up at 6.45am so we could drive back to Oban and catch the morning ferry, and you know the rest. But you're questioning me like the police did. Why?"

"We just thought Jeremy had been with you all along," admitted Dora. "You know what old people are like, we get lost in the details."

"WHAT DO YOU THINK?" DORA ASKED ETTA EXCITEDLY AS SOON AS they were alone in their flat.

"I think we won't need dinner, Eilidh's high tea was filling enough."

"True, but that's not what I meant."

"I beg your pardon, what did you mean?"

"That I – we – always took it for granted that Jeremy and Eilidh were together in London at the time of the murder."

"Apparently, they weren't," Etta said, stating the obvious.

"Jeremy only called Eilidh back after five," as she said this, Dora went to look at the brochures and leaflets Eilidh had left for them. "See?" She picked up the ferry timetable and waved it under Etta's eyes. "There's a ferry at half past one, and the next one is at four o'clock in the afternoon. If the murder took place around 2.15pm, as Debbie told me, then Jeremy had all the time in the world to drive to Tobermory, then to Craignure to catch that ferry. He didn't answer Eilidh because the sound of the sea, the crowds on board the ferry, the loudspeakers might have given him away. But by five, he had landed and he called her back." Dora felt proud that she was learning to sleuth and learning fast. But Etta brought her back down to Earth.

"Tut-tut," she said. "You're forgetting a few things. One: opportunity. This is just conjecture, not proof. If we suspected all those who had an opportunity, we'd have an infinite list of potential killers. Two: motive. I'd say Jeremy hardly has a motive. He may not have been keen on doing business with Mason, but he's as desperate as Eilidh to sell and move to London. His sister unwittingly confirmed this. Three, Eilidh said the police asked those very same questions, so they would undoubtedly have checked his alibi, which is easy to do these days as you can find out where a person's mobile phone was at any given time. And last but not least – actually, the most important objection – we're not supposed to be nosing around this time!"

Dora felt dismayed at all her theories being shattered to pieces. She would never make it as a detective, she didn't have Etta's logical brain. And that's what one needed when investigating something as serious as murder. Then a feeling of pure frustration led to an uncharacteristic flood of rage inside her. Why did Etta always have to be so stubborn?

"You might be right on all counts, apart from one: *you've* been nosing around!" she reminded Etta bitterly.

"Not this time, now things are different."

"What is different?" Dora asked as petulantly as she could. She knew Etta would find it hard to mention Rufus McCall and whatever was going on between the two of them.

"Because, believe it or not, we're not getting any younger, and it's time we acknowledged this and stopped putting ourselves in danger."

"You're not believing a single word you're saying! You're just being Mrs Contrary as usual, stubborn as a mule, determined to ruin things for me. Come, Leon, we'd better take a little walk before I say things I might regret later." With that, Dora took Leon's leash and the two strode outside into a beautiful still-luminous northern night, slamming the door loudly behind them and leaving a puzzled Etta in their wake.

WEDNESDAY

AFTERNOON

This is never ending! Gary is out of the way, but now it seems Yasmine Mason wants to carry on from where he left off. She's coming to the castle, no less, to reassure the Italian investors everything is fine.

We need to get rid of her, ASAP.

This must be why the two Italian hags are still around. It has all been a masquerade, they're not Eilidh's friends at all.

The awful thing is that L listened to the whole PP meeting, even though she wasn't supposed to be there. I don't want her to feel any of this pressure, to breathe in all the heartache and anxiety of uncertainty. I promised I would take care of her as best I can. And that means she should be as carefree as possible. I want to share with her only the best life can offer, so she has a right to be protected from all the troubles and fears and demons we have to face.

Mr T has refused to help any further. But I don't fear his mutiny. When the time is right, I will convince him otherwise. On the other hand, what if he's right? What if it's time to wait and see what happens next, as painful as that may be?

Or maybe we should just wait for an opportunity, and then be ready to snatch it when the right moment comes along. There must be a way to stop all this nonsense.

Oh Katherine, if only you were here. If we could discuss it all, you could speak to Eilidh and make her understand...

FRIDAY

FRIDAY
MORNING

All or nothing. It's today or never.

As I expected, I've managed to convince them all, including Mr T, we've got to do something. Again. But I can't brag. Even I'm starting to feel a little afraid. Not for me, mind you. I'm very much determined to have it my way or the highway, but what about the others? What have I caught them up in? I'm well into my seventies, but people like S and G have years ahead of them. I shouldn't have exposed them, nor J. What am I doing?

I read the mixture of pain and incredulity in Mr T's eyes when he said, "But what if in the end, it was one of us?"

I shook my head vehemently. "That's not the case!" But I don't think he believed me.

The worst of it is that, no matter how I look at it, the show must go on.

29

DINING WITH THE DIVA

On Friday morning, Dora indulged in a lie in. She could
see without getting out from under the blankets that it
was rainy and overcast outside, and she loved her cosy mauve
room. It was ideal for some healthy thinking.

A few uneventful days had passed. She had made her peace
with Etta, although they still both seemed to be measuring
everything they said in advance, as if half a wrong word would
see them descend into arguments more fierce than anything they
had experienced in a whole year of sharing their lives. The truth
was, Dora had calmed down a little after meeting with DCI
Findlay who, upon hearing Dora's theories about Jeremy, had
patiently requested she leave things to the professionals. Fact
checking was the daily bread of the police, Findlay told her.
Jeremy's car had not only been registered on the 13.35 ferry from
Craignure, "Which is a good 35 minutes' drive from Tobermory,"
Findlay had remarked pointedly, but the owner of Oban's
newsagent and coffee shop had remembered him being in her
premises at quarter to three. Jeremy had spilled his coffee on the
floor and helped the shopkeeper to clean it up. He'd been so
mortified by the accident, he had even bought a few books as if
trying to make up it.

"A dear lad," the shopkeeper had said. But more to the point, her testimony made it impossible that he could have been at Glengullion at the time of the murder.

From that moment, Dora had believed any suspicions she might have had were ridiculous. As Etta had said, she needed proof; she couldn't just accuse anyone who'd had an opportunity to commit the murder. Plenty of people had the opportunity, but lacked the motive, or vice versa. Even if they had both motive and opportunity, that didn't mean they would commit a murder.

For a long moment, remembering how all her theories had been shattered, Dora felt old and useless. The dark stormy day seemed to match her mood perfectly, until she had an epiphany.

Why would I become a sleuth all of a sudden anyway? That's Etta's role, but I have always had rather different interests. What's this madness all about? I was a bit shaken by the news that Etta would actually be following Rufus's request not to investigate, but I simply can't be what she used to be. I need to find my own way forward. And if the old mule is no longer interested in sleuthing, I need to find something entirely different to do. Something I have always been keen on, something that gives me joy, like hiking, or meeting and spending time with new and old friends. Something like… cooking! Like for tonight's dinner at Eilidh's.

Ten minutes later, despite the thunder outside, the rain furiously rattling against the window panes, Dora was singing in the kitchen, pulling out pans and pots, beating eggs, frying veggies. Admittedly, her mind would occasionally return to the murder and questions about whodunnit would surprise her, the whisk or spoon in her hand waving about in the air, scattering mixture all around. Then she'd shake her head, clean up the mess, smiling at herself as she kept on… cooking on!

She had been right on one thing, though: Etta was Mrs Contrary. As soon as she, Dora, had stopped mentioning the murder, Etta had slowly started coming up with conjectures. And when Dora had reminded her it was none of their business, Etta grumbled that one's words should never be interpreted too literally. On another occasion, she had gone as far as declaring that talking about murder is a matter of basic human curiosity, while poking around is a different kettle of fish.

Then came the long-awaited message from Rufus McCall, confirming that he would arrive at Glengullion on Monday. Besides the one she had earmarked for Yasmine Mason, Eilidh had another B&B room ready for guests and Rufus was very welcome to use it. He wouldn't have a kitchen, but that wasn't a problem as he could count on Etta and Dora for meals together.

This visit will clarify whatever is to come. But don't worry, old bean, whatever will be will be.

"Wow!" said Dora when she and Etta entered the Crystal Room and saw the table Eilidh had laid for her guests. It was a classic example of simple elegance. An embroidered white tablecloth with lace borders served as a backdrop to silver cutlery and white porcelain dishes, crystal wine glasses, Sheffield steel candle holders with the bases encased in dark ivy wreaths fresh from the garden. The prisms and beads of the majestic chandelier reflected the flames from the candles, and from the electric fire in the marble fireplace, creating a sophisticated yet cosy atmosphere.

"So very lovely!" said Dora, once she had finally overcome all her gasping and hand clasping.

"Are you really sure you will adapt to living in a flat in London, Eilidh?" Etta, ever the pragmatic one, asked.

"Oh, I'm sure I will," replied Eilidh, chuckling. "All of this comes at a cost. The power might go down at any time; the plumbing throws up problems week in, week out; the roof springs leaks and I'm lucky if I find them before the rainwater has seeped through and ruined whatever's underneath. And in the meantime, the bills keep coming in."

"I agree," said Jeremy dutifully. "A compact London flat will be a delight, its daily care not even requiring an hour of work."

"I can hardly wait," said Eilidh, beaming at the idea.

"I will take care of you," Jeremy said, embracing her, the grin on his face softening the passion behind the words. "I'll work hard to make our life happy, exciting and fun."

"I hope you don't mind if I kiss this man," said Eilidh and, sheltering their faces behind her open hand, she did just that, briefly but tenderly.

"WoRRRf!" Leon shouted. He didn't like someone else kissing a pretty woman whose heart he had vowed to win. Eilidh was startled by the vehemence of the dog's protest, then burst into laughter with everyone else.

"I'm sorry, Leon, if I upset you," she said, kneeling down to caress the dog's head, then vigorously massaging his whole body. "You're my first and only true love, guaranteed!"

"As for me," Jeremy jumped to attention, his hand reaching for his forehead to salute the superiority of the hound, "I will take second place."

"He's such a self-centred dog," Etta said. "He truly believes the whole world rotates around him."

"And that's exactly how things should be," Eilidh whispered into Leon's ear, "shouldn't they?" And seeing how the hound wagged his tail, his ears low on his head as he played the innocent soul, she continued, "Such a great pretender you are, Napoleon!"

"I'm sorry if I'm late," a deep throaty voice cut through the laughter from the other side of the room. Even Dora recognised that the tone didn't sound at all sorry.

The room fell into silence, broken only by the sharp click-clack of high heels across the oak floor. The lights flickered as thunder roared outside, making the windows rattle. A few more click-clacks later, Yasmine Mason came into full view. Her dress, in an attractive dark green, was as skin tight as the one she had been wearing at the fair. It was impossible not to admire her slim waist and abundant cleavage.

"I am so grateful to you for laying on this feast for me, Eilidh," said the woman with studied slowness.

"Dora helped massively, as my head chef and caterer," said Eilidh.

"You look wonderful," said Jeremy, inviting Yasmine to sit down on the sofas next to him and Eilidh.

"Thanks, Jeremy. In truth, I feel I have neglected myself," again the words came out unnaturally slowly. "Since Gary's death, I do not care much for me…"

Dora looked at Etta, worried her impatient friend might advise the woman to speak a little faster. Luckily, Etta just rolled her eyes towards the ceiling, unseen by Yasmine.

"Oh dear," said Eilidh. "Well, I'm so glad you're here now. Can I offer you a drink?"

"A glass of champagne would be perfect."

Eilidh looked lost. It was Jeremy who came to the rescue.

"I'll go fetch some, I'm sure I saw a few bottles in the cellar."

Eilidh sighed in relief and looked at Jeremy gratefully. He winked back before leaving.

"How is your room?" she asked Yasmine.

"Cold and draughty, I'm afraid."

"Oh, you see why I hate this castle? And that's our very best room."

"I know, dear, that you've done your very best. But true luxury is a totally different kettle of fish. This castle might work at present for those who like a more… rustic feel, a farmhouse kind of holiday, living like the locals. But my Italian partners know their business. They will turn this place inside out and make it into a playground for those of more discerning tastes, and then you will be my guest, Eilidh, and see for yourself what can be achieved." Yasmine smiled, sweeping her long hair away from her face as Jeremy arrived back with a couple of champagne bottles. "You'll need to ice it, dear. Don't worry, I don't mind waiting."

Jeremy flushed. "I'll fetch the ice bucket. Honey, do you have any idea where it might be?"

"Sideboard, I guess," and Eilidh sprang up to help Jeremy search for it. Dora saw the two squeezing each other's hands briefly, as if acknowledging it required a good dose of cool patience to deal with Yasmine's demands.

Then a whining cry broke the silence that had fallen over the Crystal Room. Leon sprang to his feet, pricking up his ears as much as a Basset can. As the tips rose almost to eye level, his forehead furrowed in concern, filling up with even more wrinkles than usual.

30

TWO GHOSTS?

"What was that?" cried Yasmine.

"It must have been the wind howling through the chimneys," Jeremy replied with a shrug.

"No, it sounded like... a cry," said Dora, not feeling at all reassured.

"In a building this large and this old, you will hear all sorts of noises, especially during the night," Jeremy said. "Rattling windows, creaking floors, stairs, beams. Then there's the wind in the chimney flues, and that's besides sounds coming from outside, especially on a stormy day."

"Not for the faint hearted!" Dora said.

"Yes, and let's not forget the special effects created ad hoc," muttered Etta.

"Special effects?" Yasmine asked.

"It was just a joke about an experience we had during one of our home swap holidays," said Etta, without explaining it had occurred at Glengullion.

"Let's eat," Eilidh changed the subject. "Jeremy, could you go and fetch what Dora put in the oven to stay warm?"

"I'll come too," said Dora. "I want to switch on the pot for the spaghetti."

"Spag-heh-tti?" said Yasmine, in her strange slow way, sounding more horrified by this than she had been about the weird cry. "You should never eat carbohydrates, especially in the evening. I need to watch my weight in case I become fat and ungainly," and the woman looked pointedly at the two plump Italian ladies.

"But it comes with lobster sauce…"

"Just lobster for me then, please."

"Champagne won't keep you slim, by the way," Etta couldn't help herself.

"You're absolutely right. But no one is perfect. The important thing is to choose your sins wisely, and given a choice between champagne and spaghetti, I'd definitely go for the former," she raised her glass and drank deeply.

A malicious glint appeared in Etta's eyes. So much so that for a second, Dora expected Yasmine to collapse on the floor and writhe in pain, declaring the bubbly had been poisoned. But instead, she stood up and, with the elegance of a top model, sashayed over to the table and waited for Jeremy to pull her chair out.

"We thought we'd seat you at the head of the table," Eilidh explained to Yasmine, "so you will have the fireplace at your back. It will keep you warm. But we moved the table a little to make sure you'd not be too close."

"That was so very thoughtful of you," said Yasmine breathily, but she was addressing Jeremy, not Eilidh. The chandelier overhead cast her face in luminous light, as if a Madonna had climbed straight out of a Renaissance painting.

They sat. Leon, quick as the most modern computer, ran his data, studied the diners' psychological profiles analytically and identified that the ideal spot beneath the table would be between Dora and Eilidh. Those two were more likely than anyone else to slip him a morsel of food every now and then.

The antipasto Dora served was cicchetti Veneziani, fish-based finger foods she had learned to cook during a Christmas homeswap in Venice. Yasmine picked a couple of deep fried prawns, saying how delicious they were, accusing the cook of attempting to destroy her waistline, and wondering how Eilidh – who was clearly enjoying the food immensely – could eat so much. Dora got the impression Eilidh became a little self-conscious on the back of this remark.

"I hope Jeremy won't mind too much if I gain a kilogramme or two," said Eilidh, her fingers suspending her tuna meatball in front of her face. She regarded it as if evaluating how many calories could be hidden within the small morsel, then shrugged and popped it in her mouth. "Mind you, running this place has kept me active," she added after chewing and swallowing.

"I prefer women who eat," Jeremy reassured her, seeming to have no doubts about tucking into his open sandwich with marinated anchovies.

"Men always say that," Yasmine looked at him languidly while nibbling her second prawn. "But when it comes to women they fancy, they forget all about their nice theories and always choose the slim ones."

Etta had a horrified look on her face. The hand that was reaching out to grab one more squid skewer suddenly withdrew. Surely, Dora thought, she wasn't worried about what Rufus might think? For as long as he'd known her, she'd definitely been more on the rotund side than the skinny one. Oh, dear Etta!

Eilidh coughed and chuckled. "You are one cruel woman, Yasmine."

"Just a practical one."

"I'll go check the spaghetti for you, Dora. If it is al dente, I'll give you a shout."

"Thanks, Jeremy."

He had just left the room when one of the windows behind Etta, encouraged by a particularly strong gust of wind, opened suddenly with a powerful slam that made them all jump from their chairs. The cold air and rain came pouring in as Eilidh ran to close and secure it again.

"Strewth! This crazy window. We'll have to check it out tomorrow, but I'm sure I closed it properly this afternoon."

"That was scary," Dora smiled, recomposing herself.

"The ghost is misbehaving tonight," Etta commented, looking at Eilidh.

"The ghost?" Yasmine asked.

"Etta is teasing me," Eilidh explained. "I told her that ever since I arrived, I've felt as if a kind presence is taking care of me. At night, it's like he's watching over me, wishing me well. Or helping me find things I'd lost during the day. I'm not exactly an ordered person, I'm afraid, and in a house of these dimensions, I'm too good at scattering things about wherever I happen to be. Then I spend most of the day looking for them…"

"But, listen," said Etta, holding up a hand to hush Eilidh. "Did I hear footsteps walking across the floor above?"

"No, I don't think so. It's so cold tonight, I had to switch on the electric fireplaces upstairs, and the wood in the beams always cracks as it accommodates the change in temperature."

"So, have you ever seen *him*?" Dora asked Eilidh, curious to bring the conversation back to the juicy bits.

"Once, or I think I did. I woke up suddenly – it was weird as I'd just had a dream of being a child again. Or maybe I was dreaming about my daughter, Elizabeth. I – or she – was crying and a man came over and consoled me. I never saw his face, but I knew I could trust him. Then I woke up, and I am sure I saw a shadow leaving my bedroom."

"Maybe you were still dreaming." For once, Yasmine seemed genuinely interested in something other than herself.

"Maybe it was me," joked Jeremy, popping his head round the door and beckoning to Dora. "I think the spaghetti is just right, but you may want to make sure."

"Just lobster for me," Yasmine reminded them.

"Will do," said Jeremy. "But I warn you, the spaghetti is delicious."

A few moments later, Dora and Jeremy came back in,

carrying two dishes each. Eilidh had said earlier it wouldn't do to bring the large pan in and place it on the centre of the table, as Dora had suggested. Yasmine would not approve!

"I'll come and help you bring everything else," Jeremy told Dora as he placed dishes in front of Yasmine and Eilidh.

"No, that's fine," she replied. "There's only my helping left."

When she came back from the kitchen, the talk had returned to the subject of the ghost.

"But it's really creepy," the diva called Yasmine shivered, downing another glass of champagne. Then she added, looking straight towards the only man in the room, "I wonder how I will be able to sleep all by myself tonight."

Jeremy choked, but recovered his composure heroically, joining Etta and Eilidh in complimenting Dora on the delicacy and taste of the dish.

"Truth is," she said modestly, "the fish in Mull tastes like nothing else I've tried before…"

She stopped abruptly as the lights dimmed, then went out completely. And that included the electric fireplace. The darkness was at first almost overwhelming.

"Crikey!" cried Eilidh.

"How lucky you thought to put candles on the table," said Etta, appreciating they were not in complete darkness.

"I'll go check it out, see if it's our fuse or a blackout covering the whole area because of the storm," said Jeremy. But before he could get up, a cloud of fog started to float across the floor, seeping in under the doors.

"Crikey!" the man exclaimed, echoing his fiancée and dropping back onto his chair.

The mist rose up, forming a shape. A bright flash caused them all to close their eyes for a couple of seconds. When they reopened them, a suit of armour had materialised from the mist.

The knight took a step forward, raised the arm which held his mace and pointed it towards Yasmine. "You evil witch! No good will come of it if you stay here. Begone and take your wicked plans with you. Leave this ancient abode in peace."

Then, from the door behind the knight, another figure appeared. Dressed in a sombre blue and green kilt, he had a severe face framed by long sideburns, and cruel grey eyes.

"What is the meaning of this!" he thundered on seeing the suit of armour, which turned to face him. The two looked at each other, and though the spectators couldn't see the knight's face, the agitated rattling of his armour indicated he was as surprised as the ghostly aristocrat.

At the same moment, the two moved to seize each other, but stopped in panic. In an instant, a couple of things happened. Two more windows flew open and a gale followed that was so strong, it extinguished all the candles in a single blow, this time leaving the room in complete darkness.

"Don't panic, stay exactly where you are," shouted Jeremy, his voice rising above the gasps and screams. But no sooner were the words out of his mouth than…

CRASH! The sound burst from the centre of the table where they were sitting. It was only when their ears had recovered from the deafening noise that they noticed it was accompanied by the multiple tinkling of broken crystals and loose hopping beads, while all the time, the savage wind kept howling around them.

31

IN THE DARKNESS

"My goodness, whatever's happened now?" cried Eilidh once she'd recovered enough to stammer a few words.

"The chandelier! It's the chandelier, fallen on to the table," Etta explained.

"Yasmine!" cried Dora. As soon as Etta clarified what the terrifying crash had been, she remembered who had been sitting just below the chandelier.

"Yasmine!" Eilidh had clearly realised the same thing.

Then a beam of torchlight broke the darkness. It shone on Eilidh's face, dazzling her, then moved to Etta and Dora.

"Yasmine!" Jeremy echoed the two women, his torch beam moving to where Mrs Mason should have been. Seeing nothing, he shone his torch frantically around the room. "Eilidh, where's your mobile? And let's close those blasted windows! Yasmine!" he kept hollering the woman's name all through the instructions.

The torchlight paused on a small service table near the door where Eilidh had left her mobile. She was quick to recover it, then hurried to close the two windows, moving cautiously around the crystal shards on the floor. Etta and Dora too recovered their phones from their pockets and switched on their torches, highlighting the bulky chandelier lying half on the table, half between it and the chair where Yasmine had been sitting.

"Leon!" cried Etta at seeing the mess.

"The pup's fine," answered Dora, squatting down, her beam of light finding him exactly where he had been. He hadn't moved a centimetre, the solid table providing good protection. "Stay there," she told him, "or you might hurt your paws on the crystals." Leon wagged his tail at her, agreeing that he had no intention of leaving his safe spot.

"Good dog!" said Etta, her voice betraying her relief. "But where is Yasmine? There's no sign of *her* under the table."

From her position squatting next to Leon, careful not to kneel on the floor because of the broken glass, Dora listened. She could hear a few low sobs.

A beam of light moved from the floor near the head of the table all the way to the dark fireplace, then to the armchair next to it. It was from there that the sobs and moans were coming.

"Yasmine!" Eilidh cried, running towards her. "How are you? Are you hurt?"

The formerly deep, breathy voice now rose, as shrill as that of a whining child. "No, I am not fine! That was so scary, I could have been killed."

From her low position, Dora watched the others moving closer to Yasmine, Eilidh bending down to hug and comfort her.

"Jeremy, see if it's our mains switch that has tripped," said Eilidh, turning to the man. "And fetch a glass of water for Yasmine, she's in shock."

"Champagne would be better," Yasmine whined.

Dora saw Jeremy's legs and torch beam heading for the door. Long moments later, the lights came back on. From her position, Dora could appreciate the mess: shards of crystal, food, broken porcelain, liquid still dripping from the table on to the oak floor. She distinguished Etta's legs walking towards the door Jeremy had left by, and then back again.

"Well done," she heard Etta say, and then a broom appeared

next to her.

Jeremy's feet walked over to Eilidh and Yasmine. "No more champagne, I'm afraid, but I've found some brandy," Dora heard him say.

"She shouldn't mix the two, especially in a state of shock," Eilidh reproached him.

"Babe," the slow breathy voice had returned, cutting through Eilidh's wise words, "I've mixed much worse things in life than champagne and brandy."

"How did you manage to escape?" asked Eilidh.

"When the windows burst open on that terrible ghostly scene, I was terrified, and I wanted to get away from it and find shelter. Then the crash startled me and I fell into the armchair. I guess my beloved Gary is protecting me..."

In the meantime, Etta had swept the glass away so that Dora could lead Leon out from under the table to the clearer part of the room close to the door.

"Ouch! I couldn't have held that position for much longer," Dora exclaimed, stretching while leaning against one of the chairs next to her.

"Thank goodness Yasmine is not hurt," Eilidh said, her voice rising with anger. "But this has gone too far. Those mad pensioners will hear me out this time. And, Jeremy, call the police. It seems I've been taken for a fool by the whole lot of them."

After having dished out her instructions, Eilidh rushed from the room. Dora glanced at Etta, who still held the broom as if undecided what to do next. Forestalling her friend's determination to stay away from trouble, Dora pointed to Leon.

"You take care of him, I'm not going to leave Eilidh alone."

Etta locked eyes with her. "Miss Pepe, there's no way I will let you march around this castle on your own. You keep Leon on his leash," she said, fetching the item from the floor near her former seat, "I'll bring this," and she brandished her phone, the torch still lit.

"Oh, my dearest Mrs Passolina."

"Let's go!"

"Wait! I need to be the one to follow Eilidh," cried Jeremy in dismay.

"Nope, someone strong needs to stay with Yasmine in case of a new attack."

"And to watch over the crime scene."

With that, the two women and one dog fled before the amazed man could think of any more objections.

"Where are we going?" asked Dora.

"To the car park, where I think Eilidh will start looking for the PP tricksters. They must have some means of transport."

Leon sniffed the air and sighed in relief. Yes, for once, the two women were heading in the right direction.

In the car park, they found Eilidh's car, their own yellow Fiat, Yasmine's Porsche and one more car.

"That's Jeremy's," Etta said.

They looked around, the rain pouring down and soaking them, a little lost and uncertain what to do next. But Leon – no, Leon wasn't uncertain. He sniffed the air again and, ignoring the water, the mud, the puddles and the pattering rain, he barked, pointing further into the darkness.

"He can smell something," cried Dora excitedly.

"Set him free," said Etta.

"Good dog, Leon, go find him." Dora unleashed the hound. Hide-and-seek was a game they often played during their walks, the women hiding either themselves or an object, and Leon won every time. So he trotted along without any doubts, down the road from the car park, away from the castle. The two women followed him a little clumsily as the torchlight shone against the raindrops, almost dazzling them. Still, without it, they wouldn't have seen far beyond their noses.

Groping and stumbling, they reached the main gate of the Glengullion property. There, they recognised Eilidh's figure standing in front of an old shed that in the past might have been used by a warden guarding the entrance. At this point, Leon barked as if he was at home, playing scare the postman.

"WOO-WOO-WOOOOOF!" and he pretended to attack, running past Eilidh only to stop a couple of metres beyond her.

As the wind abated a little, Dora and Etta heard cries and the jangling of metal. Eilidh, still a few steps ahead of them, was close enough for her torchlight to reveal what lay ahead.

A GROUP OF PEOPLE WERE PUSHING A BODY INSIDE THE BOOT OF A car. As Leon startled them, they turned, letting go of the corpse so that it was left hanging half inside, half outside the car, the pelvis and legs dangling.

As terrified as she must have been by the macabre sight, Eilidh pointed her torch in the faces of the criminals, recognising and naming them one by one.

"Tom. Edwina. Debbie. What are you up to?" The torch moved towards the lifeless body. "What have you done?"

Then the light shone back into Eilidh's eyes, reflected by something metallic. The body was a suit of armour.

"That explains one of the ghosts, I guess," Etta said.

At her words, Tom moved what he'd been hiding behind his back. It was an arm. Not a flesh and blood arm, thank goodness, but that of the suit of armour.

"Now, you three, put that in there," Eilidh demanded, holding her torch in both hands and moving it to indicate the suit of armour, then the open boot, "and lock the car. You're coming back with me to the castle. And just so you know, the police are on their way."

Drenched from head to toe, the trio didn't offer up any resistance. Only Tom spoke, shaking his head at Edwina.

"You see?"

"We had no choice," the woman replied stubbornly as she pushed back her sodden hair from her forehead.

Debbie trudged along, unusually quiet. The guilty three went ahead, the other three and one dog following like guards escorting prisoners. It was only once they were back inside the Crystal Room of the castle that Eilidh exploded into a tantrum of epic proportions, seeming to be addressing Edwina more than the other two.

"How could you do this to me? You knew I trusted you! Aunt Katherine trusted you, and you have betrayed us both so woefully!"

A couple of times, a subdued Edwina tried to throw some words in edgeways, but Eilidh had turned into an erupting volcano. Incandescent with rage, she hurled words out, which flowed like lava, crushing and burying anything in their way. At one point, Edwina managed to hand the younger woman a letter, but in her fury, Eilidh didn't even look at it. Instead, she grabbed it, crumpled it and pushed it into her jeans pocket, all the while hollering. She stopped only when she was out of breath, finishing with a dramatic statement.

"You almost killed your second victim!"

"We didn't kill or try to kill anyone," Tom replied soberly.

"So, dropping a chandelier on to a table around which people are eating is your way of saying hi, is it?"

The eyes of the trio rose from the mess on the floor that Etta had tried to clear away to the titanic light fitting balancing precariously on the end of the table, finally coming to rest on the ceiling where a few electric cables were hanging through a gaping hole.

"So, that was that strange rumbling crash we heard," said Tom.

"Of course, because you had nothing to do with it!" Eilidh said, her voice heavy with sarcasm.

"No, we were too busy being surprised by the other ghost," said Debbie.

"The *other* ghost?" asked Dora.

"The Scottish laird from ancient times…"

"You mean that wasn't part of your pantomime?"

"No, it wasn't," at this point, the three guilty ones managed to sound strangely innocent.

"And you expect me to believe you, do you?" Eilidh snapped.

The three nodded.

Eilidh banged her head with her hand. "Are you really convinced I'm that stupid?"

"We were behind the suit of armour," Tom stuttered while his companions remained unusually quiet. "And the other tricks to scare your friends. We wanted to show you that the ghost would still visit, even after the police had become involved, because your friend here," he nodded at Etta, "hinted his sudden disappearance was suspicious. And we wanted to scare Gary Mason's wife, so it was a two birds with one stone situation." He glanced at Yasmine warily, but she only seemed to have eyes for the brandy bottle. "But we didn't kill or try to kill anyone, Gary included. We had nothing to do with the falling chandelier and were just as scared as you were by the… um… real ghost."

"Sure!" said Eilidh, dropping down on to the sofa, but still pointing her phone at the three pranksters as if it were a gun, even though the main lights were back on.

"How could that chandelier fall?" Tom asked. "It's been there for centuries."

"And with such perfect timing, too," Jeremy said, the same tone of incredulity in his voice as Eilidh's.

"It's not been there for centuries," Eilidh said quietly. "We had it moved to sit above the centre of the table when we renovated this part of the castle."

They all fell into an uneasy silence, broken only by Yasmine's increasingly incoherent murmurs of "Silly auld killers!" in between gulps of brandy and laughter.

Then the sound of sirens brought everyone back to the here and now.

32

A LETTER FROM THE PAST

"Where was the chandelier fixed?" asked the police officer who had arrived on the scene.

"You could access it from one of the guest bedrooms," answered Jeremy, "by removing the wooden floorboards. It's a room we haven't had the opportunity to renovate. But the electrician who moved the chandelier used a robust hook, and sturdy nuts and bolts."

"We'll take a look," said the officer, indicating that Jeremy should show him the way. When they came back, Jeremy had a face like thunder.

"It seems that the chandelier had been tampered with from above," said the police officer. "We believe the nuts and bolts were partly unscrewed so that eventually, the chandelier would fall under its own weight."

"It seems the killer knew Yasmine was sitting directly underneath it," growled Jeremy, barely suppressing his fury. "While their two co-conspirators," he gestured scathingly at Edwina, Debbie and Tom, "distracted us with their ghostly tricks."

"We didn't..." began Tom, but the police officer cut him short.

ADRIANA LICIO

"Sir, if you wouldn't mind saving it for your statement," he said authoritatively. "My colleague and I need to ask you and these two ladies," he indicated Edwina and Debbie, "to accompany us back to the station." Although expressed like a request, his words left no room for refusal. The police officer turned back to Eilidh. "Ms McGullion, please would you be so kind as to vacate this room, and refrain from entering the room above, just in case we need to return to gather evidence. I can send a constable to stand guard if..."

"That won't be necessary," said Eilidh shortly.

As the police left with the crestfallen PP trio, Dora and Eilidh gently helped the very drunken Yasmine to her feet and guided her slowly up to her room, Etta walking ahead, enticing the mumbling woman with the brandy bottle. When Dora telegraphed an anxious message to her friend, suggesting it might not be the wisest idea to leave Yasmine alone with the drink, Etta held the bottle up to the light and tilted it slightly, showing the two sober women that it was empty.

On returning downstairs, Etta, Dora and Eilidh found Jeremy and Leon warming themselves by the large Aga in the kitchen.

"I will never learn who I can trust," muttered Eilidh. "I believed that woman, that wretched Edwina, was my friend. And Tom, I thought he was my friend too, and that the PP was just a bunch of nice elderly people. I've been feeling guilty for weeks that I'd decided to sell, not for my sake, but because I was letting them down. But they didn't hesitate for a second to betray me in the worst possible way by putting their murderous plan into action."

"What about the other ghost?" Dora asked.

Eilidh waved a dismissive had. "Just one more of their silly tricks."

"But he so resembled the original Lord McGullion. We should know," here, Dora shuddered, "because his painting hung in our bedroom in that awful... ahem, I mean... the turret lodgings."

228

"We had to cover him up," added Etta, "to stop him glaring at us." Dora shuddered again, recalling the feeling that the man's evil eyes had followed her everywhere.

"That's pretty easily explained," said Eilidh with a sigh. "Tom has worked for years as the special effects man at the Isle of Mull theatre company. In that role, he must have had plenty of dealings with the costumes and makeup departments too."

"We thought he was simply an actor!" cried Etta.

"So the apparitions," Dora thought aloud, recollecting all the tricks she and Etta had suffered, "the piano being played by ghostly hands, the painting's eyes moving, the fog…"

"All manifestations of one man's sick brain!" Eilidh concluded.

"Still," Etta insisted, "the two ghosts seemed genuinely surprised to meet on stage tonight."

"Maybe one was Debbie," Eilidh said dismissively, "the other Tom, but they hadn't planned it that way."

"That might be so," said Etta.

"Though you've often mentioned the benevolent presence, Eilidh," Dora whispered.

"Oh no," Eilidh said, shaking her head. "I won't believe in any presence from now on, benevolent or not. They're all too good at betraying me at the first opportunity."

"What's in the letter?"

"What letter?"

"The letter Edwina gave you," Dora said firmly. Although Eilidh seemed to have forgotten about it, Dora had been impatiently waiting to know what it said.

Eilidh reached for her pocket, feeling the touch of the paper inside. The expression on her face changed to one of surprise as she took the letter from its envelope.

"It's from Aunt Katherine," she said, scanning the letter. "Unless it's just another ingenious scam by the PP." With shaky hands, Eilidh passed it to Dora. "Could you read it aloud, please?"

"Of course," said Dora, clearing her throat.

"*DEAR EILIDH,*

"*I can only remember you as a little child with a sunny personality before a series of sad events parted us forever. I wish our lives had been easier. Now, by chance, I have come to be the keeper of a secret so much bigger than myself. It's not right for me to take it to the grave.*

"*It was my husband – your uncle, Donald – who confessed to me on his deathbed, saying that I could do with the knowledge as I saw fit. It was only then that I learned that Donald had been insanely jealous of your father, who had inherited the castle. As I'm sure you know, because of the family curse, the McGullions had always handed the property to the second born and your grandfather was the first in decades to break the tradition, favouring Duncan, your father and his firstborn. All the while, Donald was convinced he'd suffered an injustice, had been deprived of his rights, as he had been waiting for this part of the inheritance.*

"*Thus, your uncle confessed, it had been he who set the castle on fire. Worse than that, he framed your father and, even more cruelly, convinced Duncan he was mad because, of course, the poor man couldn't recall having committed the crime. Duncan merely believed he had put your life and your mother's at risk, without even remembering having done so. Your uncle was too weak and close to death to give me any more details. He just admitted to his deeds.*

"*After the fire, Duncan disappeared. He must have thought that he was cursed and wicked, that staying away from you and your mother was the only way to protect your lives from danger. Your poor mother was heartbroken and decided to move back to Australia, where I hope you had a happy life with her and the rest of her family. However, before leaving the UK for good, your mother felt she had to put things right. Respecting what the family curse demanded, she handed the castle back to your uncle. She didn't want a penny of its value.*

"*But life is full of irony. It wasn't long before, to his surprise, Donald discovered he couldn't endure life at Glengullion. Wild dreams gave him no peace and he fell so sick, we had to move to the South of France. He recovered partially, but his remorse, I later discovered, never left him. But only on his deathbed did he find the courage to confess it all.*

"To say I was shocked would be a huge understatement. Who had I been living with all those years? And more importantly, what could I do to make amends? I was tempted to get in touch with you and offer you both castle and confession there and then. But the solicitor told me the castle was in such a state of disrepair, I would be giving you more troubles than benefits. So I decided to come here myself, sort things out, and leave you with something better.

"It was tough going at first, but thanks to the success of the Mull Forest Café, shares in which I pass on to you, I managed to save enough to pay the inheritance taxes. Then, you'd be free to decide whether to sell or maintain the property.

"I was unsure whether to tell you the truth or not. Therefore, as my disease won't allow me much more time on this Earth, I will leave this letter with Edwina, the best friend I've ever had, and she can decide for me. When she gets to know you, she will be able to choose whether to reveal all or just leave you in peace, the rightful owner of Glengullion.

"We – the Pensioners' Posse – have done so much work. Josh and his cows and his cheese… after so many failed attempts, we finally learned to succeed. And as I mentioned, I'm so very proud of the Mull Forest Café. Frankly, it's been fun, so I hope you will allow those brave people to stay on your property – faithful Tom, Letitia, Sandra, Grayson and Debbie, and of course Edwina. Together, we have set up yet another ambitious plan to open the castle to the public so it can finance itself, while providing a home and community for the oldies.

"I only wish I had time to do more, to leave you with something more stable and solid, but we're not allowed to choose when we come into this world, nor when we have to leave it. I'll have to be happy with what I did. Glengullion is all yours now, and you're not anchored to our dreams and visions. It's your life and the McGullion curse has already weighed too heavily upon that, so I wouldn't blame you for a second if you simply wanted to run away. And on the subject of the

McGullion curse, among Uncle Donald's things, I found a letter from your father. It was dated many years back and had an Argentinean stamp. In it, he asked for forgiveness and wondered about you and your mother. I'm afraid Donald never replied. I tried to get in touch through a family connection Duncan mentioned in the letter, but I never got a response. I'm so sorry.

I wish you a happy and meaningful life full of loyal friends who will support you whatever you do.

Your ever faithful Aunt Katherine.

33

LOST AND FOUND

The shock ran deep. This clearly showed in the way Eilidh sat still on her chair, unable to utter a single word after Dora had finished reading the letter.

After the silence had seemed to stretch on for eternity, Eilidh finally opened her mouth. But no sound came out of it; it was as if she'd been turned into a fish out of water, gasping to breathe. She looked around, seeming to want to make sure the others had heard the same things she'd just learned. Jeremy's expression mirrored her surprise. Dora nodded at the woman to reassure her that yes, indeed they had all heard the same thing.

"My dad was innocent?" Eilidh finally managed to cry.

"Yes," whispered Dora softly.

"But then... then the other apparition – and the benevolent presence I felt – must have been his ghost!" Eilidh, it seemed, had completely forgotten her vow never again to believe in visitors from beyond the grave.

"It's such an awful story, love," said Jeremy, sitting beside her and holding his arms out sweetly for a hug. "You have to give yourself time to take it all in..."

"He protected me from those imposters," Eilidh continued, her eyes staring into the middle distance. "He scared them off before they did any more damage. My dad, the victim of his brother's wickedness. And my lovely aunt… she believed in the PP, but Edwina was never worthy of her trust. Maybe this place really is cursed after all, because the people who live here become far too greedy. Ready to commit wicked acts to get what they want. Oh, my dear Jeremy, let's leave this place as soon as we can."

She finally fell into his protective open arms and he hugged her tight.

"Let's sell it to Yasmine and her Italian investors, tomorrow if possible," she implored.

"I wonder how Yasmine's head will feel when she sobers up in the morning," Jeremy replied softly, trying to calm Eilidh. "She may have changed her mind after tonight."

"Then we will never get rid of this place!" wailed Eilidh. "Now more than ever, having seen how much trouble and pain it has caused my family, I want to leave, immediately. My dad, poor soul. He must have died all alone, believing himself to be a madman who almost killed his family. I wish I could let him know he was innocent all along. And my dear mother, she died with the same uncertainty, but I'm so thankful to her. She never tried to turn me against my dad…"

"She was protecting you," said Dora softly. "She wanted you to believe your father was a good man. Or maybe, in her heart of hearts, she knew he was innocent."

"Maybe," Eilidh looked up at Dora with grateful eyes.

Jeremy got up to leave, his face agitated. He seemed to be worried, jittery and watchful as if he knew something wasn't yet as it should be.

"Where are you going?" Eilidh asked him, maybe reading the same restlessness as Dora.

"I need to check on the electric system," he replied before the kitchen door clicked shut behind him.

The women were still chatting, wondering if, as exciting as the night had been, it wasn't time to go to bed when the door opened again. Jeremy entered, now wearing a triumphant expression.

"Eilidh, my love, I've got a little surprise for you. A gift all the way from South America."

He stepped to the side, allowing another man to appear on the threshold. The newcomer wore the old kilt in the family tartan, but it was his resemblance to Lord McGullion that was most striking. Except where the laird's grey eyes had been cold, this man's were warm and full of love. And a man of flesh and blood he certainly was, that much was clear in the well-lit room.

"The ghost!" cried Dora, her surprise consuming her common sense for a second.

"Not quite," then the man's grave face broke into a smile and in that moment, he looked so much like Eilidh.

"Is that you… Dad?" she cried.

"Yes, my darling Eilidh, it's me," he answered softly. But when Eilidh spoke again, her voice was icy.

"How is this possible?"

A long silence hung in the room, until Eilidh broke it, her words coming out in a venomous hiss.

"Why? Why did you disappear from our lives? Not a word, not so much as a note since I was an infant."

"Because, as you now know, I truly believed I was a threat to you and your mother. When the fire ravaged the castle, I was convinced it had been me who had set it alight. It was only years later, once she discovered the truth, that your Aunt Katherine tried to get in touch with me, but she wrote to an old address. Her letter didn't reach me until after her death. By the time I was able to come over, you were already here with your plans, the things you wanted to accomplish. But I wanted to be close to you, finally be able to watch over you, so I took up residence in the cottage near the lighthouse."

"Why not just show up on my doorstep? How cruel!" Eilidh said.

"It wasn't cruel, my child. Would you have believed me after all that had happened? Surely your mother told you how wicked I was and that I tried to kill you. How could I ask you to believe my word?"

"Mum never told me you were wicked or anything like that. She always said it must have been an accident, she never blamed you."

Duncan McGullion looked startled. After years of imagining his wife had hated him and believed him guilty of an awful crime, he too was finally learning the truth. Only someone as in tune with people's feelings as Dora would have noticed the tightening of his jaw, the glance at the floor to hide the emotion flooding his face.

"She was a special woman," he said once he could speak with a steady voice. "Although I'm not sure if that's what she really believed or whether she simply wanted you to have good memories, a positive image of your father. That I will never know, but I'm grateful to her either way."

"But how could you believe you had done something so awful when you didn't?" Etta asked.

"At the time, all the evidence pointed to me. It was only after I read Katherine's letter that I understood my brother had drugged me and set the castle on fire. He then left me in front of the painting of our evil ancestor, Lord McGullion, smiling in front of the homes he'd burned. Next to me were a couple of empty cans of petrol, which also covered my hands, and a box of matches. I had grown up with the story of the McGullion curse, so I had no doubt it had come back to haunt me, the firstborn."

"Oh!" It was a cry, but Eilidh's voice was little.

"I had just one thought in my mind, Eilidh: your grandfather had made a terrible mistake. He should never have opposed the curse. He should never have left the castle to me.

"I decided there and then that I had to run away, immediately. How could I have my child grow up with such a monster for a father? How could I stay close to the woman I loved after I had tried to kill her and our daughter? And I didn't even have the decency to remember a thing of what I had done! Had I been a single man, I'd have gone to prison and paid for my crime. But I didn't want that shame to ruin your lives."

"How did you manage to get away from this country?" Jeremy asked.

"I took with me the little I needed and managed to get to Glasgow. There, I convinced a homeless man to allow me to buy his identity. With his documents, I was able to apply for a passport and flee to Argentina.

"Once I was there, far away from the McGullion curse, I lived uneventfully, slowly and humbly starting to build my life. You and your mother were always on my mind, Eilidh, but the only person I tried to contact was my brother, Donald. He never replied. How could I blame him? But I understand he didn't destroy my letter as your aunt found it and knew I was in Argentina.

"As I said, it took many years for Katherine's letter to reach me because, as my circumstances improved, I moved up and down the country. But when it finally did reach me, for the first time, I knew I was a free man. I was innocent after all. I wrote back to her to ask about you, but was informed that in the meantime, Katherine had passed away. That's when I knew I had to come home…"

"And pretend to be a ghost!" Eilidh's voice still held a certain reproach, but it was no longer as icy as when her father had started to tell his tale.

"Well, no, not exactly. I wanted you to feel protected. You have grown into a beautiful, cheerful, independent woman, but still, I wanted you to know your father was watching over you. I confess, I sometimes couldn't help but overhear your conversations and I realised you didn't know the truth of the past. Would you believe my story after so many years? I thought not."

"But you could have shown me Auntie's letter!"

"And you would probably have believed it was a forgery."

Eilidh thought for a moment, obviously remembering that was exactly what she had said when Dora encouraged her to read the letter. "Indeed," she conceded, "that may be true. So it was you who played all those gentle tricks on me. I'd find a flower on my pillow, something I had lost. I felt your loving presence around me while I slept."

"It was my attempt to make up for all those lost years."

Before she could stop herself, Eilidh had leapt up from her seat and was running into her father's arms. They hugged tightly, all the love that had had gone unexpressed for years poured into that one simple gesture.

Then there was again silence in the room, but of a very different sort this time.

"I beg your pardon," it was Etta who broke the sacred moment. "But why the masquerade? Why did you decide to dress up as a ghost tonight? Were you in league with the Pensioners' Posse?"

"Once I learned the curse had played no role in our family tragedy," the man said, "I confess I felt sorry Eilidh wanted to get rid of the castle. I witnessed the PP trying to scare the Italian investors, although I realise now they were targeting completely the wrong Italians." He looked apologetically at Etta and Dora, one of whom glared, the other smiled encouragingly. "But when Mrs Mason came back on the scene, I didn't think the PP would dare use the ghost trick again, so I took matters into my own hands to get rid of the development plan once and for all."

"Oh, Dad!"

"It was stupid, I can see that now. When the time came for my apparition to start its haunting, imagine my surprise when I saw a suit of armour already threatening the woman."

"That's why you both looked so shocked."

"I guess," said the man, "I was pretty scared. If I'd just come face to face with the real ghost of Glengullion Castle, he probably wouldn't appreciate my masquerade."

"But," here Eilidh's voice quavered, "please tell me you had nothing to do with the chandelier falling and Gary's death…"

"I swear to you, nothing at all! I didn't much like the look of Gary, but I thought I should respect your choice. Murder never crossed my mind, but after he passed away, I couldn't help but think how good it'd be if you subsequently decided to stay here."

"Dad!"

"It was wrong, I know. Please, carry on with your plans to sell this stupid pile of stones and I'll come and live nearby, wherever you choose. I won't intrude on your life, of course, but I will be there any time you need me. You know that."

Dora didn't even try to hold back her tears, the fat droplets running freely over her cheeks as she clasped her hands at the happy reunion of those two souls. Jeremy stood to one side, looking pleased with himself. But every now and then, he would pass a hand over his face, as if trying – not too successfully – to prevent his emotions giving him away. Even Etta gulped a few times, her eyes suspiciously watery, as much as she pretended to be fine and in control of herself. But then the familiar impassive expression crossed her face – the one she wore whenever her neurons were processing and firing at full speed.

"We'll go now," Dora said to Eilidh and Duncan, "and give you two the space to catch up."

"I will accompany you to your flat," said Jeremy, gently escorting the two women and one dog to the main door. "Then I'll go to bed myself. I believe those two will chat all night long."

"But how did you manage to find Duncan?" asked Dora as they left the castle and walked round to the accommodation she was sharing with Etta and Leon. "How did you guess?"

"I always felt uneasy whenever Eilidh mentioned the caring ghost," he replied. "But it was only when you read out Aunt Katherine's letter that I had a flash of inspiration. Some time ago, Josh mentioned that someone was using the Smugglers' cottage. He described the man as a tramp of some sort, but he seemed well-meaning and caused no harm. Josh said he'd keep an eye on him, so I told him the man could stay as long as we didn't have to modernise or sell the cottage. But tonight, I put two and two together – the 'spare' ghost, who bore such a strong resemblance to the McGullion family, and the tramp..."

"Did you go all the way to the cottage to fetch him?"

"No, he was still in the castle, waiting for the furore to die down before leaving. I called Duncan by name as I searched the rooms, and he finally revealed himself in the Weapons Hall."

"All's well that ends well," said Dora, smiling as they reached the flat. "Good night, Jeremy."

"Won't it be great to enjoy a ghost-free sleep," he replied, grinning.

"Ghost, my tooth!" grumbled Etta.

It was indeed a serene and peaceful night. But what awoke Dora and Etta in the morning wasn't exactly what the two ladies had been expecting.

SATURDAY

SATURDAY
EARLY MORNING

T he police had to let us go in the end.
They didn't have enough evidence to charge us, or maybe it's
a trap. Maybe they're simply waiting for one of us to make a mistake.

I should have listened to Mr T. He was right and I was ~~dead~~ (maybe
not an appropriate word to use with regards to recent circumstances)
wrong. On the way back home, he gave me a good piece of his mind. I
never suspected he had such a temper, nor that he could be that mad at
me. I confess, I thought I could bend him to my will anytime I wanted,
but it seems I've confused loyalty with a lack of character. Is it possible
at my age still to have so much to learn?

I don't know what shocked me the most: the mysterious appearance
of Lord McGullion, being carted off to the police station, well aware
that I was the one who would be held responsible for everything, or the
discovery that I'm not as right as I'd believed. But too many things
went out of control all at once. Who was the apparition in the kilt?
What was he doing there? Was he a man or a ghost? And the
chandelier? Did I put the idea of murder in someone's mind? In which
case, am I not as culpable as the person who committed the crime?

But who could it be? I have a terrible suspicion that I know. Should
I do my bit to protect them? I'm worn out by this terrible doubt that I
influenced someone clearly less strong-willed than I am.

"If you have power, you need to exercise self-control, otherwise you are as dangerous as a fast car with faulty brakes." That's what Katherine once told me. She was right!

As for Mr T, I've been thinking of him all night, dreading the thought I might have lost his friendship. Did I say friendship? The very moment he walked away after venting his anger at me, I realised how stubborn I have been not to recognise the void the man has filled in my life this past year. I've loved discussing things with him, at times rather exuberantly, convincing him, having him admire me for my determination. I'd miss him awfully if he were to cut me from his life.

Oh no, I can't allow that. I need to speak to him. But wait… is that a siren? This early on a Saturday morning? In sleepy Tobermory?

Whatever has happened now?

Heaven help me.

34

A NEW SUSPECT

The sound of sirens broke the tranquillity of a beautiful morning. In accordance with the principle that in Scotland, no two days are ever created equal, this one had dawned with such a clear sky that from Etta and Dora's living room, one could admire the green plains rolling away towards the cliffs. Beyond, one could even distinguish the dark blue horizon on a foamy sea.

But this picture-perfect scene, had there been anyone up that early to admire it, was spoiled by the whine of police sirens getting closer and closer. And it's this that roused two ladies and one hound from their beds. Instead of delighting in the beauty of the view from one window, they went straight to the opposite side of the room, where they watched two police cars screaming to a halt just in front of the castle entrance.

The police officer from the previous night and two of his colleagues stepped out of one. From the other, DCI Findlay emerged. Etta and Dora assumed she must have been called back to Mull from the mainland after the chandelier incident. But if the police were back at the castle this early, with a DCI in attendance, had something else happened? What?

The main door was opened from the inside and the police

ADRIANA LICIO

disappeared from view. It wasn't long before they reappeared, Eilidh's father walking solemnly between two uniformed officers, his hands cuffed. He was helped into one car, the DCI and the attending officer from the previous night getting in on either side of him. Then the doors slammed shut and the police cars left the Glengullion grounds at speed.

"Did they just arrest Duncan McGullion?" Dora asked in shock.

"Why wouldn't they?" said Etta dryly. "He was here when Gary was murdered and when the attempt was made on Yasmine's life, yet he never thought to make himself known to the police. And he ran away from a crime all those years ago."

"But he was innocent of that crime! You don't think he was involved in this one, do you?"

"Of course. He was in the ideal position to commit all sorts of deeds while we were busy suspecting everyone else, unaware of his existence."

"But if he were guilty," protested Dora, "he wouldn't have revealed himself last night…"

"Murderers often get complacent."

"How did the police know he was here?"

"Maybe Edwina and the others, like Jeremy, put two and two together and told them. Whatever, let's check if Eilidh needs our help."

"WORF!" protested Leon. He would normally have been happy about going to see Eilidh, but he hadn't been served his breakfast yet.

"You'll get fed later, Napoleon," said Etta.

"I'm sure Eilidh will have something nice for you," added Dora.

In a matter of minutes, with just a quick stop so Leon could have his early morning pee, the trio were knocking at the main door of the castle. It was Eilidh who opened it, her red eyes and disconsolate expression showing how upset she was.

"We saw the police," said Dora.

The woman nodded. "They knocked and asked me if there was anyone else staying in the main body of the castle, besides Yasmine, Jeremy, and me. I told them about my father and they asked me if they could talk to him. As soon as I fetched him, that DCI arrested him for the murder of Gary Mason and attempted murder of Yasmine. And they took him away, just like that."

"Where are the others?"

"Jeremy went out first thing to run some errands down in Tobermory. As for Yasmine, she's still sleeping. I haven't seen her at all. But please come in. I need to talk to someone before I go mad."

She led them into the breakfast room near the kitchen. It wasn't a large room, containing just a table, a sofa and a walnut sideboard, and was rather devoid of paintings or ornaments. But it had a wonderful view over the lower cliffs and the ocean that gave it all the décor it needed.

"May I offer you a coffee?"

"I'll make the coffee," Dora said firmly. "You sit down and take it easy. I'm sure they will release your father soon."

"There's a cookie jar with a paw on the top in the cupboard, would you fetch a couple of biscuits for Leon? My dear dog, if only you knew what a comfort you are…"

Oh, my love, thought Leon, looking at her with a tilted head and furiously wagging tail. *If you could scent people the way I do, you'd know that I do know.*

"Someone has just passed the window," Eilidh said, rising to her feet. "It is probably Jeremy having forgotten something. Good! It's much better that he hears the news from me."

As Dora went to make the coffee, Eilidh crossed over to the entrance door to admit her fiancé. But when Dora returned, she found that the newcomer wasn't Jeremy at all, but Josh with Bree. The hound and the border collie were so delighted to be together again, Dora quickly suggested letting them run about outside before they destroyed the place.

"Um, I heard the police sirens as I was walking Bree and wondered if you're all alright," Josh explained.

"I'll go and fetch another mug," said Dora, nipping back to the kitchen. When she returned, there was an incredulous expression on Josh's face.

"Your father? Duncan McGullion was here all along?"

"You may have spoken to him," Eilidh explained. "He was the tramp you saw in the Smugglers' Cottage."

"Didn't you recognise him?" Etta asked Josh.

"No, I had never met him before."

"But surely the resemblance between him and the portraits in the castle would have given him away."

Josh looked puzzled. He had obviously never really looked around inside the castle.

Before Eilidh could continue with her explanations, the doorbell rang again. Edwina and Tom had seen the police car heading towards Glengullion, blue lights flashing, and had decided to brave Eilidh's wrath and come to see what had happened. Exactly two minutes later, Sandra and Grayson arrived. Having heard the news in town, Jeremy returned, followed shortly by Debbie and Letitia. Dora was back and forth to the kitchen, preparing tea and coffee for everyone, while Edwina, Debbie and Tom said they'd been interviewed by the police in Tobermory, and then released with a request not to leave the island. There wasn't enough evidence against any of them, although their latest prank hadn't been appreciated by the police.

"*One more ghostly visitation,*" Tom imitated DCI Findlay, affecting a woman's voice, "*and I'll make sure you end up in the deepest of dungeons and we lose the keys to it.*" Dora was surprised to see Edwina looking at him with an air of amused disapproval as if she were a girl again and he the naughtiest boy in her class... the one she was destined to fall in love with.

"I wonder how the police knew about my father," said Eilidh. "We'd planned to tell them today..."

"Maybe we let it slip," Edwina now seemed anxious not to hide anything from Eilidh. "We told them about the 'other ghost', but said we didn't have a clue who it was, so maybe the DCI spent the night wondering if there was an unknown guest at the castle."

"I got a glimpse of him in the police car," said Debbie. "Yer dad, I mean. He hasnae changed that much, and he looks sooo much like you, Eilidh. The resemblance is uncanny. I recognised him immediately…"

"Eilidh," said Edwina, a strange emotion in her voice, "we're here to tell you two things. We wanted you to know we're really sorry for what we did, we should have respected your choices, and that we didn't kill Gary Mason. We never even tried to harm him, or his wife."

As if on cue, Yasmine knocked at the door and entered without waiting for an invitation. She was wearing a red satin robe over a short black nightie. Even hungover, she was as gorgeous as ever.

"Did you really spend the night here?" asked Tom, once he'd recovered from the vision in front of him. "After what… well, you know…"

"Why wouldn't I? I'm going to spend a lot of time here from now on," she replied defiantly, although the way she wobbled around was a telltale sign she hadn't left her hangover completely behind.

"The police checked her room," said Jeremy. "It was fine, it has a solid lock, and it's next to ours so we'd hear if she cried out. She wasn't feeling too well and it wouldn't have been wise to move her into a hotel."

ETTA WAS NO LONGER PAYING ATTENTION. HER MIND HAD GOT stuck on one recurring theme, the 'resemblance' word hitting her like a punch in the stomach. Of course, Eilidh looked very much

ADRIANA LICIO

like Duncan, as daughters tended to look more like their fathers than mothers. That was certainly the case in her experience, with her own daughter Maddalena looking far too similar to Etta's scoundrel of an ex-husband. Luckily, the similarity stopped at the physical aspect, for Maddalena was a woman with a good head on solid shoulders. OK, at times she could be a little too *woo-woo* when she spoke of being aligned to the cosmos's energies, body and mind nonsense. But she was very practical when it came to running her tattoo business and the family finances.

Don't get too distracted, old hag, focus now on what's relevant. Resemblance, why did the word strike you? But the chatter in the room was just too much. How was one supposed to do any serious thinking in such a clamour?

She got up, locked eyes with Dora, put her hands over her ears and mouthed the word 'resemblance'. Dora shrugged, not understanding, but with her chin, she indicated towards the door. At least Dora's message was clear.

"You'd better leave before you say something nasty, you old grump." Fine by Etta. And she knew exactly where she would go.

Old Lord McGullion's painting was still hanging in the Weapons Hall, just as she'd expected. She stared up at it, wondering if she'd missed something. The police tape had been removed from around the area after the scene of crime team had finished their job during the week.

Here, close to the mantelpiece, was where the murder had taken place. One suit of armour was still there, but empty handed. Someone had clearly decided it was better for it to do without its weapons, at least until the mystery was solved. The other one had been removed, maybe by the police, maybe by Eilidh and Jeremy. Above the mantelpiece, the portrait of Lord McGullion was even more vivid than the one in the dismal bedroom in the turret flat. Etta had registered its presence when she and Dora discovered Sandra bending over Gary Mason's body, but now she wanted to give it a more thorough look.

Nature can be so weird. It was inconceivable to the human mind that a man with such cruel eyes, a picture of ruthlessness, should bear such a strong resemblance to gentle Eilidh and her father. Still, Etta was troubled by the uncomfortable feeling that the resemblance should ring a bell in her mind. But no matter how hard she looked, how deeply she thought, today, her mind was feeling rebellious and unable to linger where she wanted.

Etta sat on the sofa, her back to the garden. If there was less to distract her, maybe she'd be able to capture the thought eluding her, escaping from the back of her mind like a shampoo bottle descending from slippery hands under the shower. Oh no, now her mind had thrown her back to Iona. Had Sandra mentioned anything important? Something she had noticed too?

Hold on, could there be something there? Jenny had mentioned Tom, but he'd not only been part of the Mull theatre company. As they had learned later, his role had been that of a special effects designer. Of course, Etta had made the connection between that and all the haunting things that had happened at Glengullion. But what else was there?

At that moment, the door opened. Etta felt deeply annoyed – where could a woman go to have enough peace for some healthy thinking?

"Oh, it's you," she said none too politely, but with enough humour in her voice to soften the words.

"I saw you coming out here all alone and wondered if you're OK."

"I'm fine, just doing some thinking."

"Anything interesting?"

"Maybe," Etta replied, the fog starting to clear. Was this what she'd been looking for? Had it been staring her in the face – literally – all along? Even the days, the timings worked. Could it possibly be? Who better?

"May I ask what?"

"Of course you can ask, and I might even tell you. I'm interested in a theme: resemblance."

Her disturber's eyes filled with an expression of hate and spite, not too dissimilar to those in the painting. But Etta, typically mulish, kept on outlining her thoughts one after the other as they emerged from the mist, starting from the very beginning.

It was only when it was too late that she realised how unwise she'd been…

35

DANGER!

D ora stopped chatting to Letitia and Jeremy as soon as she saw Etta leaving the room, having signalled to her that she needed a quieter place to think. "Resemblance" Etta had mouthed before disappearing, or something similar. The exact word didn't really matter, Dora thought with a smile. This was a sign that Etta was mulling over the murder and all the mystery surrounding it. Was her friend back in sleuthing mode?

Certainly, the chatter in the room had built up, slowly at first, then buzzing louder and louder. People had divided into small groups, each discussing the latest events: the appearance of Eilidh's father and, of course, the murder attempt on Yasmine. No one mentioned the possibility, but behind each swallowed word, Dora could read the question on everyone's mind: was Duncan McGullion the man responsible for Gary Mason's death? Was it he who'd attempted to take Yasmine's life? That particular woman was no longer present, having helped herself to coffee from the pot Dora had prepared before announcing that she needed some air and was going to sit outside.

Was it just Dora's imagination, or would most of those present not have condemned the man for either deed? In fact, wasn't the buzz of conversation rather too cheerful, as if this was a party of people who had gathered for no other reason than to enjoy each other's company?

Edwina seemed to follow her line of thought and looked around, a little disconcerted. Then she cleared her throat.

"I think," she began, but no one heard her. Edwina moved quickly towards the sideboard and opened it to withdraw an antique porcelain bell. It seemed she was so familiar with the castle, she knew exactly where everything was.

She rang the bell with gusto. A piercing repeated TING-A-LING startled everyone.

"Excuse me," said Edwina, her face, as ever, not in the least apologetic. "I think we should watch what we're saying. Eilidh is facing a traumatic event, so we should support her as best we can." She didn't mention Gary. The dead man didn't seem to matter as much as Eilidh's feelings about her father's arrest. "I suggest," Edwina continued in the manner of someone used to being in command, "we make ourselves useful. Since we're all here, we could prepare a good Scottish breakfast."

Tom offered to help Edwina in the kitchen, a suggestion that seemed to suit her. Dora, Jeremy, and Letitia would lay the table, while Sandra and Debbie gave the room a light clean. Like Yasmine, Grayson had already gone outside to get some air, and Josh suggested he go and check on the dogs. Then everyone would help Eilidh with getting the rest of the house in order.

"Thanks, Edwina," said Eilidh, turning towards the kitchen. "I'll come and help you and Tom."

"No," said Edwina, "you keep Josh company. I'm sure he's already put in a few hours' work this morning, so let's encourage him to have a little rest."

Josh flushed as Eilidh followed him to the French doors.

"Eilidh, honey," said Jeremy before the two could leave the room, "we've extended the table, but now I can't seem to find any cloths long enough to cover it. Which one do you want to use?"

Eilidh grinned, seeming amused that her fiancé still didn't know where everything was in the castle

"In the cabinet, second drawer down. The light blue one with butterflies and daisies on is so cheerful…"

Jeremy left on his errand, while Dora and Letitia located dishes and cutlery in the sideboard, counted out the number they'd need and left them on the top until Jeremy had returned with the tablecloth. Dora wondered with a wry smile how Yasmine was going to cope with a full Scottish breakfast of bacon, eggs, black pudding and the carbs to end all carbs: fried bread.

When they'd finished, Dora and Letitia joined Sandra and Debbie, who had just completed their cleaning duties.

"Grayson's still enjoying the gardens," said Sandra. "He loves his morning outing along Tobermory pier, but with all the excitement, he missed it today."

"Is Yasmine still outside?" Dora asked.

"No, she's gone back to her room to fetch some pills. Guess what?" Debbie winked at Dora. "She's got a *terrible* headache. Apparently, she rather enjoyed the fizzy drinks Jeremy poured for her last night!"

"I can confirm that," Dora answered, grinning.

"What fizzy drinks?" Letitia asked. "Can I have one?"

"They're teasing, dear," Sandra explained. "They mean champagne. Apparently, Yasmine is rather fond of it."

With a number of the party now off doing other things, the room was almost quiet. While Sandra, Debbie and Letitia talked, Dora moved to the French doors to eavesdrop on Eilidh and Josh's chat. Or rather, the lack of it. Josh was still red faced, while Eilidh seemed to be trying and failing to elicit any conversation from him. In an unusually soft voice, she asked one more question.

"And how is the pup? Do you have any news on her?"

Josh's tense face softened immediately. He took out his

mobile from his jeans pocket and explained that someone called Stephanie had sent him an update from the centre.

"There she is," he said, handing Eilidh the phone and inviting her to scroll through some photos.

"Oh my goodness!" said Eilidh, her eyes warm as she browsed the shots. "She's so cute, and she must have put on some weight. And here, they're already feeding her fish. Good girl!"

Josh murmured something Dora couldn't quite catch, but it put a smile on Eilidh's face.

"Could you send me those pictures?" she asked. "I want to show them to Elizabeth, she will love this baby."

"How is she, by the way?"

"She's always enquiring after you, since you showed her that calf…" Eilidh paused, as if waiting for a particular memory to take form.

"Has she made up her mind what she will study at university?"

"She's been changing her mind every second." Eilidh laughed. "Last autumn, she wanted to be a vet; then it was a biologist. Next, she wanted to be an ethologist, before deciding on art school. For my part, I suggested she takes a business degree so she can land herself a proper job."

"You mean in a big corporate firm?"

"Yes," Dora could hear Eilidh's voice turning a little hostile. "One of those fantastic companies that pay decently for your time…"

"But would she be happy?" The question seemed to burst out of the man, and Eilidh looked as if she was taken by surprise.

"Of course! She will get all sorts of benefits, and in some positions, she could even get to travel a fair bit… which attracts her."

"And what makes you happy?"

Again, Eilidh looked startled. Josh's voice wasn't in any way accusatory, and his mellifluous tone definitely seemed to be an effective tactic in dealing with this feisty woman. Eilidh chuckled, as if she hadn't given the question any thought for a long time.

"Safety, I guess," she said after a long pause. "Yes, I hate feeling I'm in an uncertain financial position, not knowing what I can buy, spend and save. I hate wondering if I'll be able to pay the bills and support my daughter. I hate precariousness, so I guess I love safety."

"Fair enough," the man said, and he seemed to mean it. "I hope Elizabeth will be happy, she's a wonderful girl. She's told me all her news this summer, it was so good to speak to her."

"She asks about you every time we talk. You bonded, you two. I guess that's because she's loved nature ever since she was a child..."

Their voices lowered so much that to hear, Dora would have to lean too close and be noticed. But the conversation was interrupted anyway as at that moment, Jeremy came back, a light-blue tablecloth in his hands.

"You should have told me," he said, peering out through the open French doors and speaking to Eilidh, "you meant the chest of drawers in the corridor, not the one in the other room."

Eilidh shrugged. "Don't tell me you have been searching all over the castle, you silly billy," she teased, tapping Jeremy's chin affectionately. Josh shifted from foot to foot, clearly embarrassed and feeling like a gooseberry.

"I'll go check the dogs are fine," he said, leaving the couple by the French doors and heading across the lawn, whistling for Bree.

"Sorry to have kept you waiting," Jeremy said to Dora as he laid the cloth along the table, smoothing it with elaborate sweeps of his hands. "I see you've already got the dishes ready, that's great."

"I'll pop into the kitchen to see if I can bring anything through," said Dora, leaving Jeremy to finish laying the table. Letitia joined him, happily helping by folding the napkins and placing the cutlery for each diner. But when Dora walked into the kitchen, she found it empty. The pan was on the hob, but the gas was off. The eggs had been beaten, but left in a bowl on the side. The bacon had been removed from its plastic wrapping and placed in a dish ready to be fried, but there was no cook in sight. It was as if they had vanished in the middle of their tasks.

Strange. Edwina didn't seem the kind of person who would leave a job half done. But...

Yasmine! Yasmine was upstairs, all alone! What if...?

The kitchen door opened and the two absentees came in, flushing crimson as soon as they realised someone was in the room. The Ice Queen Edwina started babbling like an overexcited teenage girl.

"We've, um, been... searching for some... some..."

"...eggs," Tom completed the sentence.

Dora looked at them, feeling alarmed. Edwina was holding her left hand behind her back. Was she hiding something? Like a knife? Still, Dora managed to keep her cool and prevent herself from looking pointedly at the bowl of scrambled eggs on the counter.

"I'm sure I saw some in the fridge when I prepared the coffee earlier on and needed the milk." Dora opened the fridge. Right at the front lay a long egg box. "There they are." She looked dubiously at the two PP members.

"How stupid of me!" said Edwina, looking even more flummoxed. "And I searched the fridge thoroughly."

"It happens. Sometimes you can have something sitting right in front of you, but you just can't see it," and Dora scrutinised the two again.

"We'd better continue where we left off, everyone must be getting hungry," said Tom, a smile plastered over his red face. Edwina was only too happy to do just that, but first, she reached behind her back with her other hand and slipped something into her pocket. Only then did she reach for the bowl of beaten eggs and switch on the pan for the bacon.

"Have you seen Yasmine at all?" Dora asked, startling the duo once more.

"Not recently," said Edwina, her voice breathless with the effort of beating the scrambled eggs as if they needed to be stiff peaks.

"Then I'll check on her. Actually," she added, "I will ask Jeremy to accompany me." She wanted to send Edwina and Tom a clear message she wouldn't be going upstairs alone. If these two were still up to no good, despite Edwina's words to Eilidh earlier, they wouldn't catch her unawares. "Jeremy?" she called from the kitchen door. "Do you have a minute? I'd like to check Yasmine is OK, but feel a bit nervous about going alone. She's been gone for quite a while now, and she only went to fetch some headache pills."

"Sure," the man replied. "Letitia, do you think you can finish laying the table without me?"

"Aye, I will arrange the flowers in a vase." There were no flowers in the breakfast room, Dora noticed, but Letitia could obviously see things the rest of them could not.

Jeremy seemed as concerned as Dora felt as they went upstairs. They had certainly had their fair share of worries over the course of the last week. They stopped in front of Yasmine's door and knocked. No reply.

"Yasmine, breakfast is ready," Jeremy called.

Silence was the only answer.

"Maybe she's already left her room?" But as Dora spoke, they could hear light mutterings from inside the room. There were no coherent words, just muffled sounds.

"I'll fetch the spare keys," said Jeremy after finding the door was locked. While he was gone, Dora tried a few more times to rouse the woman on the other side of the door, but to no avail. What now? She was here in the corridor all alone. What if someone was in the room with Yasmine, keen to get out? A quick glance spotted a flower vase on a mahogany console table. There were dried flowers inside, but Dora removed them. The porcelain was heavy and sturdy. Dora would not be caught unawares.

A long moment later, Jeremy was back. They locked eyes and he understood. He didn't even waste time knocking again, but slipped the key into the lock.

They heard the tell-tale clatter as the key on the other side of the door fell to the wooden floor. That was lucky! No obstructions.

Dora raised the vase as Jeremy pushed the door open. Yasmine was lying on her queen-sized bed, her back to them, her slim shoulders writhing in agony.

36

THE DUNGEON

" . . . I'm interested in a theme: resemblance." The words resounded sonorously between Etta's temples, her head feeling as if it was about to explode.

Luckily, wherever she was, it was dark. That helped. She wasn't sure her eyes could have endured light right now. Her whole body felt weak and in pain. She knew this moment of consciousness wouldn't last long, and after all, wouldn't it be better to go back to sleep, rather than lying there on strange cold cobbles? She could feel them. Or maybe they were inside her head – her heavy, exploding head.

Her thoughts were enclosed in the prison that was her own state of excruciating pain. Was she being held hostage by a giant spider who had wrapped her up head to toe in a thick cocoon of silk-thin yet indestructible thread? Completely still, unable to move, had she been stung with a paralysing poison?

She felt thirsty. Even a few drops of water on her lips would have been paradise. Her mouth was dry and sore. She was aware it was partially open and she wanted to close it to preserve what little moisture remained, but she wasn't even able to do that. All her awareness was in her head, and in her pain. Her body, which she'd usually be able to move of her own free will, was not responding. The *only channel of communication between her mind and the rest of her body was the awareness that it hurt. It hurt awfully badly.*

Tiredness overwhelmed her, enveloping her like a thick blanket, so heavy she could hardly move beneath it, yet comforting enough that she fell into a deep sleep.

37

WHERE ARE YOU?

"Yasmine!" Jeremy cried in horror. But the woman was no longer moving. All they could hear were pathetic little moans accompanied by weird syncopated sounds.

As he reached the other side of the bed, he grasped her left shoulder and shook it gently, as if to try and rouse her in a last attempt to help. Both he and Dora jumped back as the woman raised herself into a half sitting position and screamed.

"Jeepers!" her deep, breathy voice rose as high as it could. Dora gasped for words, her heart thumping loudly in her chest. "What the heck are you doing here?" Yasmine looked in horror at the vase Dora, taken by surprise, had impulsively raised above her head, ready to attack some invisible assailant.

"Oh!" she said, not only lowering the vase, but placing it on the chest of drawers next to her. It seemed all her strength had deserted her.

"You're OK," babbled Jeremy in shock as he leaned against the bedpost.

"What?" Yasmine removed the buds from her ears. The volume was so loud, they could hear the tinny sounds of pop music coming out of them. Music she'd been listening and humming along to, explaining the strange moans they'd heard from outside the door. And her writhing in agony had simply been her shoulders moving to the beat.

"You're OK," repeated Jeremy weakly.

"I was until you scared me half to death. Are you mad?"

Dora and Jeremy looked at each other.

"Breakfast is ready. We did knock on the door, but when we got no answer, we feared you might... might be sick." Jeremy worded his response carefully, clearly not wanting to reveal they had been worried she'd become the murderer's next victim.

"I just got bored, there are too many old people downstairs," and Yasmine looked pointedly at Dora. "No offence meant."

"None taken." Dora shook her head. Better a nasty woman alive than a nasty woman dead. "I'm just thankful you're OK."

"I mean, there's only you, Jeremy," Yasmine continued, tactless as ever. "You're a good looking and pleasant man, but you're already claimed by Eilidh and I couldn't even *bear* the thought of breaking up a happy couple."

"That's very thoughtful of you," said Dora, chuckling. "Shall we go down to breakfast now?"

They arrived in the breakfast room, their mouths watering at the delicious smells coming from the kitchen. Letitia had worked her magic – a bouquet of bright flowers had indeed materialised on the table, nicely displayed in a crystal vase.

"Where did you get those?" Dora asked.

"They were outdoors," the woman replied as if it were obvious.

"Josh always brought some for Katherine whenever he came over," Edwina explained, carrying a tray of food in from the kitchen. "And as I suspected, he was up and about very early this morning. His habit was to leave them on the steps of the kitchen in a pot for that very purpose."

"They're so beautiful," said Dora, looking at the composition of white and purple cornflowers and pink roses, a few blue love-in-a-mist scattered among them.

"Glad you've joined us, Yasmine, hope you're feeling OK," Eilidh said, looking at the woman.

"I was fine before those two gave me the fright of my life," and Yasmine glared at Dora far more than at Jeremy. But it was he who explained what had just happened.

"Shall I go and fetch the others?" Dora said quietly when he had finished, thinking of Josh, Grayson and Etta.

"Please," said Sandra, sitting down next to Letitia. But Dora had no need to search for Josh as he chose that moment to walk into the room, probably attracted by the appetising aroma of bacon.

"The dogs are having fun," he told Dora hesitantly. She could tell he was a little uncomfortable with all these people around, so she smiled encouragingly at him before leaving through the French doors he'd just entered by. Once she was outside, Leon and Bree came bounding over to say hi to her. Leon was panting heavily, but pretending to be fine, although he arrived quite a long way behind the energetic Bree.

Dora spotted Grayson in the garden next to the entrance to the Weapons Hall.

"Grayson, breakfast is ready," she called.

"Coming," he replied, turning the wheels of his chair towards her. Bree ran over to him, but Leon decided to save his energy and wait for the man to join them.

"Have you seen Etta at all?" asked Dora as Grayson got closer.

"Not out here, no." The man's face was red, maybe because of the fresh air, maybe because he had been pushing himself physically. He had well-developed arms and shoulders, the veins on his bare muscular biceps standing out, a flat stomach and strong hands. Dora scrutinised the land, the cliffs, the start of the path to the lighthouse, even the horizon, but no one was in sight. On second thoughts, though, Etta must be inside, otherwise Leon would have followed her.

"I guess they will be wanting to come in," said Dora with a

grin, looking down at the wagging bodies circling her. She tried to convince the dogs to remain outside, but Leon had smelled the breakfast and was determined to claim some bacon as his own. Certainly, no human had been born yet who could deceive such a clever Basset.

"Well, I guess you've done enough playing outdoors to have earned a treat or two," Dora said, opening the French doors to let them in. Leon marched straight to the table, following the scent of bacon. Turning to Grayson, Dora added, "I will go and look for Etta, would you tell the others to start without me?"

When the man had nodded and followed the dogs into the breakfast room, Dora went to the library. The Crystal Room was still locked as the police had left it, so finding no one browsing the bookshelves, Dora checked the Weapons Hall and the small study off it, but her friend was nowhere in sight.

"Maybe she's gone back to the flat for a bit of peace and tranquillity," Dora muttered, admitting to herself she wasn't overly impressed with Etta at that particular moment. It was one thing to have a little walk outside, as Grayson and Josh had done, another entirely to disappear without saying a word. So Dora rebelled. "If that's what she wants, I will leave her to it!" And she turned on her heel and joined the others in the breakfast room.

"Where's Etta?" Tom asked, coming through the door from the kitchen with yet another tray of bacon.

"She must have gone back to the flat, I'll try calling her." But Etta's mobile was switched off.

Dora frowned. This wasn't nice. At all. Etta could at least have messaged her. This time, Dora wouldn't go and beg her to join them, only to end up on the sharp end of Etta's tongue.

"I don't want to mix with those old folks." Dora could almost hear her friend's retort and couldn't resist a smile, in spite of herself. If you didn't take things too personally, Etta could be really good fun.

But the smile didn't last for long.

The day after tomorrow, they'd be going to fetch Rufus from Tobermory. Actually, no, *they* wouldn't be doing any such thing. Dora would let Etta go alone. The two needed time together, and she, Dora, had to learn to do things on her own. As of now.

BREAKFAST WAS CERTAINLY GOOD, BUT IT HAD NO PARTICULAR appeal to Dora, who ate and chatted while pretending an indifference she didn't feel. Afterwards, she helped with the household chores, keen to do anything to take her mind off Etta's thoughtless behaviour, and the imminent end to their adventures together, but eventually she had to admit that restlessness and anxiety were creeping in. When, after washing her hands, she found Leon sitting on the threshold of the kitchen, looking straight at her and refusing Bree's invitations to play, she knew the dog was as concerned as she was. And then, she couldn't hold it any longer.

She went to find Eilidh and told her she was going to look for Etta. Most likely, Dora said, the silly woman was in their flat and had forgotten to turn her mobile on. On Dora's return to the kitchen, Leon followed her without hesitation.

Once outside in the garden, Dora looked around just in case, but no one was in sight, so she marched over to the door of their accommodation. Strangely, though, the flat was empty and just as they had left it first thing, with no sign that Etta, or anyone else, had been in since. Seriously worried now, Dora went to the car park, wondering if the inconsiderate woman had decided to drive to Tobermory. But the distinctive Fiat was exactly where they had left it after their last excursion.

Her anxiety building up, Dora repeated to herself not to panic. Instead, she kept herself busy, cleaning their flat thoroughly, then sitting in the garden to read a book, but in the end, she had to admit defeat. Putting the book down and looking at her watch, she decided that she needed to act as quickly and as rationally as possible. The first thing to do at this point was raise the alarm.

38

THE DUNGEON

"**R**un!" *Etta cried.*
*A figure wrapped in a dark cloak was following them, close
behind. She, Dora and Leon tried a door off the street. It was locked.
They banged on it with their fists, Leon raising his voice in a howl,
asking for help. An imperious voice from inside replied harshly,
demanding that they refrain from disturbing the peace of the town and
telling them to go home. Dora desperately tried to explain that someone
was following them, but the angry voice cut her short.*

*"Don't disturb me again. Just go away before the knight catches
you. You'd better run while you still can."*

*They heard the voice laugh, and then Etta no longer had any doubt.
It belonged to Edwina. She protested, banging and kicking against the
door, but the woman continued to laugh. And the door remained closed.*

*Etta met Leon's eyes and she read the terror there. For some reason,
this scared her more than the sight of the figure turning the corner, the
cloak blowing in the wind and parting to reveal the suit of armour
moving jerkily towards them. The mace in its hands rose above its head,
ready to strike.*

*Dora and Leon ran, shouting at Etta to get a move on. But Etta
couldn't; her feet were stuck just in front of Edwina's door, her legs as
heavy as towers that had been anchored in the ground for centuries. She*

ADRIANA LICIO

felt the impulse to run, her brain sending desperate messages to the rest of her body, but her limbs' only reaction was an overwhelming inertia.

The knight laughed. Etta couldn't see who he – or she – was; all she could make out was a cruel gleam behind the helmet visor, the same icy gleam reflected on the spikes of the mace above the figure's head. Then it started its rapid arc towards Etta's skull. She couldn't escape.

"Run!" she cried to Dora and Leon, who had stupidly stopped to watch. "Run!"

Ineluctably, the mace came down on her head. It was the worst pain she'd ever experienced in her life; she literally felt her head cracking on the inside as she let out a powerful cry.

And it was that very cry that woke her. She raised her head too abruptly, which seemed to cause her even more pain than the blow from the mace. She moaned, but at least she remembered to move her head more gently as she laid it back on the ground.

Yes, it was the ground. It was cold and uncomfortable, it was cobbled and obliged her head to lie in an unnatural position, but it was real. Her hands touched her bag. If she could only slip it under her head, she'd be more comfortable. It was softer than the cobbles, and not as cold.

It took a supreme effort, her icy hands clumsy. She jerked in pain as her movements were not as smooth as she would have wished, but she propped herself up on her elbow. The air she breathed in seemed cold, while at the same time particularly heavy. Or maybe it was just her body finding breathing as tiring as extreme exercise.

As she lay down again, her head found a more comfortable position on her bag. The pain hadn't stopped, but it had at least partially released its strong hold on her. She welcomed the feeling of less pain, but wanted to resist sleep, if only for fear of encountering the knight again. But her body was in command and it gave her no choice.

Back to sleep she went.

39

THE MAGICIAN'S SECRETS

"So, when did you last see her?" Eilidh asked.

"Shortly before we all decided to prepare breakfast."

"I guess she didn't fancy any breakfast, then, and went for a walk."

"That's as maybe, but she wouldn't miss lunch too. She's been gone all morning…"

"But you said she indicated to you she was leaving, didn't you?" Eilidh had clearly had enough of being alarmed over the past few days, judging by her inclination to offer a rational explanation for all Dora's worries.

"Yes, but I expected her to go for a short walk, not disappear for hours."

"There aren't that many short walks around here, most of the paths are quite long…"

"But the dogs would have noticed and gone with her…"

"I'm not too sure Bree would have followed her without Josh."

"Maybe not, but Leon would definitely have gone with her. And he is clearly worried too." Leon raised soulful eyes to the young woman's lovely face to back up his gentle biped's words.

ADRIANA LICIO

"Maybe the dogs were so busy playing, they didn't even realise she had walked past them."

"WoRRRRF," protested Leon. Not realise? This Basset noticed everything. Eilidh smiled and scratched his ears absentmindedly, before carrying on trying to convince Dora there was nothing to worry about.

"And as you've probably noticed, the mobile phone signal around Glengullion is patchy, which would explain why you can't reach her. She'll be back soon and give you a straightforward explanation for her absence."

Dora didn't say anything, but her face must have given away how unconvinced she was, because Eilidh offered a compromise.

"OK, let's do it this way. It's almost one, so if Etta hasn't turned up for lunch within the next couple of hours, then we will go and look for her. But I'm positive she's simply gone for a good walk, probably with a packed lunch, and she'll be back soon. Now, Jeremy and I are planning to meet Yasmine and the PP in the outer gardens to go for lunch in the Mull Forest Café and discuss the whole issue of the castle once and for all. You're very welcome to join us when you're ready. Dogs are welcome, too," she added, smiling at Leon.

"Thank you, I'll see you later," Dora replied, nodding distractedly, a new train of thought crossing her mind.

What would Etta do in my place? She didn't have to think too long. *She would ask why? Why might Etta be in danger? Why would someone have a grudge against her now it has become clear we're not the Italian investors?*

The answer came back almost immediately.

Because she has got too close to the truth, too close to discovering who the killer is. Now, if Etta knew something for sure, she would have told me, so she must have left the breakfast room because she wanted to check one of her theories. Someone – the killer – noticed and went after her. If I'm right, it means Eilidh's father is innocent. But it also means that… a chill went down her spine, making her skin erupt in goosebumps …*the killer is among us.*

What did Etta mouth before she left? What did she have on her mind?

Resemblance! That's the word Etta had used, Dora was sure. But what about it? They had mentioned over and over how much Eilidh looked like her father, and the two of them looked like friendlier versions of Lord McGullion as depicted in the old paintings scattered around the castle rooms. But that was natural, family resemblances were often strong. What could be so suspicious or mind blowing about that? Had the killer seen Etta mouthing her message to Dora and been worried she was on to something? Had the villain decided to follow her to make sure she couldn't do them any harm?

She would go and check the Weapons Hall, where one of the paintings hung. Leon followed, looking at her quizzically as if to say, "Hey, lady, why don't you do this?" If only she knew what 'this' was.

Once they were in front of the fireplace where Gary had been killed, Leon moved to one side of the remaining suit of armour, pointing somewhere between it and the bookshelves further along the wall and wagging his tail as if he wanted to be followed. But when Dora opened the door ahead of him, he didn't seem keen to explore that part of the castle.

Dora returned to the painting above the fireplace. Were it not for those malicious eyes, Lord McGullion would have exactly the same features as Eilidh and her father. No doubt about that. Was there something else in the painting Dora should notice? This portrait was set against the backdrop of the forest during a hunt. The scenery didn't show any particular landmark; in fact, it was rather blurred.

She shook her head and sighed.

"WORF!" cried Leon, demanding her attention, his face showing dismay at the slowness of his biped. She went to him, again asking him to go and search in the rooms beyond the door, but the dog was determined to stay there and wait for her to do something.

"What are you trying to tell me, Leon?"

"Worf!" which clearly meant… what? Dora stood beside him, but couldn't see whatever had interested him. She returned to the suit of armour and stood there, deep in meditation. Was there something Leon could see and she couldn't?

Then she had a vision of what had happened in the Crystal Room when the ghost in the suit of armour – played by Tom – had materialised, apparently from nowhere. How did he manage that when the door was too far away and, as they soon found out, was about to be used by the second ghost – Duncan McGullion? How did the knight appear? Or more precisely, from where?

Wait – could it be that there were secret passages around the castle? And more to the point, was one of those secret passages right in front of her? Could Leon smell it while she didn't have a clue?

She lifted the carpet and studied the floorboards below. Then she looked around the oak panels on the walls, the bookshelves close to the mantelpiece, but saw nothing suspicious. Leon seemed to approve of this course of action, wagging his tail and huffing encouragingly, but the outcome was the same. Nothing.

Disheartened, she was about to leave the room when she heard a cheerful whistling coming from outside the window. She peeped out and spotted Tom heading towards the main garden, possibly to join the others for lunch in the café.

"Hey, Tom," Dora called. "Do you have a second?"

"Of course," and instants later, he was beside her. "Is everything OK?"

"I just wondered, how did you appear in the middle of the Crystal Room last night? Did you come from this room? You used the fog to make your materialisation very convincing, but you must have come in from somewhere, and the door was too far away. We'd have heard you clanking across the floor."

"You should never ask a magician to reveal his tricks," he answered, serious all of a sudden. Dora took in his benevolent round face, his tanned skin testament to his love of the outdoors. Tom had such an inviting smiley expression that Dora, overwhelmed with concern, told him how worried she was about her friend's sudden disappearance, and that she was having a hard time finding out where Etta had gone.

"Why do you think she disappeared from this room?"

"Because Leon says so!"

"WORRRF!" confirmed Leon. Wasn't it time for action? Wasn't it time to find Etta? This game of hide-and-seek had gone on too long.

"I see," said Tom. "And you're right, but what I can't understand is how she would have found out about the passage by accident."

"So there is a secret passage," and Dora looked around once more for a telltale sign.

"As there is in all the most self-respecting castles…"

"A book!" said Dora, once more looking at the shelves in front of Leon.

"Will you keep the secret?"

"Of course," Dora swore solemnly.

As in any classic movie involving a mysterious haunted house, Tom moved a heavy red book from one of the higher shelves, pulling on it like a lever. The entire length of shelving moved, pivoting on its centre and opening a gap on to stairs descending into a passage as dark as it was narrow.

"Where does it lead?" asked Dora in surprise.

"It's rather labyrinthine, but you can go to the kitchen, the master bedroom, the Crystal Room and outside."

"How do you know it exists?"

"Edwina and Katherine discovered it while sorting the books in the castle and we all had fun exploring it."

"Is this how you made your appearance in the Crystal Room?"

Tom nodded.

Leon was waiting half in, half out of the passage, excitedly wagging his tail, his nose high in the air. But he'd not run inside. It seemed he wanted to make sure the others would follow.

Tom too lingered on the threshold, then he walked across the Weapons Hall, grabbed a wooden stool and climbed on it to reach for an old-fashioned gun. He checked the weapon.

"There's at least one bullet inside!" he said, satisfied.

"Does it still work?"

"Of course, Katherine used it for target practice." Tom invited her to check the gun out, but Dora, unfamiliar with and rather repulsed by weapons, refused.

"Why do you think we need that?" she asked.

"If Etta didn't go into this passage of her own accord…" the man left the sentence hanging, hiding the gun deep in his jacket pocket before searching in a cabinet drawer. "And we'll need a good torch."

Tom, Dora thought, like Edwina, was rather too familiar with the layout and contents of the castle that had been Eilidh's home, not theirs, for the past year.

Just as they were about to head into the narrow passage, they heard footsteps coming along the corridor.

"Who's there?" asked a male voice. Dora immediately recognised it as Jeremy's.

"Quick," said Tom, ushering her towards the passage. But just before entering, Dora thought again and turned round. Realising it might be unwise to go in alone with an armed Tom, she needed at least one ally.

40

THE DUNGEON

"...*I'm interested in a theme: resemblance.*" *Again, the words echoed in her head. Who had pronounced them? A man or a woman? Or – wait! – had they been her own words?*

But that wasn't the right thought to linger on now. Her hands slowly moved towards her head, which was still in pain. But the bag? It was her bag and it had turned into a little pillow, giving her a modicum of comfort. And her hands? She'd managed to move them, she remembered, when none of her other limbs had been responding.

As jerky as her movements were, it seemed she could at least use her hands and arms. She tried to flex one foot, then the other. Good, she had not been wrapped up in a cocoon of spider's web, as she had feared; she was free. Although she doubted she could do much with this freedom of hers.

"...I'm interested in a theme: resemblance."

Yes, those had been her own words, but did they matter at present? No. What mattered now was finding out where she was. What was this solid darkness? Why weren't Dora and Leon with her?

She tried to call them. But that scared her. Not only because the words fell into a silence as deep as the darkness surrounding her, but because her voice had come out unnaturally feebly, a sad reminder of her impotence.

Was she still dreaming? Or rather, having nightmares?

Earlier on, she'd dreamed about the knight in the suit of armour. Was she now having nightmares about her condition? What if once she woke, the darkness would disappear to reveal an even greater horror?

Glengullion. The name popped up from the back of her mind. She was there, in Scotland. The laughing face of Rufus came into focus. The auld country had been full of good things for her… up to a point.

Leon and Dora. That was weird, why weren't they with her? Had something happened to them? Or were they closer than she thought?

She pressed her hands against the floor and, with a supreme effort, raised her torso, sitting up and leaning her back against the wall. Her head spun as if she were on a funfair ride.

"Leon! Dora!" she managed to verbalise again. Even if they were close, she doubted they would hear her, so thin was her voice.

"Wait, take back control," she told herself. "Don't go to sleep." She couldn't even think of getting up, but she could use her arms and legs to explore the room around her.

Sitting on that cold floor, her legs stretched out in front of her, she started to slide along the wall using her hands and feet to feel what was coming. She was moving clockwise, was that an ingrained instinct? Maybe a sign she was recovering her movement and her senses, at least partially.

Her arms and hands were not only trying to make sense of this strange environment, but they were searching. She wished so much to find a bucket of water, or a bottle, or even a puddle for that matter, so thirsty did she feel.

She eventually arrived at a corner and managed to manoeuvre her body 90 degrees. Then she came to another, where the wall changed texture. It was a wooden surface, most likely a door. Stretching her arms above her head, she found a handle. Instinctively, she tried to get up, using the handle for support and a hand on the floor as leverage, but her head was spinning too fast. The pain was so acute, she knew she was asking too much of her body.

Pause, Dora would say. Take a pause, old bean. She took a few breaths, let a bunch of minutes go by, then changed tack and simply reached for the handle above her head, pulling it down.

She heard a promising click, as if the door was going to open. She pushed it, but it came to an abrupt halt with a small bump. Maybe a bar had been slid across it from the outside, keeping the door closed.

BOTHER!

What now?

Well, she'd only gone around two corners; she must have at least two more to go. Maybe there was another door.

Slowly, she resumed her exploration, sliding her bum along the floor, not daring to stand up. But even at this snail's pace, the tour was soon completed. It was a squarish room, each wall maybe 4–5 metres long. But more importantly, it only had one door, and the wretched thing was barred.

She threw her head back to howl with rage, but of course, all she actually did was shriek in pain.

"Take it easy," she reprimanded herself harshly, "and use what's left of your brain, if there's still anything inside your skull. How did you come to be here? What happened?"

She saw an image of the breakfast room, full of people, too loud. She saw herself telling Dora she needed time alone and leaving. That had been before breakfast, which had been a stupid idea. Not that she was feeling hungry; actually, she had a deep sense of nausea, especially when she moved around, but she would have welcomed even a tiny bit of water, coffee, tea or any liquid. And whoever had brought her here had left none in the room.

The killer!

Yes, Etta had been on the tracks of a killer. Gary Mason's killer, the mace, the suit of armour, the chandelier… suddenly, memories flooded her. True, she hadn't a clue yet how she had come to be where she was, but her inner cogs were whirring again. The killer was behind it.

Death! That's what the killer must have had in mind when they'd left her in this room. For good. They'd left her neither water nor food, because she was meant to die!

Gosh!

Etta began to wish her brain had stayed as dazed and confused as it had been earlier.

41

THE SEARCH

"It's us, Tom and Dora. We're looking for Etta," Dora chirped, feigning a cheerfulness she didn't feel.

Jeremy came into view and looked at her, at Tom and Leon, then finally at the open passageway. He stared at it, his eyes wide with surprise.

"What's going on?"

"Etta's disappeared. I've searched for her, I thought everywhere, but Tom showed me this secret passage. We wonder if maybe she found it by chance and has gone down there exploring. Tom told me it's quite an intricate labyrinth of corridors, so I want to make sure she's not lost her way..." Dora felt her stomach tighten at the idea of her friend wandering around in that spooky place. What she chose not to mention was that Etta may not have entered the passage of her own accord.

"Whatever will happen next in this place?" Jeremy wondered.

"Would you be so kind as to come along too?" Dora asked, her fake cheery grin still frozen in place. "Another set of eyes..."

"Yes, yes, of course," he said in a gentler tone, smiling at her worried expression.

Tom was evidently not pleased. "So much for keeping the

passage a secret," he grumbled. "Make yourself useful and hold this," and he passed the torch to Dora.

"Of course," said Dora. Now that there were three of them, she hurried with more confidence down the narrow steps that led into the secret passage.

"Didn't you know this was here?" Tom asked Jeremy.

"No, I didn't. I'm pretty sure Eilidh doesn't know either."

"So, you're selling a property you hardly know," said Tom laconically, but the sensitive Dora could hear the scathing hint of criticism behind the comment.

Once the stairs ended, the corridor opened out, but only slightly. The torchlight shone on the large stones making up the walls, the air smelled of damp earth.

"Will there be enough oxygen in here?" Dora asked.

"There always seems to be, although the circulation is rather sluggish and the air does feel heavy," replied Tom.

Was Etta really down here? Dora trembled at the idea, but if her friend had discovered the passage by chance, she would not have hesitated to look inside. But had she been alone? Dora had a vision of the empty kitchen, of Tom and Edwina returning flustered and out of breath. Could they have been aware of where Etta had gone? Tom had mentioned one of the passages led to the kitchen, so had Etta come out of it at the wrong moment? Had she seen something incriminating? Should Dora alert Jeremy to her fears? Why hadn't she insisted on calling the police?

As Tom was ahead of them, walking confidently in the cone of light Dora's torch created from behind him, she had the opportunity to pretend to slip on the stone floor. When Jeremy reached out an arm to steady her, she whispered to him, "Tom is armed, he has a gun." Then she added loudly, "How silly of me, I must have slipped on a damp patch."

"Are you OK to carry on?" Tom asked, turning round. "Would you like me to take the torch."

"No, we're OK, we'll keep up with you," Jeremy replied,

squeezing Dora's arm to confirm her message had been received and understood. She felt slightly better now as they walked along the seemingly endless corridor. Better, but not safe. She had to continue to think, to understand so she would be ready for whatever turn of events awaited her. And she knew the turn of events would come sooner rather than later.

During her fake fall, she'd grasped something from the floor, and in the light of her torch, she saw it was a brooch. It looked like the brooch Etta had purchased in Jenny's gallery on Iona.

"Etta's definitely been down here," she cried, explaining to the two men about the piece of jewellery with its Celtic design.

"Indeed, she must have passed along here," said Tom. Did he sound annoyed at Dora's discovery? Etta must have dropped that brooch on purpose, the resourceful woman. Or was he wondering if it was in fact Edwina's brooch?

"Let's go," said Jeremy, and again he gave Dora a little squeeze on her arm.

Dora was trying hard to order her thoughts. Now they were lingering on Eilidh and her father, and the painting of Lord McGullion... and Edwina. Didn't Edwina's eyes have the same cruel gleam as Lord McGullion's? Piercing eyes of steel. But nothing else about Edwina resembled Lord McGullion, just the cold eyes...

"The dog!" said Tom.

"What?" asked Jeremy. Then they saw Leon returning from ahead of Tom, trotting towards them.

"He's changed direction," said Tom. "I was heading towards the kitchen, but he wants us to go back this way."

"Leon, come here!" Dora called as the dog passed her. But, of course, Leon wasn't the kind of dog who would simply obey a human, especially when he was pursuing an idea of his own.

"Let him go," said Tom, "we'll find him later."

"No way!" Dora protested. "Let's follow him." She had the torch, she was the one in command. Well, as long as Tom didn't brandish the gun. As Dora walked on ahead of the two men, she heard Jeremy inviting Tom to go in front of him.

"No," Tom said. "You follow the lady, I will make sure we're on the right track." Those words sent a cold shiver down Dora's spine, despite the fact she was feeling rather hot after walking at such a brisk pace.

"Oh!" she cried. "Leon has taken a turn to the right."

"Is there a passage there?" Tom said, sounding surprised. Perhaps even he didn't know the extent of the labyrinth.

"Yes," Jeremy said, "it goes off diagonally and we didn't notice it on the way in. Luckily, Leon's on the ball."

"Lucky indeed," agreed Tom.

"What's down there?" Dora asked him.

"I confess, I don't know this part of the labyrinth. I think it may just be a dead end."

Dora clasped her hands, but not in her usual romantic trance. Nope, it was a completely new feeling warming her from the inside. Oh, if that killer had hurt her friend, they'd pay for it. If it was the last thing she did!

Her mind went back to the brooch. Etta had gone to the trouble of unpinning the small brooch, rather than simply dropping her purse, gloves or scarf. Why? As Dora's brain worked furiously as if it was the main computer at NASA, she forgot all her fears about being old and fragile, encouraging the others to hurry.

And then, they heard it. A feeble distant sound.

Thud-thud-thud.

Thud… thud… thud…

Thud-thud-thud.

Pause. Then again.

Thud-thud-thud.

Thud… thud… thud…

Thud-thud-thud.

As one, the searchers froze.

42

THE DUNGEON

The end.

Was this it?

As hard as she'd tried to explore, Etta didn't have a clue where she was. She didn't even have a clue what had happened after she'd left the breakfast room. But if the killer had left her alive in this dungeon, he – or she – must have felt sure no one would find her.

Was she still in the castle? No windows; all this dampness; the still, heavy air. Even with a not-so-well-oiled brain, she'd come to the conclusion she had to be underground, most likely beneath the castle.

The fact she hadn't heard a single noise was not a good sign. Had she heard even the dimmest of sounds from up above, there would have been a chance someone would hear her if she made a noise. But if all was silent, it seemed her position was too remote and isolated for that small crumb of hope.

She made another tour of the room, dragging herself on her bum, to see if there was a pipe or something similar that connected her prison with whatever was above her. But there was nothing.

Cold seized her. It wasn't the cold seeping into her bones from the floor and the walls, it wasn't the cold from outside. No, it was a freezing wave of terror.

She was going to die here of inanition.

No food, no water, no light.

How about air? Did she have enough to breathe or was the nausea, the headache, the sluggish movement a sign there was very little oxygen in here for her?

Was death already coming?

Despite her reasonably advanced age, Etta had given the idea of death no more thought than when she was thirty. Maybe that had been stupid. Truth was, she still struggled with the whole concept of the 'cycle of life', dreading her dotage. The fact life would one day come to an end was too much for her.

She'd always dreaded a painful, lingering disease or, worse, losing control of her body and/or mind and being entirely dependent on someone else. But not this. She'd never considered this!

A person, not a germ or a virus, not a gene with a sick sense of humour, had decided to send her to Our Father's Home – hopefully the nice one – before her time. Now, when she'd realised she could explore Europe and started to live her best life.

From terror to rage, it took a matter of seconds.

"Why now?" she rasped. Her voice was still weak, but grumbling helped. It made her feel alive, like Leon when he kicked his rear legs in his imitation of a powerful bull. "I was starting to have fun," she informed the all-powerful Father. "I enjoy Dora's company, and even the furry one's, as stubborn as he might be. And we had this trip all planned out. All those home swaps. Why now? Why me? Why give me a whole new lease of life, then deny me the chance to enjoy it to the full?"

She was in her sixties, so she felt she had a right to address Him a little more bluntly than she had done when she was 20. After years of trudging the paths of the planet, surely she must have gained some respect in His eyes. This was unfair, and she'd better remind Him just how unfair it was, in case He was busy and had momentarily forgotten about her – humph! – rights.

"And it doesn't matter where you place me, as you know I'm a troublemaker. Think twice – is this what you really want?" Did that sound a bit too blunt? Might He take it as a challenge? Better make

sure, just in case. You never know how touchy the Divine could be. "And that's not a threat, by the way. Just an objective statement. I know what I'm like."

She sighed. Hopefully, she had made her case as well as she could. Exhausted, she leaned back against the door, which gave way until it hit the bar stopping it from opening, making a little thud. It wasn't loud, as the door only moved a centimetre at most, but the sound it produced was more powerful than her powerless voice.

Dora and Leon, how could she not have thought of them? Those two must be looking for her. It was not like she was all alone. How stupid of the killer! She had two best friends. They'd raise the alarm.

She imagined the mysterious killer would try to mislead them, but Dora was a good sleuth. She didn't spot the same clues as Etta, but she was excellent at reading people.

Something warm started to spread inside her. Etta felt positive they'd find her. The cold temporarily retreated. She felt her hands come alive, her thirst, or at least her perception of it, decrease. She had to do something to help her friends find her. Because you've got to work for things; you can't just wait and pray.

She sat her bum a little way in front of the wooden door, angled her back against it and pushed once, twice, three times in quick succession. Then she repeated the same sequence, but left a longer gap between thuds, following that with three short thuds. SOS in Morse code, as she had learned from adventure books in her childhood.

Thud-thud-thud.

Thud… thud… thud…

Thud-thud-thud.

Then she paused.

Silence. Nothing but a thick and dark silence.

Except she knew they were looking for her. She'd help them. And it required so little effort, just leaning her back against the door. Minimum effort, maximum result.

Thud-thud-thud.

Thud… thud… thud…

Thud-thud-thud.

Pause.

"Keep on keeping on," Dora had told her once. "When you're in trouble, take a deep breath, think a little, strive to find the right direction, and then keep on keeping on."

Thud-thud-thud.

Thud… thud… thud…

Thud-thud-thud.

Pause.

Rufus McCall. She was due to see him on Monday, that fun man who'd shown her the magic of his land during an unforgettable night on Rannoch Moor, who'd danced with her during a cèilidh on Loch Lomond. The man who'd kissed her on the island of Skye.

What was that? She was sure she'd heard something. Voices? Footsteps? Merely her wild imagination?

Don't get too excited, old hag, just stay the course, keep on keeping on.

Thud-thud-thud.

Thud… thud… thud…

Thud-thud-thud.

43

THE CLUES ADD UP

T hud-thud-thud.

    Thud… thud… thud…

Thud-thud-thud.

"Someone's using Morse code," said Tom, sprinting forward. "That's an SOS signal!"

"WORF, WORF, WORF!" Leon had run ahead and was urging the bipeds to hurry up. Dora didn't need telling twice.

"Please, dear, gentle God, let me find her in one piece." But as she ran, she thought of the brooch, of Iona, of the concept of resemblance. Dora watched her thoughts streaming one after the other in the back of her mind, like still photos flicking past in fast succession to become a moving image. For some reason, they kept returning to the fact the murder had taken place on the day of the fair, a Saturday. Was that significant? And why?

She had no time to think further as she had caught up with Leon. And there, ahead of him, her torch revealed a robust wooden door that closed off the rest of the passage.

Thud-thud-thud.

"Etta, dear, is that you?" Dora cried.

Thinner than the thinnest supermodel, a feeble voice responded, "It is. Help!" So weak was the sound that Dora looked at the two men, wondering if they'd heard it too. Both nodded. Then Tom lifted the heavy iron bolt that was stopping the door from opening. Dora and Leon rushed in, finding Etta sitting on the floor, gulping in the air coming from the passage like a starving person would gobble down food.

"I'm so glad to see the two of you," she said, letting Dora hug her and Leon lick her face with his rough tongue.

Dora placed the torch on the floor so she could help Etta. The beam of light hit the two men standing on the threshold. Tom went to take a step, but Jeremy was ready and pushed him inside Etta's prison. However, Tom managed to dodge the attack, at least partially, and, as Dora had feared, he pulled out the gun.

Because Jeremy knew Tom was armed, he was ready for the man's move. He seized Tom's hand as it came out of his pocket holding the weapon. Tom reacted to the new attack with surprising strength and the two fell to the floor, rolling around the little room and fighting for control of the gun.

Dora jumped up. Jeremy had hold of Tom's arm and was twisting it, trying to get him to drop the gun, so she seized the weapon, stepped backwards and aimed it at the two men. They both stopped fighting and looked at her in surprise, their faces still illuminated by the cone of torchlight. Everyone was frozen to the spot, as if they were playing a game of Grandmother's Footsteps. Even Leon stayed stock still, watching the scene.

In a remarkably calm voice, Dora broke the tense silence. "Etta, are you strong enough to walk out of the room?" she asked.

Etta didn't reply, just shook her head.

"Who did this to you?" said Dora, her instinct yelling at her that something was wrong, that things didn't add up.

"I… I… I don't know, I can't remember anything," whispered Etta, still sitting on the floor, her back leaning against the wall. Her hands rose to clutch her head, maybe to stimulate her brain into recalling the memories.

"Dora," said Jeremy, moving towards her. "I tried to stop this man. It's a good job you told me he had a weapon on him. Clearly, he attacked poor Etta, so let's immobilise him."

"No, wait!" and Dora waved the gun, making sure both men knew she meant business.

"Don't believe him! I think it's he who's involved in this whole thing," protested Tom. "After all, you know I was in the kitchen with Edwina when Etta left the breakfast room."

"As a matter of fact," answered Dora bitterly, "I don't. The kitchen was empty when I came to see if I could help carry the food through and the breakfast was still waiting to be cooked. So, where were the two of you? Then you came back in, excited and breathless. What had you been doing?"

Tom raised his hands as if pleading and took a step towards her.

"Don't you dare come any closer," Dora spoke in a deep voice with a grit she'd never known she possessed.

"I told you so," said Jeremy. "Don't trust him. Be careful."

Dora wished she could simply help Etta leave the room, lock it behind them and be done with the two men. But the truth was, she couldn't support Etta and hold the gun at the same time, not to mention picking the torch up from the floor. Besides, she knew from what Tom had said that the weapon was loaded, but possibly only with one single bullet, so she had a problem. Even if she could overcome her natural aversion to weapons of any kind, the chances were she'd miss her target and the ricocheting bullet might hit anyone in the room.

Bother! It was so cool in the movies, when the heroine shot the baddy, but not fatally, incapacitating the villain and saving everyone's lives. But weapons really gave her the creeps, and the only reason her hands weren't shaking was because she kept repeating to herself she wouldn't have to fire the gun. She was simply playacting.

And she was acting well, because she was aware there was no Plan B.

She could hear the men's heavy breathing, Leon's pants, and Etta puffing air out like a steam train. They were all waiting for her to do or say something. This was act two of Grandmother's Footsteps.

It all came down to the answer to just one question: who was the murderer and who was her ally?

Then the images that had stilled as she had entered the room started to flow again, slowly at first, then speeding up. The resemblance, the brooch, the theatre, the special effects, the organised entrepreneur, the costume designer, the witness in Oban, Edwina keeping her hand behind her back and hiding something in her pocket, the tablecloth in the wrong chest of drawers. The flow ran faster, the single frames became as dynamic as an old silent movie. Then the irrelevant frames fell away and finally she saw the truth.

Still holding the gun, Dora picked up the torch and ran like a rugby player. Shoulders hunched, head lowered, she charged at Tom. But when she reached him, instead of striking him, she handed him the gun and pointed the torch beam right into Jeremy's eyes.

Tom seized the weapon, but instead of firing it, he bowed at the waist and headbutted a stunned Jeremy in the stomach. Jeremy fell to the floor, winded and breathless, gasping to get some air inside his lungs.

Leon ran from the small room, while Tom dropped the gun and helped Dora lift Etta and carry her after the dog. Laying her gently on the floor, they replaced the bolt across the door as fast as they could.

They had just finished when from the other side of the door, they heard a sinister metallic CLICK. Jeremy must have located the weapon.

"How could we have left the gun inside with him?" cried Dora, unable to believe their stupidity. The man could fire the door hinges off and get out. But Tom's reaction was unexpected. He guffawed.

"Doesn't really matter," he said. "One, it's not actually loaded at all, and two, it's so old, I doubt the thing would work anyway."

Click-clack. The impotent sound came from within the room, followed by a stream of expletives as Jeremy's fists beat against the door.

"But you said…"

"I wasn't sure I could trust you," Tom explained. "For all I knew, you could have been the killer."

"So, why did you help me out just now?"

"Because I saw the condition of your friend and knew she couldn't be the killer. I also saw how much you care for her and realised you couldn't be, either. But despite what I said in the heat of the moment, I had no idea Jeremy was the culprit… are you sure he didn't simply react to me having a weapon?"

"No, he's guilty alright. He and his sister Jenny plotted an elaborate plan to kill Gary Mason, and they attempted to take the life of Yasmine too, and that of my friend, Etta," Dora frowned deeply, "who had just discovered the truth. But I'll explain more later. Now, we need to help Etta out of here and get her urgent medical care. And we need to call the police."

"At last!" grumbled Etta. "I thought you two were going to carry on chattering until I passed away."

And at that moment, Dora knew Etta would be fine. She was complaining. She'd recover.

SUNDAY

44

THE NOT-SO-SOLID ALIBI

On the morning of the next day, Etta watched in satisfaction as a whole troop of people silently shuffled into her hospital room in a "special irregular admission," as the doctor had called it. But he'd had to surrender to the wishes of the opinionated strong-willed woman who had declared she'd have no peace until she could join all the dots and see the whole picture for herself. As sugar coating for the well-meaning doctor, she had added it could help her regain the memories she was still unable to retrieve.

The doctor frowned, looking at his watch. "You have just 15 minutes starting from now, not a second longer." Etta leaned back against a couple of pillows propping her up on her bed, a bandage around her head. She'd been given a CT scan and plenty of rehydration via IV. Seeing as the pain had lessened considerably, she was sure there must be painkillers among the cocktails being pumped into her bloodstream that she, for once, found rather beneficial.

"How are you?" the group chorused.

"They said it's concussion, but I should recover, and be no worse than I was before."

The visitors guffawed as quietly as they could.

"When did you realise it was Jeremy?" asked Debbie without preamble, marching straight to the point. Feeling shocked eyes on her, she justified herself. "Doctor said 15 minutes, and two must already have gone by. Let's get started, I say."

None of the others objected or pretended they had just stopped by to say hi. They all longed to hear how the puzzle had been solved.

"I didn't know for sure," answered Etta. "Our visit to Iona kept coming back to my mind and the fact Jenny knew Tom from the theatre, but once I learned that Tom was a special-effects expert, I focused on that and forgot that by her own admission, Jenny had been involved in the theatre's make-up and costumes departments. I never included Jeremy in my list of suspects as the police told us he had a cast-iron alibi. But the nature of that alibi should have raised my suspicions."

"How?" asked Sandra. "His car number plate was registered on the ferry from Craignure to Oban before the murder took place, and the woman running the newsagent in Oban remembered speaking to him at 3pm. How could he be in two places at the same time?"

"I'm too tired to speak anymore, but my friend Dora can explain it all. We might look like two separate people, but our brains work in tandem and she'd reached the same conclusions by the time she rescued me."

Dora's cheeks were on fire. She'd spent the night watching over her friend, but under the influence of drugs, Etta had mostly slept. They had only spoken a little early that morning, before the doctor had done his rounds. And now, Etta was passing the baton over to Dora. It was usually Etta who explained how the two sleuths had solved the crime – three sleuths, actually, as Leon had played an essential part in catching more than one villain. Dora might have intuition, but it was Etta who did all the hard work. Though maybe this time, out of necessity, Dora had been pushed into adopting Etta's sleuthing style.

"Well… well…" Dora started. "Let me tell you that suspects abounded, confusing us completely. Sandra and Grayson, you two have a habit of acting like co-conspirators…"

"In what way?" asked Grayson, frowning and ignoring the glares coming his way. Their time in the room may be limited, but Grayson wasn't the kind of man to let any accusation go unchallenged.

"Well, for starters, the way Sandra sometimes looks at you, as if to gain permission to speak."

Grayson laughed. "Oh, that's easy to explain," he said. "She only did it around you and Etta. Remember, for a long time, we thought you were the Italian investors with your greedy eyes on the castle, so we didn't think we could trust you an inch. But do go on."

"Right," said Dora. "So, Grayson, forgive my bluntness, but the feeling of mistrust was kind of mutual for a while. After all, we had no idea where you were at the time of the murder. Then Sandra was the one who found the corpse. Why was she in the castle in the first place?

"Then there was Tom and Edwina, two partners in crime – or, at least, trickery – who seemed to know everything and everyone." Dora turned to face the pair of them. "Your only alibi was the other's word that you were together at the time of the murder, eating a sandwich far from the madding crowd and preparing for the PP presentation planned for three o'clock. Not to mention how flustered you were yesterday when you returned to the kitchen…"

As all eyes swivelled towards the two, Edwina instinctively hid her hand behind her back.

"I'd be proud to show off that hand of yours," said Dora. Etta looked at her, not having a clue what her friend meant. Then, as Edwina finally stretched out her left hand and waggled her fingers, they all saw. A beautiful silver ring twinkled, causing a collective gasp of pleasure and admiration around the room.

"I'd say about time," said Dora, smiling as everyone burst into spontaneous congratulations and a newly demure Edwina hid her flushed face on Tom's chest.

"Then there was the ill-tempered Josh, the rather determined Debbie, Letitia so receptive to certain stimuli. Could she have felt the Masons were threatening her friends or been manipulated into killing Gary?

"Finally, there's Yasmine. True, she was accompanied to the car park by Gary before he was killed and plenty of people saw her leaving in her Porsche, but she could easily have doubled back and returned to the castle.

"These were all possibilities, but in the end, I came to the same conclusions as Etta, albeit via a different path. Where do I start? Not from the beginning, but from the moment I had to change my entire way of thinking. Which was when Tom showed me the secret passage and took down the gun…"

"About the gun," interrupted Edwina, looking at Tom, her eyes no longer cold, but warm and loving. "Why on earth did you choose that useless old arquebus? Surely you didn't expect it to work."

"You never know," said Tom, his eyes wandering around the room, a mischievous little gleam shining through his embarrassment at being the centre of attention. "What if someone had been in the tunnel? What if Dora turned out not to be as nice as she looks? At least she'd know I had a weapon on me, and I told her it was both loaded and in full working condition," and he winked at Dora and nodded, inviting her to continue.

"So, you knew all along it was entirely useless?" she asked him.

"Yes," said Tom, smiling.

"How lucky I never tried to fire it! Otherwise, I would have given the game away. I guess my aversion to weapons helped for once. Anyway, where was I?" Dora looked around, her fringe jumping merrily up and down as she turned her head, the expression in her round face a little more confident. "Oh yes, Tom had just shown me the secret passage. I was so fixated on suspecting him, I was relieved when Jeremy joined us, to the point I even told him about the gun. A silly mistake on my part. I knew instinctively that things weren't adding up, but it was only when I found Etta's brooch that my brain started to work.

"It was the brooch Etta had bought at Jenny's gallery on Iona. Why, of all the things she could have dropped far more easily, had she chosen that? It was clearly her way of alerting me that she believed Jenny had something to do with the puzzle."

Etta nodded in approval. She couldn't even remember the moment she had dropped the brooch, but knew instinctively that would have been the conclusion she'd hope Dora would reach. You could never read *Hansel and Gretel* enough, could you?

"My next question was, if Jenny was the killer, could she have acted all alone? Then a few things came back to my mind. Jeremy leaving the Crystal Room just minutes before the chandelier fell, and staying away rather longer than it would have taken him to check the spaghetti. And yesterday, when Eilidh sent him to get the light-blue cloth for our breakfast table, just after Etta had left the room, to justify his long absence, he said she should have told him it was in the chest of drawers in the corridor and not in the *other room*. What could the *other room* be? There are no rooms where one would have meals other than the kitchen, where we all thought Edwina and Tom were cooking breakfast, the Crystal Room, which had been left locked by the police, and the breakfast room, where we all were.

"So, what if the *other room* Jeremy had gone to was the Weapons Room? Not to search for the tablecloth, but to check what Etta was up to. He must have caught her mouthing the word 'resemblance' to me before she left, and that was a red alert for Jeremy. She might have been going to look at the portrait of Lord McGullion to ponder on the strong family genes, so obvious in both Duncan and Eilidh. Or she might be on the right track, which was a risk he couldn't take. There is also a strong family resemblance between him and his sister, so I surmised that if Jenny was involved, she must have been in cahoots with him."

"But they fell out over the gallery months ago!" Eilidh reminded her, the shock at finding out what a devious liar her fiancé had been still haunting her grey eyes.

"Can you think of a better way to hide the fact they were in partnership to commit murder?" Etta asked bluntly. Dora was too sensitive to poor Eilidh's feelings to articulate this particular thought.

"So, it was all planned in advance?"

"They probably only finalised the details of the plan when they were sure Gary was coming to Glengullion for the fair, but ever since he made his offer on the castle, they'd been looking for the opportunity to get rid of him. With this in mind, they decided to pretend to everyone that they had fallen out, that their once close relationship was in tatters and, by the time of the murder, had been for a while."

"How wicked!" Debbie cried. "So, it was Jenny who killed Gary…"

"No," Dora corrected her, "it was Jeremy. He knew full well how to move around the castle unnoticed, because despite denying it, he knew about the secret labyrinth and where each passage led. When he heard about Gary's plans to deliver an elaborate presentation at the fair, and that the man would have access to the castle denied to most fairgoers, he decided that was the perfect occasion to strike.

"Jeremy knew the presentation was due to take place at midday, so he made up some excuse to lure Gary a couple of hours afterwards, allowing time for the presentation to end and Gary to have lunch. Possibly, he told Gary that Eilidh's solicitor wanted to have a quiet word with him about the sale in the castle. He knew

Gary would be eager to come to the appointment, and the fair would provide the police with plenty of suspects among the island folk and the PP who didn't want the project to go ahead. It could even have been a stranger, a person with a long-standing grudge against Gary who had come over from the mainland..."

"And I must say," Etta interrupted her friend with a grin, "Edwina did a great job of helping Jeremy, threatening Gary the way she did."

"How was I to know?" snapped the woman, glaring at Etta, her eyes cold again. It seemed the two of them would never be friends. Then her sour expression softened into an ironic grin. "I never thought for one moment he would be killed for real or I wouldn't have spoken to him the way I did."

"Still," said Grayson, his logical business mind clearly wanting to march straight on to the nitty-gritty, "it seems that Jeremy's alibi was strong. His car was registered on the 13.35 ferry and at least one person spoke to him at three o'clock in Oban. It's impossible to be committing murder at Glengullion just after 2pm and be in Oban at 3pm."

"As Etta said, his alibi wasn't as solid as it seemed," Dora explained. "The registration of the number plate only means that the *car* was on the ferry at a certain time, but a car can be driven by anyone..."

"Like who?" Grayson insisted.

"Like Jenny, cleverly disguised as her brother. She told us herself that Saturday is one of the two days she has cover to run the gallery, so she was free for the day. She drove Jeremy's car to Oban, then made sure not to be seen by any of his usual contacts. She did, however, make sure that a casual witness would remember *him* when questioned by the police. Therefore, the mishap at the newsagent in Oban – spilling a cup of coffee, helping to clean it up, and offering to buy a few things to make up for the disturbance – was all contrived. No matter how many people went to the newsagent that day, the shopkeeper was bound to remember the gentle, helpful, apologetic lad called Jeremy.

"Jenny has the same features as her brother. Their faces are long and thin, their eyebrows are straight and eyelashes thick, and they share the same eye colour. It's as if they are the male and female versions of a single person. Thus, it was easy for her, using her strong resemblance to her brother, coupled with years as a costume designer and make-up artist at the local theatre, and the acting skills she would have picked up there, to become Jeremy.

"They swapped cars where the secret passage leads outside. Jenny must have left her mobile phone back home, while she found Jeremy's in his car, so if the police checked, they would have seen his phone exactly where he said he'd been at the time of the murder. Truth was, the mobile was with Jenny all along."

"How do you know that?" Josh asked, looking rather impressed.

"Because when Eilidh called him at half past four to tell him about the murder, Jeremy didn't reply. He only called her back after five, saying he'd left his mobile in the car. In actual fact, at four-thirty, Jeremy was on the 15.55 ferry, while his phone was indeed waiting for him in his car, which was already in Oban. In the meantime, Jenny had removed her disguise, returned to the island, picked up her own car and gone home."

"How could she pick her car up from the castle near Tobermory when the ferry would drop her in Craignure?"

"Because Jeremy, also in disguise, had got in Jenny's car after escaping unnoticed along the secret passage from the castle soon after the murder, driven to Craignure, left the car in the parking area and rushed to the pier to catch the 15.55 ferry as a foot passenger, just one of the many tourists."

"What if someone at Glengullion or Tobermory had recognised the registration number of Jenny's car and noticed a stranger driving it?"

"No one remembers a car number plate. I can't remember my own, let alone someone else's," Sandra said.

"And you can easily camouflage a car," added Edwina, "with a couple of stickers, a toy hanging from the rear-view mirror, etcetera."

"As for the murder," continued Dora, "while Gary was waiting for whoever he thought he was going to meet, Jeremy hit him over the head with the mace, making sure the man was dead. He then cleaned up anything that might give him away, knowing Gary's team were all still in town having lunch so it was highly unlikely anyone would enter the castle, and left through the secret passage to return to his sister's car outside.

"The body was discovered by Sandra half an hour later when Jeremy was already on the way to Craignure, and then to Oban. Once on the mainland, Jeremy fetched his own car, called Eilidh and drove to Glasgow to spend the night there, picking her up early the next morning, sure he had a cast-iron alibi. But what I still don't understand," Dora added, looking at Sandra, "is why you went into the castle."

"I was looking for Letitia. I couldn't find her outside and I was afraid she might have been wandering around the castle, as she used to when Katherine was alive. Then to my horror, I found Gary dead. After what Edwina had said, I wondered about so many things. What if the killer had been one of us? Maybe Edwina, or even Letitia, who had heard many discussions condemning Gary's plans. Maybe…" she looked at her husband shyly, a strange expression on the face of such a confident woman, "it had been Grayson. He'd come to love this castle and the PP project so much. Only when you and Etta came in did I realise the mace was the murder weapon, which is why I tried to grab it. I wanted to leave my fingerprints on it so that if Grayson's or Letitia's were found on it too, I could tell the police we had all been looking at it a few days earlier…"

"Hah!" said Etta, pleased to have one of her theories proved correct.

"OK, now I understand the mechanics," said Edwina. "The howdunnit, but why? As much as I disliked Jeremy, I'd never have suspected him of murdering Gary. He'd always wanted to get rid of the castle…"

"I wouldn't be too sure of that," Etta couldn't help intervening again. "The siblings had big ambitions. You, Sandra, mentioned what a great organiser Jenny is, so I wouldn't be surprised if they had their own contract with an investor, and wanted to have the lion's share of the new enterprise."

"But the castle was Eilidh's!"

"With Gary out the way, Jeremy would convince her to sell to the buyer he chose, and you, Eilidh, wouldn't be aware that this buyer already had an agreement with Jeremy and his sister."

The shock and hurt in Eilidh's eyes turned to blazing anger. "But he wouldn't have influenced me so easily!" she protested. "I wasn't taking orders from him…"

Dora chuckled. "That's the problem with stubborn people. You're convinced you can't be influenced, but you can easily be manipulated. Simply by telling you to do the opposite of what we want you to do, those of us around you get our own way."

"*What?*"

"If I want you to say white, I will simply tell you to say black…"

Eilidh stood there, her mouth agape, while Etta stared at Dora. She'd known this. She'd always suspected Dora used psychology on her as well as Leon!

"This is why you need to find yourself someone who's loyal to you, but not a yes man," Dora's eyes wandered around the room and settled on Josh. It was only for a second, but long enough for Josh to flush as if he'd just swallowed a whole chilli. But Dora had merely wanted to soften the blow of her next words. She was sure it would be a while before Eilidh could bring herself to trust a man again, even one as straightforward and honest as Josh.

"I'm so sorry, Eilidh, but I wouldn't be surprised if the two wicked siblings had already planned for an accident to occur after the wedding that would get rid of mother and daughter – and your father, too," she added, looking sympathetically at Duncan, who had been released as soon as the police had the true culprits in custody, "leaving Jeremy in sole possession of the castle."

"Oh!" Eilidh cried, covering her face with her hands. "I hadn't realised he could be so evil! What kind of monster did I believe I loved?"

"He had already killed Gary Mason, and he had tried to kill Yasmine. You remember when the lights went out, he told us to stay exactly where we were? That way, he could make sure Yasmine would be right below the chandelier. When he'd gone to the kitchen earlier on, ostensibly to check on the spaghetti, I suspect he went upstairs to unscrew the bolts holding the chandelier in place. We even heard his footsteps! And earlier on, he had suggested moving the table, saying Yasmine would be too close to the fireplace otherwise."

"So the two ghosts had nothing to do with the 'accident'?" Eilidh asked.

"Nothing at all. The PP and your father just happened to plan their sabotage of the sale of the castle at the same time, scaring each other half to death in the process, each wondering if they were facing a real ghost."

The members of the PP and Duncan McGullion couldn't help chuckling at the memory. Maybe laughter was their way to cope with it all, and to deal with the shocking maliciousness of the two siblings.

"When did the second ghost come into play?" asked Grayson.

"That night, I'm afraid I was the first ghost, not the second one," replied Duncan.

"Tell us quick, we went over the time we were given ages ago," said Debbie.

"Fearing the PP had given up on the idea of using the ghost

to scare off the investors, I decided it was time to take matters into my own hands. I was responsible for the crackling noises, and the whining, and the windows opening, and the blackout to make my show more convincing. Little did I suspect you guys were up to something too, until I saw the other ghost. I really thought it was the suit of armour that had despatched with my evil ancestor, the curse coming back to haunt me… again!"

"Tom, your show the previous week was really well executed, from the very moment we entered the castle," said Etta. "But how did you manage the piano trick?"

"It was a self-playing piano we'd used in one of our plays, *Mrs McIntyre and the Ghost*. It works just like an ordinary piano, but it can be set on self-playing mode. Few people would remember the play so many years later…"

"When did you write that message in the middle of the stone circle?"

"What message?"

"*Stay away from evil*, or words to that effect. How did you know we'd be up there that day?"

Tom looked blank. It was Josh who cleared his throat, calling attention to himself.

"That wasn't meant for you. It was something I'd written for myself, a reminder and a reprimand. I do have a bad temper from time to time, so I wanted to use such an evocative place so the message would stay in my brain."

"You mean it was already there when we went for our walk?"

"I guess so, as I wrote it weeks ago. As the ground is covered by sand, I just make sure the winds don't blow it away." If possible, Josh's expression became even more shamefaced, but it seemed he was in the mood for confession. "The… um, rockfall," he cast an apologetic glance at Etta, "was me too. I never meant to hurt you, I just wanted to do my bit to help the PP scare you off, because we thought… well, you know…"

Josh looked so mortified that even Etta found it in her heart to forgive him. "It's fine," she said as robustly as she was able. "No harm done, thanks to the quick thinking of Leon. But going back to the stone circle, I could have sworn the writing hadn't been there when we first looked. I guess we were still digesting the shock of the previous night. Such is the power of suggestion, we didn't even consider that it might not have been meant for us."

"Talking about suggestion," Dora chimed in, looking at Tom in an attempt to draw the attention away from Josh, who was now squirming with embarrassment, "what about the marble busts in the corridor whose eyes seemed to follow me everywhere?"

"I substituted Lord McGullion's marble bust with a polystyrene one. When we get back to the castle, I will show you. It's hollow and not convex like a normal sculpture, a trick used in haunted houses to create the effect of the eyes following you..."

"And the painting in our former bedroom?" asked Dora, remembering another couple of eyes staring at her.

"I admit, I had a little fun there. I had cut out the painting's eyes so I could slide them away and peer through the holes, but I made sure to do so when only one of you was watching. I beg your pardon, but I intended to undermine your confidence in each other."

"You even winked at me!" Dora said, making everyone chuckle.

"What about the face we saw floating outside the window?" asked Etta, being careful not to shake her head or gesticulate as much as she would normally.

"Just a pepper's ghost, reflected from the room next to yours..."

"A *pepper's ghost*?"

Tom winked at Dora. "Och, I've told you before, a magician doesn't like to reveal his secrets. But I'm sure Mr Google will tell you all you need to know. Anyway, where was I? Ah yes... we knew you wouldn't go in there after Edwina had suggested you might not want to use the most haunted room…"

"Perfectly executed, Tom," said Etta with a grin. Dora clapped her hands and the others joined in.

A knock sounded on the door, then the doctor popped his head in and reminded them bluntly to be a little more quiet in the hospital. And more to the point, their time was up.

SUNDAY

EVENING

My dear Katherine, I've done my very best and made a mess of it all. Mr T is right when he says at times, I should let things run their course and be confident they will take care of themselves. The problem is that I like to take action, and it is difficult to know when I should act and when I should pause.

Life is such a complex thing to deal with. I finally realise that Mr T, being a man with a completely different mindset to my own, will be a great help to me in the future. Och, this sounds so wise and rational. But... I'm not being totally honest here.

Truth is, after the debacle at the castle, getting caught by Eilidh and arrested by the police, Mr T was so angry with me. I was scared – horrified – when I realised I could lose him. All of a sudden, I became aware of how much... I love him. Well, after the police released us, I apologised like I've never done before – my dear Katherine, you know the word 'sorry' doesn't come easily to me, but it did then. Thankfully, we made our peace.

When the sound of sirens cut through the quiet morning, Mr T was the first person I thought to call. Together, we went up to the castle to find out poor Eilidh had seen her beloved father arrested – the father she had just been reunited with. But the morning held a far more pleasant surprise for me. While we were meant to be cooking breakfast, Mr T led *me out into the beautiful garden and, in the morning sunshine, he got down on one knee and offered me the loveliest ring I have ever seen, asking me to marry him. I was swept off my feet, I simply couldn't believe it.*

I blushed, my heart went pitter-patter as if I were a teenager again. Poor Mr T must have thought I was struggling to find the words to refuse him, yet again, as he looked straight at me.

"I'm not going to ask you a second time," he said sulkily.

I burst into my happiest laughter of the whole year and said, "You won't need to." And would you believe it? I kissed him. This old spinster found a passion she didn't even know she had while imaginary fireworks exploded in an array of sparkling colours all around us. Even at my age, it would seem romance is alive and well.

As for everything else, I'm not totally sure what will happen now. What will Eilidh decide for the future of Glengullion? With Duncan back on the scene and firmly on the side of keeping the castle, I have my hopes... but I promise I won't let those hopes run wild.

And mostly, I want to celebrate this: no one in the PP was involved in the murder of Gary or the attempt to kill Yasmine. I was so worried that our heated meetings had influenced dear Letitia to do something awful – something she wouldn't understand to be a heinous crime. It's such a relief to know we're just a happy, high-spirited, harmless bunch of old people, striving to make this world a better place... one island at a time.

MONDAY

45

RECONCILIATION

"I won't be sharing a bedroom with him, I hardly know him!" Etta definitely looked better and stronger by Monday morning, propped up in her hospital bed, munching on a croissant.

"I thought you said you kissed him."

"Firstly, what I said was that *he* kissed *me* on Skye, not the other way round. And either way, it was just a kiss. Secondly, I don't think I'm ready for more. Maybe he and I need to discuss our feelings... or maybe adults don't speak of such things. That's silly, of course they do. Anyway, where was I?

"No, no, no, don't tell me, I know where I was. Thirdly, Eilidh has offered him his own room and he can be happy with that. For the moment, at least."

"As you wish, but we can sort the finer details out later," said Dora, smiling at seeing Etta back to her belligerent best. "For now, let me go and fetch him."

"If you're planning to bring him here, do I look presentable?" and Etta touched the bandage around her head. The paramedics who'd arrived on the scene on Saturday had medicated a cut on her scalp and applied ice to help reducing the swelling on her forehead. Apparently, when Jeremy had hit the back of her head, she had fallen forward and banged her forehead on the hearth. Drifting in and out of consciousness, she'd had a fleeting moment of inspiration and had unpinned the brooch not just to give Dora a clue that she had been in the tunnel, but also to implicate the woman from whom she had bought the jewellery in the first place.

"You look fine." Dora smiled sweetly, adjusting the bandage and handing Etta the lipstick she loved.

"Thank goodness!" Etta applied the lipstick generously over her mouth, admiring the result in the hand mirror Dora held up for her, then looked at her friend. But this time, she wasn't happy with what she saw. No matter how Dora tried to hide her feelings, Etta could read her like an open book. "Before you go, I need to know what your sad mood is all about. You've not been yourself since we arrived on Mull."

"Oh dear, it's nothing to worry about. Just me being silly…"

"Silly, eh? It's more than that and it's time for you to open up. If you still trust me, that is."

"Oh, Etta, I'm very happy for you and Rufus, believe me. But I guess I'm a little sad for myself as well. I've already phoned Pietrapertosa to see if the owner of my former flat is looking to let it out, I don't think he found a new tenant when I left."

"Pietrapertosa? Tenant? What are you talking about?"

"Etta, let's speak frankly. It was in our contract that if you ever wanted me gone, I would move out of your house without argument," Dora referred to the agreement they had signed when they'd decided to live together.

"There's a load of rubbish in that contract and you know it," Etta said. At the time, she'd written in black and white that they'd sell the Fiat 500 and use her comfy saloon car for their travels, and that not even a stuffed cuddly toy animal would ever pass the threshold of her house. But then they had adopted Leon and brought him home in the very Fiat Etta had wanted rid of, so as things had turned out, 75% of that contract wasn't worth the paper it had been written upon.

Dora looked at her, unconvinced. "But you will need the house for yourself, when you and Rufus marry. And... Leon..." here, Dora bit her lip, determined not to make things harder by crying at the thought of the hound, who was being spoiled rotten by Letitia while Dora was at the hospital, all under the watchful eyes of other members of the PP.

"How could you think for a second I would throw you out on the streets for the sake of a man?" Etta considered her words and decided an *erratum corrigendum* was needed, if only for clarity's sake. "Even though I must say Rufus is a cut above the average. Still, that's no reason to throw a friend out of a home we've agreed to share."

"But it's natural that you'd want to find romance..."

"Natural, my tooth! We're not some hot 20-year-olds. And frankly, even if things should work out as Miss Matchmaker believes, I doubt a Scottish man could survive the heat of summer in Southern Italy. He might come for a visit, as I might visit Scotland from time to time, but I truly believe we should keep things as they are back home. We can all have our privacy – it's such a large house, it can easily accommodate the four of us."

"Mrs Passolina, do you really understand what you're saying?"

"How can you doubt it, Miss Pepe?" Etta roared.

"Because I can endure the present sadness, it's the hope that will kill me if it proves to be a false one..." Dora was uncertain whether she should explode with happiness or wait until she was absolutely sure she had understood properly.

"You're telling me you believe that a woman who's a real pain in the neck like Edwina could live in a residence with I don't know how many crazy oldies around, but I couldn't live with my two best friends ever and maybe a Scotsman?"

"Oh, Etta!" Dora cried, clasping her hands in the most exquisite happiness that she, the ever-happy woman, had felt in her entire life.

"Come here before you go into one of those trances of yours!"

Etta hollered, opening her arms for a bear hug. Dora rushed over to her, sat on the bed and let her friend hug her. And that was how the nurse found them, laughing and crying and sniffling all at once.

"It's time for all visitors to leave before the doctor does his rounds," she reminded them.

"And it's time for me to fetch Rufus!" Dora cried, noticing that the bus from Craignure was due at Tobermory coach station very soon.

When Dora arrived in Tobermory, Rufus was already there, waiting by the pier. She saw his tall, sturdy frame from afar, his red hair ruffled in the breeze, but only noticed that his laughing eyes were dark and worried when she got closer.

"Hello, Dora," he said in his gruff voice, kissing her on each cheek and holding her hands in his. "How is she?"

"She's doing fine, the doctor says she's headstrong," they both chuckled at this statement of the obvious, then Rufus bent down to greet the wagging Leon with a series of scratches and rubs. "There doesn't seem to be any damage following her concussion," Dora went on as man and dog were reunited, "although the cut on the back of her head needed a few stitches. She's not recovered all her memories of what happened, but otherwise she seems to be as sharp as ever. Her tongue certainly is!" Dora chuckled again as she led Rufus and Leon towards the car.

"Such a relief to hear that. I've never met a woman as stubborn as Etta, or as prone to getting into trouble."

"Well, she's an expert at getting into and out of trouble, and she's managed to help quite a few people because of her perseverance and intuition."

"Perseverance rather than stubbornness, interesting. I see you're her perfect partner in crime, I will have to keep a watch over the two of you. I confess, I thought you were the quiet one of the trio, but I understand you can be as belligerent and tough as your friend, if not more so."

Dora smiled, feeling strangely happy at having the opportunity to get to know her friend's man a little better.

"Well, after all, friendship is about exchanging ideas, learning from one another. I have no doubt I've changed a lot since I met Etta, she has helped me become stronger, grittier and less whiney."

"And she says you've taught her to be kind to herself, to trust in people, to be more indulgent with the world. In all honesty, with such a strong bond between the two of you, I wonder if I stand any chance of winning even a little place in her heart."

"Love doesn't come in metres squared. A person's heart can expand as required, and the larger and more accommodating it is, the happier and healthier he or she will be." Dora said this maybe more to herself than to Rufus, who was distracted by trying to fold his tall frame into the passenger seat of the Fiat 500. It was Leon who responded with a "WoRF" of approval.

Before Dora started the engine, Rufus handed her a white envelope with a curious blue image stamped on it. The image showed a picture of a whale.

"What is this?" Dora asked, tearing open the envelope with the impatience of a child at Christmas.

"Three tickets for a tour of the island of Staffa," Rufus clarified.

"That's so kind of you, but I'm afraid Etta doesn't really like boats. And now with the concussion…"

"In fact, it was Etta who asked me to buy those tickets as a surprise for you. She said you'd love it, even though she was sure she would regret her impulsiveness and fail to follow through on the idea. So, she asked me to do it for her."

Dora clasped her hands in wonder. It was lucky she hadn't yet started the car as she was in one of her trances for quite a few minutes, which could have been tricky to manage had she been driving. Leon sighed deeply, knowing how long it would take before his gentle biped recovered. The male biped, who seemed to know about this particular brand defect, smiled and waited patiently. The feisty one must have warned him.

Fancy that, an inner voice was singing like an angel in Dora's ears. *My friend was thinking of me rather than planning to spend her time exclusively with Rufus. All along, she wanted me there too. And doing something she hates, because she knew I'd love it. How could I have ever doubted her? Such a perfect friend. And Rufus was so happy to oblige, it seems that far from losing one friend, I have gained another.*

As for Leon, he wasn't entirely annoyed by the turn of events. It had been a long time since Dora had had one of her rapturous trances, so this meant that the sweeter biped was recovering in her own way from a deeper and more damaging wound than the feisty one in the hospital had suffered.

All's well that ends well, thought the wise Basset, already looking forward to the next adventure. Hadn't the gentle biped mentioned a cute cottage in the Lake District, and a garden belonging to a rabbit called Peter? Not that Leon was as interested in rabbits as he was in falling in love with the most charming she-Basset ever, but didn't a district dedicated to lakes seem to be the perfect place to find her? Border collies are fascinating dogs, but they're a little... um... over the top.

The hound sighed. Matters of the heart were always so complicated. His eyelids fluttered, and soon he was in dreamland, running over rolling hills and craggy fells, bathing in an infinite expanse of crystal-clear waters and chasing powder-puff tails emerging from the heather carpet of a rabbit's garden...

THE END

~

Dear Reader,

I hope you've enjoyed this story, but if you want a little extra, to find out what happens next at Glengullion, you can access it *for free* here:

WWW.ADRIANALICIO.COM / GLENGULLIONEPILOGUE

AUTHOR'S NOTE

My story with the Island of Mull

I arrived on Mull many years ago, around 1994 when I was a student at Glasgow Caledonian University. I took a coach to the ferry port and loved the journey over the sea, surrounded by seagulls catching the chips the tourists and locals alike threw for them, hovering over the heads of anyone who was snacking on the deck. Nowadays, you're advised not to feed the seagulls, who can become quite aggressive when they descend en masse, so let me hasten to say here that this is GOOD ADVICE. Please don't feed the gulls, then blame me for encouraging you to do so, because I'm actually warning you, these birds have changed. Decades ago, they only took food that was offered to them, but nowadays they prey on everyone, whether you want to share your meal or not. So to avoid an unpleasant battle of wills, it's best not to encourage them in the first place.

Anyway, I digress. On arrival on Mull, the coach carried on to Tobermory. With its famous promenade of colourful buildings lined up in front of me, the town rose to decorate the gentle hill behind them, and in minutes, I had fallen head over heels in love with the place.

The first shop I entered was the Chocolate Shop, which didn't simply sell chocolate; the people working there made it themselves. And it was irresistibly good. When I talked with the owner, she told me how proud she was of living in such a great place. Intrigued, I asked – as Etta did – what the inhabitants of Mull did to pass the time in winter when the tourists had all gone back home, and she gave me an answer that has stuck with me for almost three decades.

"That's our time, when we come together as a community and organise things. It's when we have activities going on not for the tourists, but for ourselves. We're very grateful to the tourists who visit throughout the year, but winter is when we rekindle the relationships within our community, do things together, relax and recharge before the next tourist season."

So yes, I got much the same answer as Etta received almost thirty years later. The seagulls might have changed, but the good folk of Mull have not.

The Chocolate Shop owner also showed me the mysterious little path that passes through the woods, telling me it leads to a lighthouse. I left my backpack at the youth hostel and went for a walk that very evening, despite the sun setting and the shadows lengthening. It was a fairy-tale place that inspired my usual daydreaming. Well actually, it was night dreaming as it was so late in the evening by then, but I was still awake. The moon was peeping from behind the clouds every so often, but when I tore my eyes from the ocean and its lighthouse and looked for the path, it was so dark, I could hardly see where it was.

It was even worse when I entered the forest again, I could barely see the tip of my nose. And this was the time before mobile phones and their handy torches. How would I be able to return to Tobermory without stumbling over the cliffs?

It was only when my eyes adjusted to the darkness that I noticed there were a few white pebbles shining under the intermittent lunar light filtering through the branches. Like a rerun of *Hansel and Gretel*, following these gleaming natural signposts, I reached the hostel safely. What a magical experience.

That evening in the hostel, I described my adventure, and many others, to John, a father of two young children. A teacher by profession, he had a passion for all things environmental. He had recently lost his wife, but he was a splendid dad, doing his very best to bring up his two precious little ones to be happy, compassionate and healthy human beings. We spoke until the early hours, and many years later, he became my inspiration for Flemming, the widowed father of two children in *An Ærø Island Christmas Mystery*.

All of this goes to show what an inspiring place Mull is, and what wonderful people you can meet there. So, although I had initially planned to set this book on the Isle of Skye, I was irresistibly drawn to Mull, and now that the book is finished, I've realised it could not have been otherwise.

REAL OR FICTIONAL BUSINESSES?

As my dear readers know by now, I love to use real places and businesses whenever I can, but populated by fictional characters. So, for example, the **Tobermory Fish Co** is a real place selling the freshest food imaginable, but the premises is actually on the A848 just before you enter Tobermory itself. However, in order to tighten up the arrival scene, I wanted all the businesses welcoming our trio to be on Tobermory Main Street, so I moved the shop accordingly. If you're looking for the real place, just Google it; it's well worth a visit. And yes, you really can order a delicious Seafood Platter!

The same goes for the dark brown building housing the **Tobermory Chocolate Shop**, which, for similar whimsical creative reasons, I had to move further down the Main Street so as to give Etta and Dora a little time to appreciate the town before they drilled in with local encounters.

· · ·

THE TACKLE AND BOOKS BOOKSHOP

This is where Dora stops to find some solace from the weird sense of forlornness seizing her. Again, it is a real place, this time in its real location. The building is beautiful, its shop windows dreamy, but more importantly, on the bookshop's website and Facebook page, you will always find plenty of suggestions for intriguing books to read. I, very much like Dora, have discovered many new books and authors thanks to them.

You can support the store by buying online through bookshop.org, a tremendous resource helping independent bookshops to keep striving.

THE ISLE OF MULL CHEESE AND MULL FOREST CAFÉ

Josh McIntosh's cheese-making enterprise was inspired by the real-life story of the Reade family and their Isle of Mull Cheese. I was totally drawn into it. It's such an amazing tale of passion, determination and hard work, going back to 1979 when a British family of five fell in love with the place and decided that Mull was where they wanted not only to live for the rest of their lives, but also to make their dreams come true and set up a dairy farm.

It took years of sacrifice, living in a caravan while restoring stone by stone what remained of Sgriob-Ruadh, a "derelict collection of buildings". Years later, they were providing milk for the whole island. Fast forward to today, and they now produce one of the best cheeses Scotland has to offer.

And I owe the family not only for the dairy farm idea. You see, from Chris Reade's passion for beauty, the incredible **Glass Barn Café** was born. I had no choice, I instantly fell in love with this beautiful conservatory. For the sake of my story, I conveniently moved it closer to Glengullion Castle where it became the Mull Forest Café, but truly, it's a creation of the Reade family.

· · ·

MULL HOSPITAL

There is a 66-bed hospital on the island of Mull, which can offer quite a lot of treatments, but not a CT scan, for which Etta should have gone to Oban. But I just couldn't send her there to recover, so far from Dora and Leon, Rufus, and her new friends...

So once more, life in my book differs a little from reality, but that's not necessarily a bad thing.

ABOUT GLENGULLION CASTLE

The closest castle to Tobermory is Glengorm. You can read about the engaging family endeavours to preserve it, making it sustainable in a variety of ways that have changed through the ages. It was a B&B, but at present, as this book goes out, it's only possible to rent a few charming cottages or castle apartments with stunning views, as after Covid struck, the family decided it was time to pivot once more. They breed Highland cattle and Blackface sheep, preserve the surrounding natural areas and organise splendid tours led by biologists.

Undoubtedly, Glengullion Castle was created by moving Glengorm closer to Tobermory. No planning permission required, no taxes to be paid when you do such things in books. Then I started to spin a story, involving characters that bear no resemblance to real people, but are the fruit of my own imagination.

To the best of my knowledge, there's no ghost at Glengorm, though in Scotland, you can never be too sure. Bogles abound!

THE ISLAND OF IONA

There's not much more I can say here beyond what has been shown by the story. Iona is a magical, spiritual place; it doesn't matter whether you're a believer or an atheist. Try it and let me know how it moves you.

· · ·

THE ISLAND OF STAFFA

I was disappointed not to include a trip to Staffa in the story, but I was already worried about the length of this book (my longest to date!), so I had to be happy with just a mention. This island is a haven for so many wild birds, the beautiful clown puffins in particular.

When I took my trip there, the sea was so rough, we couldn't land, much to my deepest regret! But during the cruise, we spotted several dolphins, a mink whale, cute seals as curious to study us as we were to look at them, and mostly, the adorable puffins diving in and out of the stormy waves as if they were in a theme park.

THE NINTH WAVE RESTAURANT

The Ninth Wave is another very special (and real!) place I was only able to mention in passing in the story, unless I wanted to turn the book into a saga. It is not simply a restaurant serving delicious food; it's the culmination of a lifetime of passion, dreams and love.

Imagine a young woman by the name of Carla Lamont, a Saskatchewan Canadian living in Vancouver, applying to work in a restaurant in the middle of nowhere. In her own words, it was "an island as large as a pea in my mom's atlas as there was no Google Maps at the time." This was where Carla bravely went and met a local fisherman, who invited her to stay in his home (no electricity, no running water, just four stone walls and barely a roof). May I remind you that all this happened in Scotland, not in the warm Canary Islands.

This house would have scared most guests off, but Carla fell in love with it for three reasons. 1) The 'almost' house was perched on the cliffs, overlooking the wild sea; 2) the fish from the island was delicious; and 3) the fisherman, John, who eventually became her husband, cooked divinely well.

Most unexpectedly, Carla was hooked, even though she

didn't believe John's estimate that it would take as long as two years to transform the cold stones into a proper house. Turned out she was wrong – it took seven!

Over the years, the Ninth Wave, where Carla cooks the fish John catches, has become a famous restaurant and a place where people gather to have fun. I'd give almost anything to be there, savouring a meal and enjoying one of the funny Steampunk Tuesdays, meeting Mr Lobster King in his top-hat and monocle, and Carla wearing a giant lobster clip in her candy-floss pink hair as if it were the most fashionable coiffure.

~

I HOPE YOU NOW SEE THAT MULL IS A VERY SPECIAL PLACE THAT attracts very special people.

Thanks to the **What Do We Do in the Winter podcast**, I have heard stories that have fired my imagination and rekindled my bonds with the island. Please listen to this podcast if you want to know more.

BREE, THE BORDER COLLIE

During a book-writing project, it often happens that I can't come up with the right name for a character. I'm lucky enough to have a mailing list of keen readers (you can subscribe too at www.adrianalicio.com/murderclub) whom I can ask for help. Thanks to Debbie Fredericks for suggesting the perfect name for Bree, in memory of her own girl:

"Our sweet girl, Bree, had many of the traits you describe. She was so loving and loyal. Her family was the most important thing in her life. She loved her mom and followed her everywhere.

"She had what we referred to as her 'Elvis smile'. Whenever she saw one of her family after any time apart, we were given her Elvis smile. I think Bree would be a great name [for a cheese maker's dog], *and a play on Brie!"*

Thanks so much, Debbie, I couldn't have come up with a more suitable name!

SEAL RESCUE AND INTERACTION

While we were talking about Bree and Storm the baby seal, one person suggested that a seal pup stranded on a beach may have been scared of a full-grown border collie. I sent her this video to watch: https://www.youtube.com/shorts/R46C7p7GN0M

The truth is, interspecies animal behaviour is an unpredictable and wonderful thing :)

Of course, as hard as this can be at times, interactions with wildlife should be avoided. We humans need to leave wild animals in peace and not encourage them, for their own good, to become too familiar with us. If you see a wild animal in distress, call professional rescuers where possible.

To the best of my knowledge, there isn't a seal rescue on Mull, but there are a few of them in Scotland. As ever, as an author, I felt free to set up a new one where I needed it to be. Most of my inspiration came from the Cornish seal sanctuary: https://www.youtube.com/@cornishsealsanctuary8635

These guys do an awesome job and always manage to convey a positive feeling in all they do and show, and their centre is amazing. I haven't visited in person yet, but I hope to go to Cornwall sometime soon! Feel free to browse through their videos and make a donation if you so wish. Storm would thank you :)

MORE BOOKS FROM ADRIANA LICIO

AN ITALIAN VILLAGE MYSTERY SERIES

0 - And Then There Were Bones. The prequel to the *An Italian Village Mystery* series is **available for free by signing up to www.adrianalicio.com/murderclub**

1 - Murder on the Road Returning to her quaint hometown in Italy following the collapse of her engagement, feisty travel writer Giò Brando just wants some peace and quiet. Instead, she finds herself a suspect in a brutal murder.

2 A Fair Time for Death The annual Chestnut Fair brings visitors from far and wide to the sleepy village of Trecchina. This year, one will be coming to die.

3 - A Mystery Before Christmas A haunting Christmas song from a faraway land. A child with striking green eyes. A man with no past.

4 - Peril at the Pellicano Hotel – A group of wordsmiths, a remote hotel. Outside, the winds howl and the seas rage. But the real danger lurks within.

5 - The Haunted Watch Tower – The doors are locked, the windows shuttered, but still he comes. Dare you set foot in the haunted watchtower?

THE HOMESWAPPERS MYSTERIES SERIES
Travelling Europe one... corpse at a time!
0 - Castelmezzano, The Witch Is Dead – Prequel to the series
1 - The Watchman of Rothenburg Dies: A German Travel Mystery
2 - A Wedding and A Funeral in Mecklenburg : A German Cozy Mystery
3 - An Aero Island Christmas Mystery: A Danish Cozy Mystery
4 – Prague, A Secret From The Past: A Czech Travel Mystery
5 – **Death on the West Highland Way: A Scottish Cozy Mystery**
6 – **The Ghost of Glengullion Castle: A Murder Mystery** *based in Scotland*
***

An Anthology: *A Christmas Mystery in Venice and Other Winter Tales – 3 Short Stories*

More books to come!

ABOUT THE AUTHOR

Adriana Licio lives in the Apennine Mountains in southern Italy, not far from Maratea, the seaside setting for her first cosy series, *An Italian Village Mystery.*

She loves loads of things: travelling, reading, walking, good food, small villages, and home swapping. A long time ago, she spent six years falling in love with Scotland, and she has never recovered. She now runs her family perfumery, and between a dark patchouli and a musky rose, she devours cosy mysteries.

She resisted writing as long as she could, fearing she might get carried away by her fertile imagination – she was already renowned for living in the clouds. But one day, she found an alluring blank page and the words flowed in the weird English she'd learned in Glasgow.

Adriana finds peace for her restless, enthusiastic soul by walking in nature with her adventurous golden retriever Frodo and her hubby Giovanni.

Do you want to know more?
Join the **Maratea Murder Club**

You can also stay in touch on:
www.adrianalicio.com

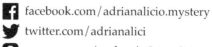

facebook.com/adrianalicio.mystery

twitter.com/adrianalici

amazon.com/author/adrianalicio

bookbub.com/authors/adriana-licio

FREE EBOOKS

Subscribe to Adriana Licio's Murder Club and you'll get exclusive content:

Adriana Licio Murder Club

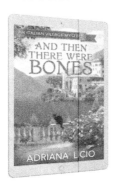 

- **The *FREE EPILOGUE to the Ghost of Glengullion Castle***
- **Book #0,** *And Then There Were Bones,* the prequel to the *An Italian Village Mystery* series featuring travel

writer Giò Brando and her sister's perfume shop in quaint Maratea, a real sea town in Southern Italy

- **Giò Brando's Maratea Album** – photos of her favourite places and behind-the-scenes secrets
- **A Maratea Map** – including most places featured in the series
- **Adriana Licio's News** – new releases, news from Maratea, but no spam – Etta would loathe it!
- **Cosy Mystery Passion:** a place to share favourite books, characters, tips and tropes

Sign up to **www.adrianalicio.com/glengullionepilogue**

Made in the USA
Las Vegas, NV
16 May 2023

72130777R00198